MITZI BYTES

MITZI BYTES

· · · · · · · · · · · · · · · ·

KERRY CLARE

HARPER**AVENUE**

Mitzi Bytes
Copyright © 2017 by Kerry Clare
All rights reserved.

Published by Harper Avenue,
an imprint of HarperCollins Publishers Ltd

First edition

HarperCollins books may be purchased for educational, business,
or sales promotional use through our Special Markets Department.

HarperCollins Publishers Ltd
2 Bloor Street East, 20th Floor
Toronto, Ontario, Canada
M4W 1A8

www.harpercollins.ca

Canadian Cataloguing in Publication information
is available upon request.

ISBN 978-1-44344-922-9

Printed and bound in the United States of America
LSC/H 10 9 8 7 6 5 4 3 2 1

This book is for Stuart,
and for Harriet and Iris.

Naturally, you put down the truth in your notebooks.
What would be the point if you didn't?

—Louise Fitzhugh, *Harriet the Spy*

Still Byting after All These Years:
Blogger Mitzi Bytes Looks Back on a Decade of Life Online
Jennifer Anderson, *The Star Weekly*, April 6, 2010

Mitzi Bytes is not an easy woman to get in touch with. She doesn't do face-to-face interviews, and phone calls are arranged well in advance via a network of publicists. My conversation with her, in connection with the promotion of her new book, *Hot and Heavy* (named for the wash cycle), was rescheduled twice before I finally heard her voice, which is softer and sweeter than her sardonic blog might suggest.

"I get that a lot," she laughs. "People think they know me, and then they're always surprised."

I suggest that her readers might have a right to think they've achieved a degree of knowledge. Bytes has been writing her blog for a decade, documenting the progression of her life from diving back into the dating pool as a sassy divorcee in the city, all the way to stay-at-home mom strung out on fabric softener fumes, these days high on domestic bliss.

"It's been quite a winding road," she admits. "I make my own yoghurt now." She laughs again, then qualifies, "Okay, I made it once."

Her fans are familiar with the story. At the tender age of 25, after two years of marriage, Bytes's lawyer husband left her for his (male) secretary. Heartbroken, Bytes picked up the pieces by displaying the sordid details of her dating life on her blog, whose audience quickly grew to hundreds of thousands.

"The appeal was like watching a car crash," admits Bytes. "Impossible to look away from." Memorable posts include the one about the man who pulled out a tape measure before they had sex and made her record the length of his penis, in a notebook he kept in his back pocket, and the night she was performing oral sex in the back of a taxi that was rear-ended. "The guy was fine," she explains. "I've got smart reflexes, but then I ended up with this really complicated kind of whiplash. The doctors were baffled."

When she found love again, it was in an unlikely place. "The Programmer" was the name she gave to a neighbour she'd encountered in their condo building's laundry room. The peculiar contents of The Programmer's basket resulted in a 1,500-word screed against "tighty-whities" and many amusing posts about his awkward gestures and obvious affection for her. When she finally declared their love, Bytes's readers were aghast, and the relationship made newspaper headlines.

But even with such hoopla, The Programmer remains unaware of both his own online celebrity and his wife's: Mitzi Bytes, of course, is not her real name.

"When I started out, nobody used their name," she said. "The culture has changed so much—back then, the Web was more intimate, anonymous." She admits that she's been lucky to keep it that way. "I'm like the Dooce who never got dooced," she says, referring to the popular blogger whose online handle became common parlance after she was fired for writing about her boss and co-workers.

Though the public outing didn't hurt Dooce's popularity. So why is Mitzi Bytes still afraid to come out of the closet?

"I'm not afraid," she says. "It would just get complicated. I like my life the way it is."

And who can blame her? The blog these days depicts an online idyll, all blue skies, cupcakes, and clean sheets hanging on the line. Bytes's artful photos suggest a comfortable home, happy children, and cozy dinners with the husband once the kids are tucked into bed, though all of this is filtered through her signature acerbic perspective.

"It is a good life," she agrees. Her blog nets a respectable advertising revenue, and *Hot and Heavy* is her third book, a collection of blog-like domestic vignettes.

But doesn't it seem ironic, I ask her, that a blogger who's made her name out of being forthright should go about her own life as if under a shroud? It must seem like a lot to hide.

She shrugs off my concern. "We all compartmentalize," she says. "My husband gets that. He actually insists on it. It's why we're so good at being married."

But doesn't her brand suffer for her anonymity?

"I'm not a brand," she corrects me. "I started blogging in the 20th century, remember? People didn't want to be brands."

She levels with me. "I've got my work, but I keep myself for myself. And I appreciate that."

It's a refreshing point of view in this age of full disclosure.

CHAPTER 1

· · · · · · · · · · · · · · · · · ·

When Sarah Lundy woke up that morning, the first thing she felt was relief, one eye opened and taking stock of the room around her, the soft light from outside muted by the curtains. Still here. White walls and carpet, the whir of the fan on the ceiling up above her. Her clothes from yesterday all piled on the floor, the teetering stack of books on her bedside. She held her breath for the sound of her husband beside her, the quiet sound of his breathing while he slept, the way he never snored. Just one of many things she had reason to be thankful for, and she was. You could almost hold this. The stillness.

But then the alarm exploded, 7:03, in the middle of the news. She woke up just before it every day, and she wondered if the clock radio had some kind of mechanism that clicked into place before the alarm, if the click was what awakened her every morning and not some uncanny ability to be alert to the morning before her clock was. The radio reporting on bombings some-where far away, a shooting someplace closer, plummeting stock prices, melting Arctic ice, but also declining childhood mortality rates in sub-Saharan Africa—one thing for which to be hopeful. Then the noise as the house was beginning to wake up around her. Whisked-open curtains revealing morning, small voices shouting from down the hall, the spray from the shower turning on in the adjoining bathroom. The world returning, but with it also the dawning remembrance of the reason she'd slept so uneasily, the email that had arrived like a sock in the gut shortly before bed. Sarah burrowed under the covers.

But before she could begin to contemplate her trouble, Gladys arrived, jumping on the bed, Sarah anticipating her landing just as she'd anticipated the alarm, and oh yes, here she was, forty-five pounds of force bounding up and pummelling her mother.

"Good mooooorning," Gladys shout-whispered into Sarah's ear, and Sarah pulled away from her daughter's manic embrace, rubbing her ear. It hurt. Gladys had leaped onto her mother this way nearly every morning since she'd learned to climb out of her crib, which, now that Gladys was almost five, had made for a lot of mornings. It was possible that Sarah awoke just before her alarm each day just to experience the rare pleasure of the sleeping world for a moment or two, the quiet before the wheels began to turn. And the rest of the day would be a race to return there, list items checked, work done, the house set back in order, the children in their beds, a few good moments of everything in its place, all right with the universe, before she dropped off to sleep in spite of herself.

Sarah moved slowly in the mornings. She didn't like to speak until a shower had revived her. By the time she'd shaken off Gladys and swung her legs out of bed, pushed her tangled hair out of her face, Chris was already out of his shower, half-dressed.

He smiled, rolling his eyes as Gladys skipped a circle around him while he buttoned up his shirt. All Chris's shirts were the same, more or less, and so were all their mornings.

Except for this one. The matter of the email had shaken her wits, though it was reassuring to wake up today and find the world still standing. But the relief didn't make her trouble less present, she was realizing now as she massaged soapsuds into her scalp and then tipped her head back to let the shampoo run down her back, to let the water fall over her face like a film. Going through the motions of her life, nothing outside of ordinary, and she felt extra conscious now that here she was, a woman playing a role.

Did it always feel like this? she considered. Yesterday when she'd stood where she stood now, inhaling her fruity shampoo scent, what had she been thinking about? Probably nothing. She found it difficult to think about anything so early in the morning, even as the water from the super-turbo showerhead pounded her scalp, her back, awakening her senses. A force that felt so good.

But here was something. Sarah opened her eyes to find Gladys peeking around the shower curtain. No surprise there—Gladys regarded her family members' showers as open invitations. She liked to lean in and feel the mist fall on her face, and then her hair would frizz up even more than usual. Somehow between her parents' room and the tub, she'd lost her pyjamas, and now she was naked, brandishing her tiny nipples, her sleek slender form. She was climbing into the tub. "Oh, no you don't . . . " said Sarah, picking her up, dropping her back over onto the bathmat. She pulled the shower curtain closed again.

A futile gesture, really, because moments later came a pounding on the door frame, although the door had been left wide open, steam billowing into the hall. The knock, Sarah supposed, at least a gesture toward her privacy being respected. She peered around the curtain—it was Clementine, already dressed, wardrobe being her main preoccupation of late, head-to-toe purple, which as far as she was concerned was the only colour that counted.

"I have to go to the bathroom," Clementine announced, never mind that the girls had their own bathroom down the hall, but then nobody else would be in there. And arguing with Clementine would only mean she'd pitch a fit, so Sarah didn't bother. She let Clementine step over her sister, who was lying face down on the bathmat playing dead, then pulled the curtain closed for the indulgence of just a few more seconds alone.

"What's wrong, Mommy?"

For a few more seconds without someone asking her that, or demanding anything at all.

"What's wrong?" they asked her again.

Not that anyone ever really wanted to know the answer. The precise response they were looking for was and always would be "Nothing."

•　•　•

But it wasn't. Sarah had just spent eight hours racked with torment, her dreams that night of elevators mostly, ones that lurched sideways, got stuck, and threatened to plummet but didn't, bringing her so close to testing the theory of whether it was impossible to die in a nightmare. Or else the dreams in which she was commanding teams of horses, thousands of reins, runaway and out of control. She'd been dreaming haunted bungalows, psychopathic men in hot pursuit. She'd had the one in which she'd just killed somebody, the weapon in her hand. Who had it been? She couldn't remember but recalled watching blood drip off a blade and noting that here was the point at which her whole life had come apart, that tapestry of days, places, and people that mattered, all painstakingly stitched together now unravelled, and utterly lost to her. All the king's horses and all the king's men. Like that.

Sarah's trouble, the email, was sticking in her mind like a spot in her vision. Halfway to the shower, she'd run the text through her mind, and now she was ruminating on the message. None of it made any sense, she was thinking as she made her way back to her bedroom, still dripping, a towel wrapped around her hair. Gladys was not yet dressed and now was lying sideways across the mattress, thwarting her father's attempts to pull up the duvet and declare the bed made. His coffee was waiting downstairs, and once he'd gulped it, he'd be gone.

Sarah picked up her glasses from the bedside table, put them on: some clarity. But still not enough. She picked Gladys up by her ankles, dangling her for a moment before dumping her on the carpet, where she landed shrieking in a heap. Chris edged by, breezing a kiss that landed somewhere on Sarah's hairline. His feet on the stairs—going, gone. She could breathe now.

"Go get dressed," Sarah said to Gladys—most days nearly an impossible request. These were the same lines she ran through every morning, and she tried to sound convincing now as she delivered them.

"We've got to get going. Now. Come on, move it, or we'll be running late."

•　•　•

At the playground, Sarah leaned against the chain-link fence, catching her breath, hoping it looked like a casual stance. You had to take your moments of peace where you could find them, and here was one now, the sheer luck of arriving at school three minutes before the bell rang. She hadn't even had to park illegally, and now she slouched like the weight on her shoulders was nothing, taking in the scene while her children bounded about on the pavement.

Her phone had been waiting for her downstairs in the kitchen, where it had been charging all night, on her mind like a beacon, but there'd been no new messages. She checked again now—still nothing, but she stayed intent upon the silent screen, transmitting her own message to the people around her. She didn't want to talk to anyone this morning, to make the small talk, answer polite inquiries. This was the morning she'd offend everybody with her reticence, even more than usual, so Sarah kept her head down, tried to blend into the fence. To disappear.

The scene before her was unfolding in the usual fashion; she didn't even need to see. The same thing happened every day. Cars pulling up at the curb and delivering more and more children, the gathering throng thick with bikes, balls, and ponytails. Backpacks. And so much noise. Parents like Sarah sticking around on the perimeter, chatting like with like, school drop-off en route to yoga class or the office. Kids on scooters wearing helmets, others in their wide-brimmed hats, now that fleece and woollens had been retired with the winter chill. It was April, so the sun's kiss was now the kiss of death. She'd forgotten to pick up a tube of that organic sunscreen, the kind without carcinogens that sold for twenty-five bucks a pop. Oh, what a beautiful morning.

Her phone buzzed in her hand, stirring her out of her daydream; it was Chris. Him, she could talk to.

She said, "What is it?"

He asked her, "You got off okay?" He was walking to his office from the subway. She could hear blaring horns and construction, a different cacophony than the schoolyard. Chris could have taken the underground pathway to work from the station, but he preferred surfaces of things.

"Of course," she said. "What's going on?"

He said, "Nothing. Sometimes I can just call, you know."

"But you don't." Most days, once Chris left the house, he'd be spun through the revolving door of his building and whisked up to the forty-third floor, absorbed into a busy day of tasks, projects, and demands, that she wouldn't hear from him again until the sun was down.

"I'm just checking in," he said. "You sure you're okay?"

She said, "Yeah."

He asked her, "Anything I need to know?" Which might have been a strange question, but not from Chris, even if the call itself was unexpected. Chris got by on prompts and reminders. What he was asking her was if tonight was the night he had to leave work on time because she had her book club, if she wanted any groceries picked up on his way home, and if there was something else she needed him to remember. These were practical things. He was certainly not inquiring as to the status of the depths of her soul, the reason for her fear and dread, about her strange mood this morning. He didn't want to know any of that. He wouldn't have noticed the strange mood. That much she took for granted.

So she said, "Nope," which was true. There was nothing that Chris needed to know. "And there's the bell gone." Their moment squandered—she was clumsy this morning. But it was too late now, so they said their goodbyes. And she didn't have to tell him that she loved him because of that he was already certain.

· · ·

She'd almost made it, the kids dropped off in kindergarten and Grade 2, and she was halfway to the car, when somebody called her name. Not her actual name, but she knew to answer. It was what anyone called her who knew her from her kids' class lists. It was their last name, their father's name. The name she'd consciously not taken, but she owned it when required.

"Yoo-hoo, Sarah Bennett, yoo-hoo," shouted Starry Fiske, whose *yoo-hoo* was making her sound a little woo-woo. Her name was Starry for reasons that Sarah had never been able to discern—it seemed unfitting for someone so earthy, in the root vegetable sense. "I knew that was you," she said. "You and that *hat* of yours," as though the hat was something remarkable, even vaguely disgraceful. A perfectly ordinary pink ball-cap, its brim perfect for keeping the sun off Sarah's face and for hiding beneath. Though not perfect enough for the latter.

"You know about the fundraiser? For the gala?"

"I thought the gala was a fundraiser."

"Well, a gala can't put itself on, can it?" said Starry. "Can we count on you?"

"Well, I'm not sure what I can do," said Sarah. "These days I'm really pressed for time—"

"Oh, but who isn't?" said Starry, taking Sarah's hand and squeezing it as though she were commiserating. It was all too much. Starry leaned in confidingly. "I was hoping we could use some of your media connections."

Sarah took her hand back. "That's a bit of a stretch," she said.

"After that piece you wrote about the gymnastics tournament? I emailed that link to everyone. Did you check your stats? Your traffic was probably huge that week."

"Probably," said Sarah.

"We're selling olive oil. Organic. These cute little bottles—you can use them again. Fair trade, sourced from the most incredible orchard in Palestine. I'm thinking you could make it into a travel piece."

"Not quite my beat, Starry."

"Well, what angle were you thinking, then?"

Sarah said, "I wasn't."

Starry said, "You sound . . . *dismissive*." This was what made Starry Fiske an indomitable fundraiser. An indomitable every-thing. Sarah wanted to *domit* her now, though. She wasn't going to apologize. She wasn't going to submit.

"Listen," said Sarah. "This is really not a good time."

"I'll send you an email, then. We'll set a date. I'm open to an interview—something casual. Over coffee at my place?"

"An email," said Sarah, fumbling in her bag for her keys. "Olive oil."

"We've got so much to talk about" Starry was yelling as Sarah beelined for the car.

• • •

When Sarah had said she was really pressed for time, Starry hadn't believed her. No one ever did. People imagined her days stretched out wide, with hours of lying on couches, coffee dates, and pedicures. They imagined that all this time was how she got so much reading done. A vision that was wholly incongruous with how the hours really went, the tedium of running back and forth to school, how fast those hours flew, and how they were usually crammed with grocery shopping, household chores, and doctor's appointments. Two afternoons a week she taught a literacy course. And somebody had to be home to wait for the appliance guy to arrive, she still had to e-file their taxes, and who else would mop the mess from snotty noses when the girls were home with a cold? It wasn't just getting Clementine and Gladys out the door, taking them to and from school. A checklist, never-ending, but most of the time, she knocked off every item, one by one.

But even if she'd explained all that, they wouldn't believe her, and the mothers with the full-time jobs would only roll their eyes, and it wasn't even enough for Sarah herself when accounting for her time, so she'd preserved a few choice elements of her life pre-kids, adding these to the mix. Formerly a journalist, she still dabbled in online freelance work, mostly writing articles ("Top Ten Easy Dinners Your Kids Will Eat") for parenting websites run by old colleagues, but most of these articles came without a byline. The writing Starry was referring to was of the old-school variety, committed to actual newsprint, the column Sarah wrote for the community paper delivered free each month to every mailbox in the neighbourhood before being redirected to every recycling box. Even with its paltry web presence, the *Maplewood Village Sentinel* had fewer readers than her Easy Dinners did, and if Starry Fiske—with all her flattering lines about media connections—had regularly been among them, she would have known Sarah's last name.

So why did she bother? If called upon, she'd probably explain how the paper prided itself on being a last bastion of democracy, all justifications for its existence (in grant applications and fervent pleas for ads to local businesses) emphasizing the importance of independent media, supposing media to be an end in itself. She believed all this. Never mind that nobody ever read it, that its finger was so far off the button that the April issue came out with a front-page story on December's ice storm. That *democracy* was probably in trouble when you could only pay the *demos* twenty-five dollars for eight hundred words.

Obviously, she didn't do it for the money. One of the benefits of having married a computer genius was that she didn't have to do anything for the money. But an extension of this luck was not doing anything, a terrible trap. Having no reply in hand when people she met said to her, "So tell me about yourself—" Falling back on dentist appointments and waiting for the appliance guy.

Motherhood was not the answer. Or not the right one. She needed a different answer, not only because being "just a mom" was beside the point. Plus the phrase itself was so fraught—"just a mom"—the quickest way she knew to shut down a conversation. Implying a lacking, less than whole, undermining the way that being a mom was always *everything*, no matter how you pulled it off. Motherhood was an all-enveloping vortex. During those first few minutes of Clementine's life more than seven years ago, when that furious baby had come out screaming at the world and Sarah had taken her in her arms, the baby locking her tiny mouth to her mother's nipple, Sarah had gazed at her, thinking, "You could totally devour me." The opposite of what she'd been expecting, a yearning to nibble on fat baby thighs and toes. But appetites were a two-way street, she realized as her baby sucked like she'd been born to take and take. It was always going to be about cannibalism, and Sarah resolved that she would not disappear.

On the rare occasion she was ever asked to expand upon her reasons for working in community news, Sarah would say, "It's a foot in the door." Recycled or not, there was still something substantial about print. Even Starry knew it to be true. Sarah, though, had once upon a time written features for major papers and glossy magazines, so the *Sentinel* was more like the door to the supply closet, or perhaps it was a trap door, journalism these days pretty much tantamount to career suicide.

But it was an outlet, a response to "So tell me about yourself," and the column gave her a connection to the community. She was a personality, allowed a degree of differentiation. Not that any of this mattered. But it secretly did. And mostly because of the other secret she harboured, her chief pursuit, the occupation that mattered more than the rest of the ways she filled her days but that nobody knew about at all.

• • •

So they were a cover of sorts, her easy dinners and community news, all the more important now that both girls were in school and needed her less. Lately she was also absorbed by a project with the Maplewood Village Heritage Association, transcribing old audiotapes from the 1980s and '90s of interviews by wives of Second World War vets, work that actually meant something.

She'd gotten the gig through a contact at the *Sentinel* who'd applied for a grant. The tapes had turned up in a local basement, perhaps part of an oral history project long abandoned. Most of the people speaking on the tapes were dead now. These days Sarah worked from digital files, so she had to pick up a second-hand tape player at Goodwill. And she'd been working steadily over the last two months, committing these disembodied voices to text, preserving stories of the home front. The woman whose boyfriend shipped out a few weeks before she realized she was pregnant; another who'd gone to work as a welder while her husband was away, while raising their four children alone; a war bride who'd spent the 1950s receiving shock treatments after several suicide attempts. The extraordinary ordinary stories that only get peripheral treatment in the history books. These women had raised their families in the neighbourhood, walking the same sidewalks, living in the same houses, dragging tired feet up and down these narrow staircases. And Sarah kept getting lost inside their stories, forgetting to type—caught up in the spaces between sentences, how words trailed off, the nuance and tone, all that stayed unsaid beneath the surface. Rewinding back and starting over again, until she was sometimes typing faster than the voice was speaking. She wanted to know what would happen next. Usually she arrived home each day and bounded back upstairs to her desk to get back to work and find out.

But this morning was different. Her mind was on other things. She didn't want to get lost, and she couldn't have. She was lacking focus to go deep into anything. The kitchen was still in shambles, breakfast dishes piled in the sink, the front hall torn asunder after the usual scramble for shoes and bags that morning. Theirs was an old house, and usually shambles didn't look so bad. It could be homey. But today it felt as though the mess couldn't wait.

She took a moment first. She brewed a cup of tea and sat down with an issue from the pile of magazines on the coffee table—subscriptions were her weakness. But she couldn't concentrate. Flipping through pages—home decor, a humble literary mag from her alma mater, one of Clementine's comic books—was like passing time, poorly, absorbing nothing. Outside, she could hear the knife-sharpening truck crawling by, its dinging bell a most familiar sound, but never a comfort, always jarring, disturbing the peace. Sarah imagined the look of that bell, all tarnished and dented. Tin. She listened to the truck going all the way up the street, and coming back now one block over, so much fainter but not quite gone.

She had checked her email three times in the half hour since she'd returned home. She resisted the urge to check it again. There was nothing she could do anyway until Seattle started its business day on the edge of the continent. Under other circumstances, she might have sat down to write a blog post, her usual go-to in a moment of crisis, but now that seemed inappropriate. She had no idea what kind of game she'd be playing.

By the time the sharpener's bell had faded away, she had already started on the kitchen. It was easy to be preoccupied while rinsing bowls, loading the dishwasher, removing soggy Cheerios from the bottom of the sink. She turned on the radio but had to turn it off again—a story about a baby found dead in a bathtub in the suburbs, its mother taken into custody. Standing at the counter, Sarah took stock of the tension in her neck, her back. Closing her eyes, she rolled her neck slowly, first one way and then the other.

She opened her eyes again and caught a flash of movement out the window. It could have been a bird or squirrel, but it wasn't. Moving her basil plant aside, she peered right up at the glass, leaning over the sink, squinting to see behind the trees— either somebody or something. Black and bright orange, the most exotic bird. But not a bird. She took off her glasses, put them back on. Someone was there, standing behind the trees that separated her sister-in-law's backyard from her own. Which made no sense, because Frances and Evan were both at work, Charlotte at school. Their cleaner came on Thursdays. Sarah knew their schedule as well as she knew her own. And if the schedule had changed, Frances would have let her know. Sarah would be involved somehow. Frances had her household schedule running like clockwork, but clock mechanics are fallible, and then she always needed Sarah to step in. Evan was basically useless.

It was probably only Evan out there anyway, or something related to his goings-on—none of her business. The hush of these weekdays made her mind stretch too far. A bird in the bushes, and then she'd be thinking of burglars. It could have been a woodpecker, one of the huge ones. Or she was just imagining things. But then the things she imagined weren't only in her head. There had been a spurt of garage break-ins lately, and arsons in back laneways only blocks away. Sarah was thinking too about the email she'd received the night before, her whole world slightly askew ever since she'd read it. Things she'd always considered safe suddenly vulnerable, suddenly out in the open.

Drying her hands on her jeans, Sarah stepped into her wellies, overpriced rain boots with their insulated inserts, boots she was ashamed to have purchased, twice over even (for she owned a pair in red and another in green), as though she had occasion for such apparel. As though she were constantly tramping in gardens and jaunting down muddy lanes. The very same boots all the mothers had.

She unlocked the back door, and tramped out onto the patio. She could have used one of Starry's *yoo-hoos* right about then. Something was certainly visible behind the trees, a most extraordinary orange. A hat? It was the colour of a hunting vest. Did Evan have a hat like that? Was he worried that somebody might want to shoot him?

Sarah settled for "Hello?" instead of "Yoo-hoo." She clomped down the steps onto the grass, the ground soft and sinking underneath her feet from last night's rain. Perhaps she needed her overpriced boots after all. Everything was starting to thaw. She was not looking for a confrontation, but something was unfolding over there, and she wouldn't just stand by and let it happen. She felt for her phone in the pocket of her hoodie; she wasn't a complete fool. She was connected to the world.

Sarah called out again, "Anybody there?" She could see nothing out of the ordinary now. She'd reached the lot line, the hedgerow. There was barely a gap in the trees where they wiggled through from time to time, just at the space where the tumbledown fence was especially tumbled, and Sarah made her way to the other side.

"Frances?" Frances was a bank executive. She worked downtown. She hadn't been home on a weekday morning for years. She didn't even get sick. Frances's immune system was as steely as the rest of her.

In Frances's yard proper now, Sarah took a look around. It was empty. That huge house shut up and quiet, the backyard tidy. When she stood still, she heard nothing, not even birdsong. Not even the sound of a car going down the street.

So she went home, feeling foolish. Disappointed, even. She wasn't sure what she'd been looking for, but there had been a fantasy of somebody caught red-handed. Orange-headed.

Back in the house, Sarah locked the door behind her. She felt extra attentive to these details today, as though somebody had their eye on her. There were no new messages on her phone. By all measures, the day was unfolding in an ordinary fashion. Surely she had enough on the go—the point she'd tried to underline to Starry—that she didn't have to stand staring out the window, inventing local crimes?

Her phone buzzed in her hand—a message from the school about the olive oil fundraiser. She'd never escape these people and their insistent campaigns. And then she signed out of her main email and back into a different account, the one she tried rarely to check from her phone, but this morning she couldn't help herself. These were extraordinary circumstances. Not that anybody was snooping, but after years of experience, covering her tracks had seemed like a reflex. Until now.

She'd had thirty-four new messages that morning, which was nothing out of the ordinary, most of them from readers whose names she recognized. Benign, often tedious, and sycophantic messages of solidarity and support. A few she appreciated from real online friends. Some more from the regular trolls, people who responded no matter what she wrote and were united in their tendency to confuse "dribble" for "drivel" in their comments. One reader threatening to call Children's Aid because she'd written about walking around the house without clothes on, the implicit lesson for her daughters that bodies were nothing to be ashamed of. And because of an old post on sexual consent circulating around social media that week, she received the obligatory comments from men's rights activists telling her she was a fat and ugly lesbian who no one would ever want to fuck, except to rape her eyes.

Delete. Delete.

She'd grown accustomed to Internet vitriol, and rarely did these messages ever surprise her. No, what had been weighing on her all day was something altogether different, a message like none other she'd ever received before in nearly fifteen years of life online.

Scrolling down to find it in her archives, she found it sent the evening before at 8:37. She hadn't come across it until after the girls' bedtime. No identifying details in the name, sent from "Jane Q" from a Gmail address made up of numbers. The subject—*Who do you think you are?*—and she read down to the first line to see her name there, so casual and familiar, until she realized the implication. She'd stopped breathing for a second, and then her heart started beating so fast that her head got light, and then the weight sunk down to the pit of her stomach, where it had remained ever since.

She was glad that she'd been alone when she'd received it, that her daughters hadn't been around to see the fear it had struck in her, Chris downstairs, completely unaware, because she never would have been able to hide her response if they'd been nearby. The depth of her dread—she'd felt a chill on the back of her neck, where her ponytail tickled her skin. She shivered, and shivered again now just thinking about it.

The rest of the message had done nothing to calm her fears. *Guess what—this game is over. You're officially found out.*

From the Archives: Mitzi Bytes
Other People's Mothers

Before I had children, I was afraid of other people's mothers. Once I momentarily blocked a small boy's view of the Mother Goose float at the Santa Claus Parade, and his mother clocked me in the head with a huge plastic candy cane. She hit me so hard, I couldn't see straight, and when I told her so, she said, "Well, now you know how he felt."

I had imagined that my relationship to these women would be different once I became a mother myself, that perhaps I might cross over to the other side. While I didn't see myself clobbering strangers with plastic confectionery, perhaps they'd stop attacking me? But I was wrong.

K is the mother of a child in my Big Girl's Grade 1 class. I don't know her well, because she terrifies me, and any time I'm in her presence, my wits are wholly occupied with trying to get away.

And so it was awful to have her bearing down on me in the playground this morning. She was blocking the sun. She said, "Mitzi, we've got a little problem regarding your holy terror."

"I don't know what you mean," I told her, and this is a phrase I often find myself uttering to mothers at school. I'm getting a reputation for being stupid.

Which K could probably attest to, but she didn't look confused now. She looked as though she knew me better than I did, shaking her head, her narrowed eyes with a peculiar gleam. "Oh, but I think you do," she said.

I asked if she was talking about my daughter, who is many things, some good, some bad, but does not deserve to be called a holy terror, in particular by someone who is using the name with the explicit purpose of trying to get me riled. And so it was in deference to my daughter's honour that I refused to give in to K and her military-style tactics. I didn't even cock an eyebrow.

"I some heard rumours," said K. "Talk of a party."

But I am sure my face moved at that, eyes rolling skyward, crossing my mouth the slightest grimace. So there was something to this after all. There are no secrets within the confines of our school fence—I don't know who I thought I'd been fooling.

"It was just a small party," I said to K. I sounded defensive now that I had something to defend. I had indeed violated a sacred tenet of elementary-school social politics. There would be no atoning for this. "A casual thing, last minute." But from her expression I could see that this point only served to implicate me further. What kind of mother was I? "Just three girls—one of them was her cousin. It really wasn't a big deal. We gave them hot dogs." K looked disgusted.

"The numbers aren't the point," she said. "Or the menu." She had her keys in her hand, and I was imagining them as nunchucks. She was turning them over and over, with a flip of the wrist. "It's the way that word gets out, leads to other kids feeling excluded. You have to agree—that's not a positive thing."

"Well, no," I said, "but it's not that simple. And I wouldn't have called it a 'menu'—we just pulled the wieners out of the freezer. They'd been there since the summer." I have trouble not talking when I'm nervous.

"But it is simple," she said. "It's the reason we have a practice—which I know you know about because I'm sure you've seen the school handbook—that birthday party invites should include the entire class list."

"There are thirty-two kids," I said, trying to get her to see my point. There was still a chance for us to be sensible here.

But K figured I was just quibbling. Her concern was that her daughter had come home from school traumatized at having not been invited to the party. She was a sensitive child—"an orchid," K had previously described her, though I've seen that child, and any floral reference would be misleading. She'd also recently been identified as Gifted, the matter of the party only compounding the alienation she'd been experiencing from her peers ever since.

I suggested this alienation had come about because she actually was excluded every afternoon for special academic programming.

K said this was beside the point. K seemed to see the birthday party as part of a plot.

She said, "She was heartbroken, you know. I do think you need to know the implications of the example you're setting."

"Me?" I asked.

"Starts in the home."

"What does?"

"Let me just say that little pitchers have big ears."

But enough with the cryptic clichés. Stop talking about jugs. I wanted to yank K's horrible daughter over by the lobe and say, "Speaking of big ears." This conversation had been taking up far too much of my precious morning.

"You want me to talk to her?" I said to K. "About your orchid? Tell my terror to look out for her, keep her in the thick of things?"

"How you handle these things is your own business," said K. "It's not my place to say."

"No, I'm not sure it is," I said.

"I've been witness," she continued. "In the classroom. It's the great benefit to volunteering. These glimpses of our children in different contexts."

This was another rub. I don't volunteer at the school. I refuse to. The Board of Education fired twenty-five educational assistants from our school two years ago, expecting local parents to step into the roles, as uncompensated as they were untrained, which they were only too happy to do. I had ethical issues with this, which, you might remember, I voiced at a parents' meeting, only to discover that boat rockers were most unwelcome.

I told K, "I am her context."

She said, "That's what I'm saying."

And there, having been walloped with my own words, I had the rare experience of speechlessness. K figured it was because her message had sunk in so deeply; really, I was just confounded. It was a kind of surrender, the whole thing so ridiculous. It seems that in the company of the mother people, I'm as hopeless as ever.

CHAPTER 2

· · · · · · · · · · · · · · · · ·

At noon, it was finally nine o'clock in Seattle, so Sarah dialed the number she knew by heart. She'd never even bothered programming it into her phone.

"A momentous occasion," said Andrea. "A call from you."

"Something's up," said Sarah.

Andrea said, "I had a feeling."

"Have you heard anything out of the ordinary?" Sarah asked.

Andrea said, "You'll have to be more specific."

"I got a message yesterday," said Sarah. "On the blog account. They knew my name. My real name. It said, 'Who do you think you are?' And that I'm 'officially found out.'"

"By whom?"

"Whoever wrote it. Whomever."

"And therein lies the mystery."

"Exactly."

Andrea said, "I don't know what to tell you." Then she said, "Well, actually, I do." It was nothing she hadn't told Sarah already, about the risks she'd been taking for years, about the things she stood to lose, the things she had lost already, and the things she'd never get. What she was missing out on with her insistence on anonymity, keeping her profile small, limiting her reach. Plus, Andrea warned Sarah, an anonymous platform was unsustainable. "The Internet is the last place you want to keep secrets," Andrea told her over and over. "At least if you want them to stay that way."

Sarah listened to the same admonitions all over again, sitting at her desk in her office on the third floor of their narrow house. Her *office*. Leaning back in her ergonomic chair that had cost twice what her first car did. Bookshelves lining the walls, the big window behind her letting in light from the backyard. The antique tape deck was set up on her desk. Here was the room of her own, whose symbolic size was so much larger than the space inside its walls.

"But what do you *do* in there?" Gladys had asked her not long ago when Sarah had barred her access again, reminding her that it was Mommy's space.

"I write. I think." It was another reason for the *Sentinel* and her other work. That she could justify the space, though other moms she knew needed no such justification. The last vestige of the careers they'd left behind, what they still felt entitled to after years of training and experience: a room with a door that shut.

She'd pointed this out once to her best friend, Beth-Ellen, whose room with a door that shut was actually a closet. "I had a cubicle before, though," said Beth-Ellen, who used to be a journalist. "Which was actually smaller. And didn't even have a door. So in a way, I've been promoted."

Andrea in Seattle was saying, "Surely you knew this was going to happen sooner or later. I can't believe it took so long."

"So what do I do?" Sarah asked her.

"I'd wait on it," Andrea says. "You don't know what they're really all about. They could be bluffing."

"They knew my name," said Sarah. She didn't like this unspecified pronoun, which suggested there was more than one person behind the message. She didn't like that at all. Correcting herself, "He or she . . . But it's probably nothing. I might never hear from this person again."

"More likely than not," said Andrea, who stated things so resolutely that they always seemed statistically true, which was why Sarah liked her. And she was often right, as right as she'd been in 2003 when her name turned up in Sarah's email inbox, suggesting that books made out of blogs would be the next big thing, and was Sarah interested in signing with her literary agency with the intention of obtaining a publishing deal?

There had even been a word for it—*blooks*—though the concept had had more leverage than the neologism. Years later, no one knew what a blook was, but Sarah's were on sale at the airport, and in grocery stores, and in bookstores all over the world.

The first two books sold well—they were considered good reads among the set who usually didn't like to read; they were just the right mixture of provocative and universal, so they made a good gift for anybody; they had received fawning reviews in the pages of gossip magazines. She had been a bestseller on a few of the bigger bestseller lists. Hers was not a bad definition of success.

So she was probably entitled to her desk, Sarah thought, spinning her chair around to look out the window. Out through the trees at Frances's house, where everything was still. Soon the leaves would be in full bloom, and she wouldn't be able to see through at all.

Her desk. "Moms with Desks" was a thing she'd seen online

recently, a page in a slideshow on decluttering and personal organizing. "We know what it's like . . . " the text had read, accompanying a photo of an electric mixer, of all things, with a stack of papers mostly takeout flyers, heaped inside its bowl. "You've got a desk somewhere in the house, but you never use it. Why not move your 'business' down to the place you frequent most—the kitchen?"

Sarah spun around again, full circle, and knocked on her desk's wooden top. Oak. She'd found it on the street years ago and sanded it down and finished it herself. For a while it had been the most solid thing in the universe.

"I just wanted to let you know," she said to Andrea. "If you could keep an eye out for anything that seems unusual . . ."

"Well, I've heard nothing," said Andrea. "I doubt that it's the big time. If it was a journalist or a gossip blogger, someone wanting to expose you, I don't think they'd go about it this way. They'd have blown it all up out in the open." Andrea was probably disappointed this hadn't happened, actually, just as she was continually annoyed by Sarah's refusal to come out of her shadow, to join Twitter, Instagram, and Snapchat. To spread herself thin across the web. Underlining the importance of *exposure* for a writer, when it was the very thing that Sarah and Mitzi both wanted to avoid.

"If anything, it's probably personal. Sounds like a vendetta. I don't know," said Andrea. "Made any enemies lately?"

·   ·   ·

Sarah had started blogging during the loneliest time in her life. Everything she had understood about herself—she was a rising star in the PR industry, a wife, a winner, she was one of the lucky ones—had been revealed to be a fiction. In the final summer of the last year of the old century, her husband, whom she had fancied herself in love with since she was sixteen years old, had broken down and confessed he was gay, and she hadn't even been surprised.

Her first thought, looking down at the coin-sized spot of skin visible through the thinning hair on the back of his head, was "Oh honey. Couldn't you just keep pretending?" Because she was willing. She wanted to have a baby. If she only had a baby, she would have something tangible to take away from all this. Something to prove the years she'd put into their relationship had somehow been worthwhile.

But Greg didn't want to have a baby. It had been the notion of a baby that had driven him to this breaking point. Time stopped while he knelt on the floor beside their bed, weeping, falling entirely apart, and taking her whole life down with him. And then after that, time only moved very slowly.

"You're still young" was what everybody told her, as though this was some kind of consolation. She'd never felt so old, ancient in her rented bachelor apartment with mould crawling up the bathroom wall. The place was all she could afford without her husband's financial support, which she was determined to do without, but her career choices were cast in a different light now that she was on her own. Her place was above a fish shop, and it was summer, and when the windows were open, the air didn't smell like the sea, like she had imagined it might. Grouper kedgeree plaice. When they were rotten, every fish smelled the same.

Grouper kedgeree plaice. Words were so much easier to grasp than thoughts, whole concepts. Words were easier to stack on top on one another, like blocks in a game of Tetris, coming up with something that almost made sense, or something that sounded good, at the very least. If nothing else, she could have euphony.

So she started writing the words down in a diary, an online diary, which seemed particularly private since nobody else she knew spent any time on the Internet. The only people online were lonely just like she was, other people who couldn't sleep at night. It seemed like there was just a handful of them, all networked on the online diary site. This was when she'd never heard of a "blog," let alone a blook.

She wrote about insomnia, the fish shop, the depressing corner into which she'd painted her life. She signed up for dating websites and began to write about that too, the triumphs and the horrors of attempting to begin again. When she finally had sex with a man who wasn't her gay ex-husband (whose condo she had been turning up at regularly for sex, pathetically, in order to satisfy her appetites and possibly to change his mind), her online friends had showered her with jubilation. This was the post that had indicated that perhaps her online diary had some resonance with the wider world. A bunch of popular blogs had linked to her post, which she'd called "Notes on Finally Sleeping with a Heterosexual Male," and the resulting traffic had crashed the server of the online diary site.

The owner of the site had gotten in touch with her after that, suggesting she move her diary to her own domain. He'd designed and built her very own website, which she'd christened *Mitzi Bytes* for a few vague reasons. She liked the Germanic tones of *Mitzi*, which suggested a dominatrix in big leather boots (far from her actual identity, so far that it was more of a joke), and *Bytes* because it had only recently stopped being the 1990s, and she'd intended that her writing have teeth.

Her traffic continued to grow, her candour and humour drawing fans. The Twin Towers had not long ago fallen in New York City, and this had been a peculiar, dark, and despairing time for everybody, her brand of candour a welcome diversion. Her minor Internet celebrity pushed her out of her fishy apartment and into the world, to take chances and go after things to write about. Usually, those things were sex and dating, but behind the scenes, other parts of her life were coming together. She left PR, tired of rebottling other people's words, and got a job writing for a fashion magazine, quickly moving up through the ranks, her performance made all the more impressive for the storytelling skills she'd acquired through blogging. She moved out of the place above the fish shop into her very own condo, into which she'd carried that wooden desk she'd found in the street. She'd borrowed a dolly and brought it three blocks all by herself. It got stuck in the elevator, and her foot had nearly been crushed in the doors, the entire experience wrought with peril but worth it when the desk was finished, wood gleaming in the pot-lit glow of her place. She was beginning to triumph after all.

When people in her real life asked her what she did, it was here she began to tell them, "I'm a writer."

And nobody ever knew where it had all come from. At first because she'd had nobody to tell about Mitzi Bytes, and the grouper kedgeree plaice certainly weren't listening. She learned to cook and found out that kedgeree wasn't even a kind of fish but instead a seafood dish cooked with haddock. And now there were people she was cooking kedgeree for, but she wasn't going to tell them either, because she was starting to no longer be the kind of person who gave head in a taxi. These stories were getting old now, and she didn't want to have to tell them all over again.

Mitzi Bytes may have been famous, but Sarah Lundy wasn't doing too badly either, and it didn't seem in the interest of either for the two personalities to meet. Each could be nurtured independently. Sarah's tendency to fade into the background was what allowed her to absorb the stories all around her. And this way, Mitzi Bytes didn't have to answer to anyone. When has a woman ever been so free?

"So what's the point, then?" the reporter had asked her when her last book came out—*Hot and Heavy*, a collection of domestic tales (sort of ironic, because she had a cleaning lady, but it demonstrated how much her focus had shifted since her *Sex and the City* days). "What do you get out of this?"

To which she hadn't had a definitive answer, except that she couldn't stop writing it even if she'd tried.

And she had tried. Way back when the attention had all got to be too much, and she could sense that she was starting to envision her life as a performance, so focused on picturing herself from the outside that she had forgotten what it meant to feel things, when she despaired for a single thought to go unexpressed, she'd tried to go cold turkey. She wanted the space to get back inside her head, but then being in her head was just too overwhelming without a place for all her stories and thoughts to go.

She had tried proper journals, paper ones and locked journals online, but she missed the engagement. She missed the way her worries could be halved with a good online rant, and then halved again when, not long after, the messages started piling in: "Exactly," they'd tell her. It's like you're living my life. You're reading my mind. You are not alone.

Every time her life had changed—new jobs, moves, getting married, having kids—she'd thought perhaps the time was right now, that here was a natural time for her to shut down the blog. But instead, the blog came with her, growing and evolving as her life did. Where it had once been a place for performance, it was now more for reflection, a change that hadn't been popular with advertisers who didn't like their brands being associated with some discomfiting or controversial topics she wrote about, but her traffic remained strong. The readers were reading because they'd been growing up alongside her, and she continued to write because the world around her never ceased to inspire.

"How do you find the time?" interviewers always asked her. The time for this secret self on top of all the other things a person had to be. But Sarah didn't even have to look for the time—it was right by her always, as long as she reached for it. Going about spending her days, she spun blog posts in her head, and then to finally sit down and type them out was like a reflex, a release. As Mitzi Bytes, she had nothing to prove, no one to impress or be held accountable to. That voice was her voice, the distillation of her purest self.

"Made any enemies lately?" Andrea's question echoed in Sarah's mind after their conversation was over. Andrea had been joking but not entirely—Sarah's whole blog persona was based on being at odds with the world. After she had logged on to Facebook and scanned her Friends list, though, no one immediately came to mind. Half the people there she hadn't talked to since high school.

While she saved her astringency for Mitzi Bytes, Sarah Lundy herself was only regarded as a mildly disagreeable human being. Most of the time she blended into crowds, didn't talk too much, and tried not to rock the boat, her flouting of expectations for school volunteerism aside. And even that manifested in just not showing up, which was the easiest way Sarah knew to cause no offence. No one in her periphery cared about her enough to online-stalk her so thoroughly that they'd connect the dots between Mitzi Bytes and Sarah Lundy. The people she knew were too busy for that.

The connection was unlikely anyway. Back when Sarah had written magazine profiles, she'd discerned that few people were wise enough not to be surprised by how they were perceived by the world. She was confident the people she wrote about on her blog would never recognize themselves, but even so, she tried to hide identifying details—she used bright and vivid photography, but with images that were abstract, of the way that sunshine fell upon the wood grain of a table, the dimple on her daughter's elbow, a sopping red umbrella dripping in the hall. She tried for a similar effect with her writing. Mitzi Bytes was an any-woman whose wit was as sharp as the focus on the startlingly good camera on her phone, and this had always been her chief appeal.

And Sarah Lundy, a less charismatic figure, did her best to counter her extraordinary secret fortunes, which had been born from often-uncharitable points of view, by putting good karma in the world. She was an excellent wife, mother, and friend. Usually. She tutored teen moms; delivered lasagnas when her neighbours were in the hospital; tried to remember to call her own mother, and sometimes she did. She used her *Maplewood Village Sentinel* platform in the name of social justice, speaking in favour of keeping open the local shelter for abused women, and highlighting worthy charitable projects.

At least this was the CV that Sarah called to mind when presented with a question of whether she'd made any enemies lately. This was the kind of track record she had to remind herself of after making a small but tidy financial profit from secretly skewering the lives of others. How to counter the notion that she was indeed, as many a commenter on her blog had suggested, "one nasty piece of work."

· · ·

By the afternoon, her fears had started to fade. Talking to Andrea had put the previous day's event in perspective—it was an email, it could be nothing, probably harmless, another crank. She'd known plenty of those. She felt settled enough to have lunch. She finished tidying up the kitchen, reset the kids' bedrooms, took deep breaths periodically to steady herself. She still couldn't face the blog, but she had an hour and a half before she had to pick up the kids, so she went up to her office with a big cup of tea and transcribed the words of one Betty Sullivan, who'd started a babysitting co-op for local mothers who'd worked in the factories while their husbands were overseas.

"And these girls turned out to be the loves of my life," Betty Sullivan was explaining, exhaling. She must have been smoking. She had a hacking cough. Sarah could just imagine the state of her lungs. "The greatest friends I've ever known."

Sarah brought a novel to school pickup—Virginia Woolf's *To the Lighthouse*; she was reading it for book club—looking forward to reading on the playground sidelines while Gladys and Clementine played with their friends. But there was too much company, so the book stayed in her bag. She ended up on the bench beside Cherry, who was Gladys's best friend Paige Kincardine's nanny.

"I am motherfucking Mary Poppins" was how Cherry presented herself when she met people for the first time, because she had a Canadian boyfriend who had taught her to swear. Cherry cared for Paige three days a week, the other days Paige's mother, Claudia, fetching her at the end of the school day, a switch-off that Sarah appreciated because of how talking to both women gave her such a vivid picture of the life they shared.

"All I ask" is how Claudia started most of her sentences, which were always about Cherry, the drama fraught between them. "All I ask is that if she starts a load of laundry, she finishes it. Nobody likes to find a washer full of wet clothes that have been sitting there all day."

"All I ask," said Claudia, "is that she show a little initiative. If there are dishes in the sink, wash them. Something's on the floor, pick it up."

"I am motherfucking Mary Poppins," said Cherry, snapping her gum and not letting her conversation with Sarah slow her flying thumbs as she texted message after message out into the world. ("Who are you talking to?" Sarah had asked her. "My fucking people," Cherry said.)

Cherry wasn't wrong with the Mary Poppins reference. Her considerable talents did not end with flying thumbs but extended to an ability to stare down children into good behaviour, beatboxing, a knack for cat's cradle, and even the magical bag she carried, unremarkable-sized but which always seemed to contain sidewalk chalk, skipping ropes for everyone, washed and sliced organic fruit, and a freshly baked loaf of something.

"She's going to fire me," Cherry said to Sarah, still texting, not taking her eyes off the children, who had turned the space under the slide into a bakery counter and were selling sand-cakes, using wood chips for currency. She offered Sarah a Tupperware of cantaloupe ripe to perfection, artisanally sliced, the rinds removed.

"She's not."

"For real, this time," said Cherry. "I asked for five weeks off. To go see my mom." Cherry's mother had been ailing for a while, and most of her earnings went back to the Philippines to care for her and Cherry's children, who were being raised by her sister. "Do you know how long it takes to get there? The cost? I want to make it worth it. Five weeks, I say. I'll take it unpaid. I need the time. And she's so mad now."

"She says, 'All I ask is that you take the vacation time we agreed on.' Four weeks, she said, and not all in one chunk. And I told her that my mother was sick, and this was different. She said, 'Cherry, I can't just take five weeks off from my job.' She said, 'That's what a job is. You go to work.' She says I'm acting entitled. Unprofessional."

Sarah had heard it all from the other side the day before. She doubted that Claudia was going to fire her, but she was upset. Claudia was one of the mothers who liked to claim that their nanny was a part of the family, until she had the nerve to act familiar, to ask for anything at all. Having your nanny disappear for five weeks was inconvenient, but then so was having to travel halfway across the world to watch your mother die.

"She'll get over it," said Sarah. "Just do what you have to do, and don't press the point. She needs space to rage away in, but then she'll settle down."

"I don't know," said Cherry. "I make her mad all the time, but this was different. She was serious. I could tell by her eyes."

"You mean how they turned red, then smoke started coming out her ears?" asked Sarah. She ate another melon slice. They were full of flavour, at the peak of perfect ripeness. "And the matter of the forked tail? The horns?"

"See, you know exactly how it is," said Cherry. "None of the bullshit." She called out into the playground, "Paige, stop hitting the little girl. And get off the ground. You'll get wood chips in your underwear." She turned back to Sarah. "She gets wood chips in her underwear. Your kids get that?"

"And grass and sand. Unimaginable filth. Disgusting children. One of these days, I'll show you between their toes. You won't believe the things I've found there."

Cherry said, "And there you go again. I love it. The way you hang your laundry out so everyone can see."

●　●　●

Managing the house between 5 p.m. and bedtime called for a certain kind of acrobatics, frenzied feet keeping the wheels on and turning, all the while her arms busy juggling multiple balls. Sarah had dinner on, sorting out school bags and homework assignments, waiting for the phone to ring, Chris providing an estimate for his homecoming. Packing tomorrow's lunches, and getting the kids fed and bathed, indeed an epic endeavour, the scrubbing required to remove the sand embedded in Gladys's scalp, shaking the wood chips out of *her* underwear.

And then, finally, there was time to be still, and she and the girls collapsed onto Clementine's bed with a pile of books. Books by Virginia Lee Burton, Marie-Louise Gay, Shirley Hughes, and Bob Graham. Jillian, Jillian, Jillian Jiggs. *Mabel Murple*, about a purple girl in a purple world—still Clementine's favourite even though she was into chapter books by now. These books were all their favourites, the picture books both girls shoved into their mother's hands, even though they could read themselves by now. And then *Harriet the Spy*, which Clementine appreciated for its wickedness, most of it going over Gladys's head, but not entirely, because she'd lately taken to carrying around a notebook of her own, most of her notes illegible on account that she hadn't yet learned how to write.

"I want a tomato sandwich," said Clementine.

"Tomorrow," said Sarah, kissing her big daughter's forehead, then scooping up the little one to deliver her to her own room.

"Sweet dreams," she said, leaving Clementine in bed reading *Zita the Space Girl*.

Sarah deposited Gladys in her bed, pulled the covers up to her chin. She heard her phone vibrating on the table in the hall, and she just knew that this was it—another message from Jane Q. Lingering in Gladys's room because she really didn't want to know, but Gladys's eyes were falling down.

"'Night," she whispered, a kiss on the softest cheek, and then she went out into the hall, closing the door behind her on account of the monsters. Clementine liked hers open for the very same reason. Her monsters were apparently claustrophobic, while Gladys's were deterred by the dark. Either way, both girls were safe.

∙ ∙ ∙

She had her phone in her hand when she heard Chris come in. He was later than he said he'd be. She'd stayed logged in to her secret Mitzi account—her stress was making her sloppy, threatening to expose her tracks. And sure enough, there was another message from Jane Q. *Have been reading your archives. You're like a monster, some kind of vampire. You can't do what you do, can't take what you took, without paying some kind of price. I'm going to make sure you do.* A second message sent just moments after the first: *Are you nervous yet?* This was a bit persistent, if nonsensical—what exactly had Sarah taken? But not a person going nowhere.

"Hello?" called Chris from the hall downstairs.

Sarah shoved her phone in a drawer and went down to see him.

"Stop it," she called as she overlooked the railing.

"What?" He looked alarmed.

"Your hair." Chris had mad scientist hair, and he liked to rake his fingers through it. But his hairline was beginning to recede, and she was concerned that all the raking would hasten its demise. "Never mind," she said. He was looking at her funny, as though she wasn't quite in focus. She grabbed his ears so she could pull him down and kiss his forehead. She felt him relax in her arms. "Welcome home," she said.

He kicked off his shoes into the pile by the door and dumped a pile of papers on the table. "How are things?" he said.

She said, "Thing-like. Ever much the same, I mean. The girls are fine." And Chris was home. She curled around him like a cat, tracing her hand across his chest, his back. "It's good to see you." He held her tight, inhaling her scent. She said, "They're probably still up if you want to go. They were waiting for you. Why don't you run upstairs and say good night?" And he did, the pad of his sock feet on the stairs, the stairs' familiar creaks, the sound of him and their home. At this time of day it was dark outside, but their rooms were full of light. Looking out the window, her existence was confirmed in a series of images a thousand times over.

From the Archives: Mitzi Bytes
Part of the Family

My neighbour's nanny sleeps in a closet. A generous-sized closet, but it's closer to a cell than a bedroom, no window or ventilation, and a door that doesn't lock. And if that weren't bad enough, my neighbour has taken to complaining that her nanny doesn't spend enough time in the closet. That she is forever encroaching on the family's space, getting in the way and apparently undermining my neighbour's ability to parent.

"Sometimes we just want to sit down to dinner as a family," she says. "But she is always there. Looming."

I've suggested to my neighbour that perhaps she get a nanny who lives out. I've suggested to their nanny that she get another job, she but doesn't have her visa yet, and the family is her sponsor. The arrangement works well for my neighbour because she gets to pay less for childcare and still have it available at odd hours in accordance with her shift work at the hospital.

Next door at our house, the closets are closets, but that doesn't make the childcare problem any simpler. My girl is in daycare, an arrangement that devours a sizable chunk of my respectable salary each month. So yes, I have become one of those people with good reason to complain about the cost of childcare . . . as performed by people (women!) who are themselves paid minimum wage.

Could you honestly think of a way to make this system any worse?

And that's why, when all the middle-class mommies start arguing with all their stupid acronyms—SAHM, WFHM . . . not to mention the full-time moms, and what about the half-time moms, because there is such a thing, right?—I am sure there is an evil bureaucrat somewhere cackling with glee at this state of affairs. He (and he is certainly a he) came up with this plan to keep the mommy wars in perpetuity, in order that nobody ever notices the truth. We've got nannies in the closets and fetuses on daycare wait-lists, with the people who care for them getting paid next to nothing. It's a labour issue, it's a women's issue, and we're all blind to it, calling each other names over the playground fence, failing to see that the childcare problem is not just matter of personal choice but instead a symptom of systemic failure.

Okay, I'll get off my stump now. And obviously, I'm not calling for an end to name calling over fences, because I've made a career out of that. But can't we please keep an eye on the bigger picture? And if you must keep your nanny in a closet, please don't bitch about her where I have a chance to overhear you. Or I will have to write about you on my blog.

CHAPTER 3

· · · · · · · · · · · · · · ·

I f there had been a book subtitled *Looking for Love in All the Wrong Places*, Sarah could have written it. Or rather, there was such a book, and Sarah *had* written it (her first), documenting the various locations to which she'd gone searching for love and been sorely disappointed.

The book's chapters were as follows:

1   Weddings
2   Ultimate Frisbee
3   Wall Climbing
4   Frat Houses
5   Dance Clubs
6   The Library
7   Canoe Trips
8   The Internet
9   Church
10 The Dentist
11 The Dog Park

When love finally did show its face, she'd been least expecting it, which was what everyone had been telling her all along, and it didn't make their advice any less annoying when it turned out they were right.

It happened in the laundry room of their building, a subterranean hideout whose musty smell was overwhelmed by the scent of fabric softener.

"I'm allergic to perfume, and whenever I come in here, the smell makes me want to die" was one of the first things she'd ever said to Chris.

"What smell?" he'd asked, looking up from his whites, which was her first introduction to his general obliviousness.

And it's true that while the attraction wasn't immediate, the first time she saw his face, she couldn't look away. He needed a haircut, he was curiously dressed for the laundry room in a button-down and jeans that she could have sworn were pressed, plus he was sorting through a basket containing a mountain of once-upon-a-time-white briefs. But none of that mattered as much as his eyes, which were watching her intently. She felt like she'd never encountered anyone who paid so much attention, who gave her all he had. He was so tall, a stature that could have been imposing, but his eyes were gentle, and his smile was real. He'd asked her a question and was waiting for the answer. Simple as that.

"You really can't smell it?" she asked him, and he shook his head. Smiling still, folding his underwear. "It gives me the most incredible headache."

They'd chatted while she waited for her cycle to finish, introducing themselves at the end. She said she'd see him around.

On Monday after work, she'd gone to check her mail and found a printout of all the laundromats in the area, each of them plotted on a map, with details about one in particular that was fragrance-free.

When she was coming out of the mailroom, Greta, the concierge, waved her over. "He was asking about you," she said, gesturing toward the paper in her hand. "Wanted to get that to you, but he didn't want to cross any lines. He knew your first name, and I knew who he meant, so I delivered it for him."

"Christopher Bennett," Sarah said, saying aloud the name she'd been thinking over and over since the night before, but every time with a brief hesitation, as though to suggest she were tentative. She held his message with both hands. "What unit is he in, Greta?" she asked. "Because I'd like to thank him for this. That is, of course, unless *I* shouldn't cross the line."

"Oh, my friend," said Greta, "you'd make a good man very happy if you crossed the line. He's in 303."

She went down later that evening, knocked softly on his door. This was a big move. People never just dropped in to condo units. She'd probably give him a heart attack. But he didn't look disturbed when he came to the door.

She said, "I wanted to thank you for this. This is . . . useful."

He hung in the door frame, reluctant to let her see inside, let alone invite her in. But he said, "We could go together sometime, you know. A laundry date. Are you free next Saturday?"

It was unbearably perfect. The geeky neighbour, those manky off-white briefs, Saturday night exploring the local laundry scene, and she wrote the hell out of all of it. Never had she been presented with material this good that wasn't somehow harmful to her mental health or putting at risk her physical well-being. Her readers loved it, or at least some of them did, and then others left messages informing her of what she'd known from the start: she was going to break The Programmer's heart. Because clearly, he'd fallen in love with her.

So for six months, they were friends. She'd given it to him straight: she wasn't looking for anything more, it hadn't been long since her divorce, she still had a lot of recovering to do. Though this wasn't the whole story. Fundamentally, she wasn't attracted to Chris, which was at the root of everything, never mind the cow eyes and his kindness. She wanted what every girl wanted, as she wrote on her blog: she was looking for a spark.

And then Chris got a girlfriend. Unlikely, or maybe not unlikely because he was the kind of guy who was thoughtful enough to deliver printouts of local laundromats to a woman with fragrance issues. But still, Sarah was shocked. First, that here she was, still single, after all the trouble she'd taken to remedy the problem, whereas Chris had just stumbled onto full-blown romance with a woman from his office. She'd met the two of them one afternoon for coffee, and the girlfriend hadn't even been pretty.

Sarah had had to suffer watching them kiss goodbye, and then summon a smile herself and lie, "Nice to meet you." Though it had not been nice at all.

"Did you like her?" Chris asked her as the two of them walked back toward their building. He'd been anxious about their meeting. "I want you to like her," he said. "It's important to me." He stopped walking and faced her, waiting to hear what she was going to say. He had such unlimited patience about the things that really mattered. He would have stood there forever.

Suddenly, she couldn't be polite anymore. Even at the best of times, she found it difficult, but now was just impossible. She said, "No."

"No?"

"Would it be so terrible?" she asked him. "If maybe I've fallen in love with you?"

Which should have been the end of it, straight to Happily Ever After, but this was Chris, who wasn't primed for fairy-tale narratives and unexpected twists. There in the street, he'd actually cried, and then said he couldn't be friends with her, and that he didn't understand why she had to make things so complicated.

Now, it wasn't strictly true that Sarah had fallen in love with him, not at that point, but what she'd fallen into instead was an awareness that she possibly could. It wasn't a spark but something slower, quieter, and persistent. The feeling she got whenever she found him at her door—that this was home. He liked her for her very best self, drawing out the person she wanted most to be: strong, confident, smart, and funny. A person who was more or less the same on the inside and out—it was a revelation that this was possible in a relationship. So she was despondent to find her great confession had driven Chris out of her life altogether.

Until three weeks later when he'd shown up at her door on a Thursday night. "She broke up with me," he said. The girl had accused him of having other things on his mind. "So how about now?" They'd gone to bed, and the rest was blog history.

•　　•　　•

Chris came downstairs now, more than ten years older but exactly the same in all the fundamental ways. He was the opposite of every other interesting person she'd ever known, whose layers were peeled back to reveal a series of surprises but also incongruities and disappointments. With Chris there were no layers, but instead an uncomplicated solidity she liked to throw her arms around.

She was sitting in the kitchen, having poured them both some wine, when he walked in carrying her phone.

"What are you doing with that?" she asked, and he didn't notice the edge in her voice. Chris didn't pay much attention to tone. This was sometimes useful and sometimes not.

He dropped it on the table before her. She turned it off before she turned it over. "It was buzzing in the drawer," he said. "I could hear it." He sat down beside her and took a sip from his glass. "Gladys is asleep already," he said. "Clem's on her way."

"Tonight she asked me what a Gestapo was," said Sarah. "It was in the book we're reading. I told her they were really mean police."

"More or less the truth," said Chris. "What are you reading?"

"It was out of context," said Sarah. "A throwaway remark. It's just an innocent book."

"An innocent book? That doesn't sound like you." Sarah smiled. He said, "Your hair looks pretty." He reached out to touch her cheek. She took off her glasses. Her hair was pulled back in a ponytail as usual, but strands had come loose around her face. He'd learned to pay attention to those details because it was important to her to know that he really saw her, and that he could attempt to articulate his vision. She would tell him things, and he listened, took notes. He delivered. He said, "How was your day today?"

"Fraught."

"More than usual?"

"Not just with the girls. With everyone I talked to, there was just this tension. And then I thought I saw somebody in Frances's yard, somebody trying to get into the garage. So I made this big deal of wading through the muck to find out what it was, and it was nothing. I'm like Neighbourhood Watch, but there is nothing to see. I'm wasted here. Plus I'm getting paranoid."

"You need to get out more."

"But whenever I get out, I end up fighting with somebody. About olive oil. You see my dilemma?"

"About olive oil?"

"More wine?" She topped up their glasses. "How are you?" she asked.

"Glad to see you." Lately, Chris had been developing Android apps. The ins and outs of his day were less scintillating than even hers were. The facts and details he worked with were intangible to the average mind, and she didn't understand them at all, which he was fine with. He would say that he came home so that he didn't have to be at work. He didn't need to talk about it.

At first Sarah had interpreted this attitude to mean that he was unhappy at work, but he'd set her straight. "I love it," he told her. "It's great to do. Just not to talk about."

"But isn't it weird," she asked, "that there is this whole side of your life that I don't know about?"

He shrugged. "Keeps me interesting." She smiled. "No, I'm serious. If I started talking about work, I would bore you to death. This is something I worked out the hard way." So she said nothing now, took a sip of her wine. They were so content in silence. It was a perfect arrangement, but maybe it was fragile. She didn't know. They'd never been tested.

She said, "Everything is okay, right?"

"How?"

"I mean, if there was something wrong or strange, you could tell me, right?"

"What's going on?"

She said, "It's nothing."

"What is?"

"I mean *there's* nothing." He wouldn't press the point. The thing about Chris was that he thought nobody else had layers either. If you couldn't see it, there was nothing there. The forest and the trees, perhaps, but that would be the entire story. He accepted things, he was unflappable. And if that unflappability had a limit, she hadn't got there yet. She hadn't even come close.

•   •   •

Are you nervous yet?

She turned on her phone, and there it was, the latest message. Taunting her. And she didn't have to consider the question long to know the answer was yes. Which was a curious thing, because she'd never been nervous before. She had always been so assured, confident in her justifications. "I'm only ever honest," she'd written a thousand times, and reported to journalists who dared to wonder how she thought she could get away with a double life.

Though she wasn't even being honest about that. She was only honest by matter of a technicality, which was that Chris never knew enough to ask about her work, but honesty wasn't a technical matter. Or at least it shouldn't be. She'd have no truck with such things if she was on the receiving end of it all, but she and Chris were different people. Wasn't this the very point?

What would it take? she wondered, still sitting at the table, watching the back of his head as he watched the TV. How far could she go before he didn't know her anymore? She put down

the phone—this person wasn't going to get a rise out of her—
and leaned on her elbows, massaging her head.

He said, "You know, I see you."

"What?"

"I can see you," he said. He turned around, and there
was his face. Full on. "Your reflection in the screen. I see you
watching me."

"So?"

"So nothing. But why don't you come over and sit down?"

From the Archives: Mitzi Bytes
An Unexpected Twist

Well, the earth moved. First, like the shifting of tectonic plates, the ground beneath my feet undertaking a brand new composition. It's like that line about never
stepping into the same river twice, except I'm walking down the street, and I've
walked down this street a thousand times, but the pavement is different now,
stronger and more solid, and it seems to be holding steady. The tectonic plate
comparison ending when it comes to fault lines and cracks in the ground—every
metaphor has its limits. But really, there's nothing here to trip me up, for the first
time in my life. And as with any earthquake, I didn't see it coming.

But I am going to have to back up here. Gentle reader, get ready for the
longest post I've ever written, or at least the longest I've posted since the Tighty-
Whitie screed. I regret you've been out of the loop. It's possible that even I have
been out of the loop, all this time I was loping through marshes after birdwatchers,
having sex on fire escapes, and not having sex at all with anyone at horseback-
riding school, though not for lack of trying. All the while I was looking for love, not
knowing that love was in front of my face. Or at least as close as a ride in the
elevator, and a short walk down the hall.

Though perhaps I don't have to lay it all out for you after all. It's possible that you knew better than I did. That as of very late on Thursday, I am very probably in love with The Programmer. That somehow, even with his unfortunate under-attire, this man has programmed his way into my heart.

It had been platonic between the two of us since last spring, when he kissed me and I went along with it, just to see where we might go, but then I realized that his feeling for me extended beyond idle curiosity. And that wasn't fair, so we stopped kissing, I started riding horses, and we still hung out, being neighbours after all. I liked him, but I didn't *like* him; there was considerable warmth, but there was no spark. And I thought that was the end of it until very recently.

It turns out that minds can change, though, that a woman might not know her own self, that plans can alter, the earth can move. And oh my, did the earth move.

We've had a complicated few weeks, The Programmer and I, as we struggled to work out where we were standing. There were bumps in the road and mis-understandings. Hearts were bruised and everyone cried, and then he knocked on my door on Thursday, just days after I'd accepted that I might never see him again. While at the back of my mind, of course, I kept the secret hope that things would come to pass exactly as they did. (Sometimes it is impossible to wonder if I'm not actually the architect of the universe after all.)

So I knew it would be him when I answered the door. We'd been waiting so long—weeks or months, depending on your vantage point. He said, "How about now?" and I had no reason to argue. He stepped into my place, and he kissed me, sure of himself this time. And I wasn't even curious, because I knew very well where all this would take us.

The kiss itself was the first sign, like the meeting of minds. The meeting of mouths? In this way, we seemed to be immediately compatible. He was taller than anyone I've ever been with, and the only problem was that standing there in the hall, he had to lean down to kiss me, and I was straining my head looking up, so I migrated us to my couch, where he sat down and I straddled him.

It occurred to me that I must have dreamt this already. Because it all seemed so familiar, though I swear I'd never contemplated it once during waking hours.

Just how it would be, I mean, negotiating with the realities of this particular body, its edges and contours. But there was no negotiation about it. I unbuttoned his shirt, because as ever he was wearing a shirt with buttons, never mind how I longed for a garment I could whip off over his head in an instant. He leaned forward so I could pull it over his shoulders, push it down off his back, his head in my neck, breathing deeply as though to absorb the entire moment. And then here was his chest, its small dark nipples and springy hair, the smoothest skin, this body I'd been working toward my whole life.

I was kissing his shoulders, licking his nipples. I felt him hard where my legs were wrapped around him, and I pulled myself closer. I helped him pull my tank top over my head, and he reached around to unfasten my bra. Suddenly, his mouth was full of me—he was a man ravenous for tits, and then his face was smothered between them, licking my sweat with a tongue that drove me crazy.

He was reaching for my jeans, the waistband.

"We can slow down," I said.

He shook his head. "I want to get you naked."

Keep in mind that this is The Programmer, the world's most considerate and gentle soul. I'd never known him to want a thing in his life, except for a general level of human decency and perhaps a pint of beer at the end of a long day. It's not that he's a bland guy, although he sort of is, if you're not looking hard enough, but instead that impulse control was basically his religion. He called it civility.

But where was civility now as he tore off my pants? We moved down to the floor, where I shook them off, and he shimmied out of his own neat khakis and the white briefs I'd been prepared for. I tossed them both aside. And what had just been revealed was most impressive, though perhaps my impression is just coloured by love (love!), but it really was the most beautiful penis I'd ever seen. Smooth, hard, and perfect, I thought, as I kissed its length, and then I took it in my mouth, thinking this man deserved what he wanted because he'd waited all this time, but that wasn't it, it seemed.

He said, "I want to fuck you." (And I'd never even heard him swear.)

I said, "We need a condom."

He said, "Go get one." Breathing hard. We were trying to manage this conversation whilst molesting every inch of the other's body.

"I don't have one," I said. This was true. I'd been seeing Rod the Rod on the weekends, and he always came with his own equipment. It was Thursday night. I'd forecasted a night in with the TV, which was still playing on the screen just above my head.

"I've got to turn that off," I said, fumbling up on the table for the remote. There was no sound, but the movement was distracting. "Haven't you got anything?" I asked him. "Even downstairs?" Though the truth was, I was willing to forgo all caution. It was The Programmer after all. I was thinking, *And I'm going to have your babies one of these days, so why not now instead of later.* I had him in my hands, and I wanted him so bad.

But he was The Programmer after all, even if he said *fuck*. He didn't want to fuck me bad enough to take a chance, to do the wrong thing, which was the opposite of human decency. He said, "Never mind, there will be time for that," and then he buried his head between my legs, his tongue deep inside me, displaying an oral dexterity I'd never known. His ability to be in all places at once, a fluttering tongue that rubbed me hard. And it was nearly instantaneous. I was airborne, exploding. It went on and on and on, and when it was over, he sat up, wiped his face. I started to cry.

He said, "What's wrong?" Becoming deflated in every sense. I tried to tell him I was okay, but I was crying too hard. He said, "What happened? Wasn't that all right?"

"It was so all right," I told him, then I sputtered, "but but but." How to put it. That all this time I'd been thinking about his terrible underpants and bad haircut, imagining the two of us as two worlds colliding, except that he was kind of the Third World, socially speaking. That I was brightening up his world by merely being in it, when here he was outranking me in this fundamental way. "Whatever that was," I said, "I've never felt that before."

"No one's ever gone down on you?"

"Not like that," I said. "Like my entire body hurtling in space. Like every nerve was attuned to a separate sensation. It was terrifying, enormous. It was wonderful. And I can't do that to you."

"You can't?"

"Oh, I can do it. But nothing special. And that was special." I was crying again.

"Seriously, do you even know your powers? Has nobody ever told you?"

"So it was good, then?"

"Good?"

"Please, just stop crying." He leaned over and he kissed me. "You're so great but you're acting crazy," he told me. "You're making me scared."

CHAPTER 4

. . . .

S arah liked to imagine that she had a talent for friendship, though it might have been by virtue of the friends, Janie and Beth-Ellen, who had been her friends for decades. Janie was a chemist, which had been her ambition since long before Sarah met her during their first week at university. The only person Sarah had ever met whose aspiration was to build bombs. Everybody else she knew wanted to ban them, but Janie said the bombs were going to be built, so why shouldn't she be the builder, with improved accuracy, less toxicity, and minimized casualties no less. Besides, the Cold War was over, and warfare was going to be theoretical anyway.

Sarah listened to all this as they walked together in the Frosh Parade, appalled but also fascinated. She'd preferred to spout political nonsense gleaned from T-shirt slogans and buttons on anarchists' backpacks. She realized that she'd never had an original thought in her life.

Yes, Janie. *Jane Q*. Sarah had skipped the connection. At first. Her friends weren't like that. There were a lot of Janes, and her Jane's surname did not begin with Q. Plus, anonymous email seemed oddly passive for someone who built weapons, and anonymous emails were also the mark of insanity. Janie herself was a model of rational thinking, sometimes insufferably so, and she would have picked a better pseudonym.

Blackmail wasn't Beth-Ellen's style either. She was too forthright. Beth-Ellen had been Sarah's first-year roommate, small and unassuming, and looked twelve, which had been strange when they were eighteen, and now that they'd reached their forties was uncanny. Her looks meant that she tended to be underestimated, and this was always a mistake, because she saw everything, Beth-Ellen, behind those same round glasses she'd always had, that were bigger than her face.

As she entered the restaurant, Sarah saw Beth-Ellen waiting at their table, reading a book, so self-contained even when caught unaware. Looking up from her reading as Sarah approached, her expression avid with something. Sarah stopped. She was nervous now. She was tempted to turn around and run. Was this an ambush? Was she going crazy?

And she probably was, because Beth-Ellen only wanted to talk about the book in her hand. She waved it in the air. *To the Lighthouse.* "I have to get it done," she said. She had two-year-old triplets, which made it difficult to get anything done. She'd only recently come back to their book club after a very long hiatus. "I haven't read it for years," she said. "I haven't read anything for years. This is so wonderful."

Beth-Ellen indicated the pot of tea at Sarah's place at the table. "It's been steeping," she said. "Should be ready by now." Back to the book, which would be under discussion at their next book club gathering. "I was worried that everybody might hate it. I don't know if I could bear that." The book had been her choice.

"No," said Sarah, pouring her tea, which was a fragrant Cream of Earl Grey. "It was a very good pick." She held the cup to her lip and breathed in the scent. The tea was still too hot to drink. "Anyway, happy birthday." She put down the cup and reached to squeeze her friend's arm. "You've gotten old again." Beth-Ellen was the eldest of the three, and her birthdays always felt like a milestone. A few months down the line when Sarah reached the same age, she'd be accustomed to it. Sarah pulled out her phone—there were no messages. She noted the time. "Did Janie say she'd be late?"

"A few minutes," said Beth-Ellen. "She texted."

Sarah looked out at the other diners in the restaurant—everyone looked suspicious in a certain kind of light.

"You're distracted," said Beth-Ellen. "What is it?"

"Nothing," said Sarah.

"Uh-huh?" Beth-Ellen was calling bullshit. She was skilled in this department, which had helped in her career as a political affairs reporter, but she was less intimidating since her boys had been born. It was easy now to steer her off course.

"So, how's the sleep?" Sarah asked. Beth-Ellen's favourite subject, and Beth-Ellen launched into an agonizing description of recent nights. She had an entire library at home devoted to sleep books, a sign of her faith in the power of the written word. That in one of these books she'd find the magic solution to getting three small boys to slumber at the same time.

"So I feel like a zombie," she explained. "But it's my birthday. And I'm out in the world. *Lunching*." A great indulgence. Her parents had come over to watch the boys. "I got to read Virginia Woolf on the subway." Not a sleep book. "Except that I'm so tired, it makes me fall asleep."

And there was Janie, leaning over to kiss Beth-Ellen's cheek.

"Wake up," she said. "Happy birthday." She sat down in the third chair. "Sorry I'm late."

"I was regaling Sarah with my sleep woes."

"Sorry I missed that," said Janie. "I thought you'd order me a coffee," she said, signalling to the waiter.

Beth-Ellen said, "It would have been cold by now."

"I have had a day," said Janie. "Not to detract from the occasion, of course. But, jeez." Professionally, Janie was frustrated. War in the twenty-first century had turned out to be far from what she expected, and she dropped out of the weapons industry a few years in, leaving behind her humane bomb-making dreams and the accompanying huge salary. Her industry success had won her a prestigious professorship at the university, but she was forever stymied—layers of bureaucracy, cuts to funding and her academic freedom, plus the students who cheated on assignments by sharing their answers on Facebook.

"Right there on the class page," she said. "And they see nothing wrong with it. They all think they're so damn smart with all of their eighteen years. Eyes gleaming, and they shoot back at me, 'Well, is a calculator cheating?' Nodding, arms folded, as though they've really got me there. And then I get called out for being a bitch. They write that right there on Facebook too. And each of these children is so remarkably stupid, but not enough people have ever told them so."

"It's the problem with parents today," said Beth-Ellen, light shining off her lenses. "We should all go home tonight and be sure to tell our kids they're idiots."

"A little of that might go a long way," said Janie as her coffee arrived. She gulped half of it, then leaned back in her chair and sighed. She hadn't addressed Sarah directly, not even once. Was she consciously avoiding conversation?

But no, this was farfetching. Janie had only just sat down. From her corner, Sarah could observe no evidence that anything was wrong in their triangle. And she would have sensed it, she was sure, with these friends she knew as well as she knew herself. But then they'd probably say the same thing about her. And the whole problem—what she feared the most but also clung to—was what if they actually did?

They were watching her. "You look worried," Janie told her.

"Doesn't she?" said Beth-Ellen.

"The lines on your forehead," said Janie. "What is it?"

"You're worried," said Beth-Ellen.

Sarah said, "Do you want me to be worried?" She assured them she was fine. Just wrinkled. She'd had trouble sleeping the night before, she started to say, but Beth-Ellen gave her a dirty look. She took a deep breath and attempted to relax her expression, and they were still looking at her. Beth-Ellen said, "What now?"

She threw her hands in front of her face and hid. "Stop it." But they would not accept this.

"You're acting crazy," said Janie.

"You're driving me to it," Sarah said.

"Maybe we should leave her alone," said Beth-Ellen, who then embarked upon an analysis of the complexities of toilet training three children at once. "I'm doing everything the book says, but it's still not working."

Sarah was relieved but disappointed to find the subject so rapidly changed. It would be something, actually, to get to the point.

Talk had gone on. "Fuck the book," said Janie. She'd been a stepmother for years, and considered the concerns of biological parents tedious. Her situation, she said, afforded her the necessary perspective. "*I* should write a book," she'd been known to say, but right now she was explaining, "They're going to piss on the floor, and then one day they won't, and it's got nothing to do with you."

She looked for support from Sarah, who nodded, but a second too late. It was hard to keep up. One would suppose that after all these years of duplicity, she'd be well versed in faking, but she'd never had to try before. It had always been so easy to keep Mitzi Bytes separate from the rest of her life, but now the borders were blurred, and Mitzi was everything.

Her friends. How much of their stories had she mined, and to what ends? It was getting very difficult to keep everything straight. You could keep spreadsheets upon spreadsheets on all this stuff. Would either of them fall under a category called "People I've Betrayed"?

"I get the feeling you're not all that interested in the ins and outs of triplet toilet training," said Beth-Ellen.

"No, it's scintillating," said Sarah. "Really."

"So what, then?" asked Beth-Ellen. They all paused.

But it was other people, obviously. They started talking about their friend Michelle, with the propensity for married men; about their mothers; about Beth-Ellen's feuding neighbours. Suddenly there was nothing stilted about their conversation at all.

Sarah said, "And I'm seeing Leslie, on Friday." Poor Leslie. The three of them sighed in harmonic concern.

"How's she doing?" asked Janie. If Leslie was doing well, there'd be nothing left to talk about.

"The same, I think," said Sarah. This was confirmed by Beth-Ellen who'd seen her a few weeks before. So they could go on to address Leslie's poor choices, their consequences, and how she never asked for help.

"It's too much," said Beth-Ellen, whose triplets were a handful, but she had plenty of support. Her boys had arrived after years of struggle with infertility—a blessing. Whereas Leslie was raising her severely autistic son alone, no relief on the horizon.

"She doesn't make it easy on herself," said Janie.

And the whole scenario reminded Sarah of Betty Sullivan and the heritage tapes, what her friends had termed her Old Lady Project. She filled them in on the babysitting co-op, how these women had supported each other, about the marvel of decades-long female friendships. "Though I think they ended up with emphysema, all of them."

"Remember my cousin Patsy?" said Beth-Ellen. "Used to smoke like a chimney?" Patsy had since quit smoking and also her entire career to stay at home with her kids. "She's started a Simple Living blog."

"A Simple Living blog—is that a thing?"

"She's trying to monetize it," said Beth-Ellen. "She's written an e-book about decluttering."

"Your cousin's an idiot," said Janie.

Beth-Ellen said, "I know."

Their food arrived—quinoa burgers for Beth-Ellen and Sarah, and a beef burger for Janie, who didn't believe in quinoa.

"The worst part of it, though," said Beth-Ellen, "is that I can't stop reading. The mundaneness is fascinating. Do you know she did a three-parter itemizing the contents of her kitchen drawers?"

"Three parts doesn't sound very simple," said Sarah. She was trying to sound cool. Her own drawers were a mess.

"She gets very philosophical. Where does one lay one's melon baller? It says a lot about the kind of person you are."

"Couldn't she use a spoon?"

"But life *isn't* simple," Janie told them. "Think of Leslie." They nodded sagely. Exactly.

Beth-Ellen lowered her voice. "I keep leaving comments," she said. "Not nice ones."

A dry chunk of quinoa stuck in Sarah's throat.

Janie said, "Oh Beth-Ellen."

"Don't chastise me—she's just the worst. Someone needs to tell her so."

"I wasn't going to chastise," said Janie. "It's just not a very productive use of your time."

"I'd like to sic triplets on her," said Beth-Ellen. "That would really fuck up her simple life."

"What do you write?" asked Sarah, after she'd had a drink of water. "In the comments?"

"Well, I don't mention triplets," said Beth-Ellen. "She'd know it was me. I just itemize instances of hypocrisy. Like while it's really great that stealing her neighbours' Wi-Fi saves her money, perhaps it's unethical. Or that growing your own vegetables doesn't work when your life is so simple that it doesn't have a yard. Or that it's easy to live simple when your husband's family is fucking loaded."

"She sounds bored," said Janie.

"Mostly bor*ing*," said Beth-Ellen. "My mother thinks she has postpartum depression."

"Your mother thinks everyone has postpartum depression," said Sarah.

"That's true."

"Oh god," said Janie, talking with her mouth full. "But that story about the baby. The dead one, and the mother . . . In the suburbs. Did you hear—"

"Please don't," said Beth-Ellen with her hand up. Shaking her head, she added, "Because I'll cry. And it's my birthday."

Sarah wanted to stay on topic. She said, "Does she ever respond? Your cousin, I mean."

"She deletes the comments. But she reads them—she gets really defensive in subsequent posts. It's unbearable. And I can't quit her. Even if I tried to, I've ended up on some list that delivers her posts to my phone, and she's always linking on Facebook. I fucking hate the Internet."

And Janie said, "Hear, hear." Sarah poked her burger. It was inedible. She should have stuck with beef.

Beth-Ellen said, "Apparently she's big in the frugal vegan community."

"Where they have their melon ballers all in order," said Janie.

Beth-Ellen said, "Precisely."

"It's so smug, though," said Janie. "A 'lifestyle' blog. How is a lifestyle different from a life?"

"But you read them," offered Sarah.

"Hate-read," said Janie. "Definitely not the same."

"I don't know," said Sarah.

"You sure you're okay?" Beth-Ellen asked Sarah. "You haven't finished your burger. Usually, you eat and hate everyone."

"Just peachy," said Sarah. Took another bite, but no one noticed. Beth-Ellen started to explain how Patsy sewed her children dresses out of vintage pillowcases, and now Sarah rolled her eyes and shook her head in all the right places. She knew the script, how to be in the company of these women who had been her friends since before she'd heard of blogs, let alone written one.

•   •   •

It was with Janie and Beth-Ellen she'd developed the art of weaving legends from her tragedies. Apart from herself, there was nobody better in the world than Janie at telling the story of the night Sarah's hair had gone up in flames while she was singing

"Lover of Mine" by Alannah Myles at a karaoke pub downtown, howling out her angst as she shimmied too close to a tea light. And it had been Beth-Ellen who hadn't minded the smell, staying with her in the bathroom after, helping to pull out all the singed bits.

Their friendship was the one thing that lasted from that time when Sarah's whole life had been a series of disasters, the flaming hair one of the more benign episodes. She'd been so sure about things then, in particular that she was going to spend the rest of her life in the corporate world and married to Greg. And she'd been wrong about *everything*, except Janie and Beth-Ellen. She'd been miserable, the worst friend, and they'd never left her alone, taking her out for meals and walks, getting her away from the fish smell and back in the world. Not even so that they could remind her either that they'd been right all along, because they never, ever did.

What luck that this one thing she hadn't screwed up—her friends. Her best bits, the characters in all her favourite stories, and she wondered how they'd read them. Yes, one of them was an expert bomb builder, possibly dangerous, but Sarah was getting ahead of herself. She had nothing to fear from her friends. She could lay it all down, and neither one of them would raise an eyebrow. They knew her that well, and she knew them too.

Right?

Although maybe that was somebody else's friends.

"Fucking cross-stitch," said Beth-Ellen. They were still talking about Patsy.

"You could crochet a noose so she could hang herself?"

"I'm not sure violence is the answer."

"She makes her own granola bars."

"It's pretty nauseating."

"In real life," said Sarah, "is she really so unbearable? Or is it the blog that makes me come across as somebody you'd crochet a noose for?"

"You?"

"I mean her. Patsy."

"Funny thing to say."

"Slip of the tongue. But really?"

"In real life, she used to do heroin and has 'No Angle' tattooed across the bottom of her back. Her taste is as bad as her spelling. The blog's a lie."

"And that's the problem?" said Sarah. "Not the pillowcase skirts."

"Thrifted organic-cotton pillowcases."

"Sheared from free-range sheep."

"Is there any other kind of sheep?"

"If I were a better person," said Beth-Ellen, "I wouldn't mind so much."

"No," said Janie. "It's because you're a better person that you do." And then after a pause, "Or maybe we just don't get it. Maybe we'd feel differently about simplicity if we knew where our melon ballers were."

And Sarah said, "But I never even had one. Does life get any simpler than that?"

From the Archives: Mitzi Bytes
An Occasion for Cake

When I went over to G's last night, it wasn't for sex. I've sworn off booty calls. Mostly because it doesn't count as a booty call when your partner has to close his eyes and imagine you're not there in order to rustle up arousal.

"But doesn't it mean there's still something between us?" I'd said to my best friends, J and B. And they told me, "It means that he likes having his dick sucked."

Which I hadn't considered. For me, all of our intimacies are still so tangled up in love. But I was willing to see things from my friends' point of view—part of the reason I went to see G this one last time. To test their theory. To show off my hair. And also because he has the Bundt pan, and I wanted to bake a cake.

He was home. He's always home. One of these days he's not going to be home, and they've warned me about that, my friends. That his habits are going to change, and he's going to start living outside of the frame of the life that was ours, but in the meantime, he's there alone—the guy he's seeing is a waiter and works nights—so I always know where to find him. Which isn't really helping with the project of moving on.

I still have my key, which isn't helping either. I knocked once and then unlocked the door, and he was there in the study against a backdrop of files, books, and paper. It was just like coming home at the end of the day, because this place had been my home for so long, and his expression like he'd been expecting me.

"Just passing through," I said. "I need a thing." The key in my hand, but it felt heavy and wrong. I held it up. "You want this back?"

But G waved away my concern. "No, no," he said. "It's easier like this. And I was meaning to ask you anyway—I was hoping you'd come by." I closed the door behind me. "You cut your hair," he said.

"Well, not really," I told him. "Mostly it caught on fire, but yeah. After that, I got a trim. You like it?" I shook my head like a woman in a shampoo commercial. He looked uncomfortable. He couldn't tell if I was joking about the fire. I'd never joked much when we were together. I'd never set myself on fire either.

"You need a thing?" he asked.

"A Bundt pan," I said.

"I don't have one of those."

"You do. We did."

"It was ours?"

"It was yours. But you never used it. So I kind of thought."

"Oh, no, go ahead," he said. There's almost nothing he'd say no to now—bending over backwards, always an awkward contortion. I don't know if he's feeling guilty, or if our breakup has made him a better person, but I'm entitled to any benefits I can get from this arrangement. Hence the Bundt pan. It would have only just sat in his cupboard anyway.

"So, what's the occasion?" he asked me.

"Why I'm here?"

"No, the cake."

I said, "Because I'm hungry." And I wondered why he really wanted to know. Maybe this was something. Did it bother him, the prospect of me having something of my own? A cake-worthy occasion that had nothing to do with him?

He said, "Listen, I was wondering if you'd be able to come by next week. Not every day, but maybe every other?"

"What do you have in mind?"

He said, "I'm going out of town. We're. I'm going skiing." I got the point now. This wasn't company. Or at least not mine. He said, "I need somebody to come in and water the plants. And the turtle. And I thought since you're always passing by the place anyway, and you know it." Perhaps he could tell by my face that I wasn't so keen. "You know, and you could help yourself to anything else that you wanted. Any other Bundt pans."

"There was only ever one."

"Never mind," he said. "I was joking."

"About me watering the turtle?"

He said, "That part was real. Could you do it? I'll be back on Saturday night."

And I was getting the picture. Though things had been this clear before, and it hadn't stopped me then.

"You're going away with Levi?" The waiter. He shared stories of his dates, and I shared stories of mine, imagining this put us on the same level. Like we were cool. Me supposing that if we were on the same level, then anything might still happen between us—it was a question of proximity. But we weren't. He was going skiing with Levi, and I was going to water his turtle, and it really was that simple—no matter how deeply I read things, these facts wouldn't change.

So I didn't try to kiss him when I left, which I suppose was a kind of a triumph, an occasion for cake if ever there was one. I got my Bundt pan and got out of there. Hightailing it over to J's place, and she was home, and she let me lie on her bed and cry and sleep over, and we baked the cake in her tiny oven in the morning, and ate it even though it didn't rise.

CHAPTER 5

. . . .

On Tuesdays and Thursday afternoons, Sarah tutored teenage moms at an alternative school. It was part of a bridging program to get the girls back into education. Childcare was provided, and the girls who showed up pulled their chairs into a circle in the library, where they worked on reading and writing. They read magazine and news articles together, and over the course of the program, they'd conquer an entire novel. The girls shared thoughts and reflections in their personal journals. It was interesting work, if only indirectly rewarding. It was the kind of work whose successes you had to measure by every little step rather than by great goals achieved.

Today's little step is that all the girls were present, Lolo, Audrey, Tasvir, and Candice. Four spirited girls who, if lacking in social graces and academic skills, were unusually blessed with powers of human perception. Just now, Sarah was trying to lead the group in an exercise in narrative, the composition of a collaborative story on the whiteboard told in the format of text messages. Teaching required all the skills and concentration of performance, but Sarah's mind was elsewhere today, and the girls could see where she was falling down.

"That's not what I said, miss," said Audrey, Sarah's title more a slur than a sign of respect. It was the way she hissed it; they all did. When they dropped the *miss*, that was always when she felt like she was making progress, connecting with them. "You've got that wrong, miss." Audrey got up from her seat to correct her, rubbing out *what* and replacing it with *WOT*.

"I'm not sure that it matters."

"It matters," said Audrey. She sat back down in her seat and folded her arms. She was sixteen, and her daughter was three. She'd just been given her own apartment, a ticket out of foster care. Attending the literacy program was the terms of her staying there. Her daughter had ADHD. Every class, someone from the nursery would come knocking on the door to get Audrey to come and calm the toddler down. "You've got to get the details right," she said with her head cocked, a dismissive shrug.

Candice, mostly sleek and entirely beautiful, folded and unfolded her legs beside Audrey, smiling, rubbing her big round belly. This was her second baby. She was perpetually pleased with herself in a way that frustrated all the do-gooders like Sarah who were trying to fix her. If the other girls had looked like Candice did, they could have gotten away with anything. She was elegant and articulate in a way that belied that undeniable fact that she couldn't read or write a word, that she had severe dyslexia that no one had ever been able to get to the bottom of. And today, her smug smile was irritating. "What do you think?" Sarah called on her. "Candice, what comes next?"

"I don't know, miss," said Candice. "I don't follow."

"You don't?"

"Texts on a whiteboard."

"It's a story."

She shrugged. "Exactly. I don't see the point."

Sarah decided to move on. It was essential that this moment not be turned into a power struggle, especially since Candice could out-struggle her any time. She sighed, though. They all heard it. And this would be the moment from which everything would go wrong.

The other two were Lolo, mother of Baby Divine, a sad and homely girl who, in casual sex and frozen grocery-store cakes (both were recurring themes in her poetry), constantly sought the comforts which life had not seen fit to deliver her from elsewhere, and Tasvir, mother of Aleesha, whose pregnancy had been her conservative family's first and only clue that their daughter was not quite the shy and studious girl that they'd imagined her to be. She *was* shy and studious, though, the latter point making her incongruous presence in Sarah's classroom both welcome and tricky. Tricky because Tasvir didn't see the point either of these gimmicky exercises either. She'd never sent text messages because her family hadn't allowed her a phone, and now she couldn't afford one. She'd prefer to write a thousand-word essay on a Shakespeare play. She wasn't impressed with the company she was keeping in this class.

"Okay, open your journals," said Sarah. "Let's hear your personal responses now." The girls were most partial to poetry, short poems with fractured sentences. It was easy to do and hard to do demonstrably wrong.

Audrey went first with a surprisingly evocative poem inspired by a story from the news—a mother who'd abandoned her baby in a parking garage stairwell one cold night last February. She had a talent for rhyming couplets. "I was out turning tricks just to score some blow. But Jesus loves me, this I know." Next was poor Lolo with a poem about her boyfriend. All her poems lately were about her boyfriend, a fiftysomething trucker who lived in Tennessee whom she'd met online but never in real life, who had a YouTube channel dedicated to videos of him singing her covers of "Kiss from a Rose." So Sarah was listening with less than half her mind. Another message had arrived while she was having lunch: *Why so quiet? Ignoring me won't make any of this go away. It's all going to be so much bigger than both of us, and there's nothing you can do about it now.*

In iambic pentameter, Tasvir had written an ode to a ceramic jug. The poem was boring, but Sarah had a feeling that this was a comment on her assignment. She listened to the poem, eyeing her bag on the chair beside her, wondering if she was just imagining the sound of the buzz from her vibrating phone. She glanced at the clock on the wall—just five more minutes until the class was over, and then she could check.

And finally, Candice, whose journal was empty. Showing up to class was one of the terms of her probation, so she did, not that she ever contributed. It had taken a few weeks for Sarah to realize the problem was more than just a bad attitude—Candice would stare at text with her eyes unmoving, and then say she'd forgotten her glasses. She always forgot her glasses—Sarah had never seen her glasses. She'd say she'd do the reading later and take it home, where someone would obviously read it to her. She was smart and had a good memory. She'd come to the next class knowing what was what, but then the next reading would flummox her. Sarah would ask her a question, and she'd just stare back with that assured tiny smile, as though she had something over her.

"Nothing today?" asked Sarah.

Candice tapped her head. "It's up here." This was new. But communication was the point of the exercise. This was okay. Flexibility was crucial in dealing with these kids.

"Go ahead," said Sarah.

Candice smiled, hauled her awkward body from the chair. The group was small, but she basked in their attention, the strangeness of her shape making their stares much more riveted than they might have been if she were just merely beautiful. Candice was fascinating to consider.

She spoke just quietly enough that they had to strain to listen, leaning forward. "I wandered lonely as a cloud," she began, which was enough to turn Sarah's thoughts away from the clock. She sounded as though she were speaking from a stage. "That floats high over vales and hills. When all at once I saw a crowd of golden daffodils." Continuing through the poem, Wordsworth's, just bastardized enough that her classmates would think Candice had actually written it. "When often on my couch I lie, in a vacant mood, they flash upon the inward eye, which is the bliss of solitude, and then my heart with pleasure fills, and dances with the daffodils."

She stared at Sarah, just daring her. To do what, though? Sarah bit her lower lip.

"That was amazing," said Audrey, breaking the silence in the room.

"Whoa," said Lolo, and even Tasvir looked impressed.

"Nice . . . *delivery*," said Sarah. "All right, everyone—see you next week." The girls gathered their things. "Just stay a minute, would you, Candice?" They shuffled out. Candice stood with her hand on one hip, her head cocked to the side. "You know, that was fantastic," Sarah told her. "Reciting the whole thing—that isn't easy."

"Uh-huh."

Standing beside Candice—even Candice at nine months pregnant—was to feel like a schlub. But Sarah would not let herself be intimidated. She was the authority here. "The assignment, though, was to write something, not pass off somebody else's work as your own."

"I didn't pass anything," Candice spat.

"Don't shit me, okay?" said Sarah. Candice just stared. "Or at least don't do it while reciting Wordsworth. Do you know how little Wordsworth I know, but I knew that one."

"You wanted a poem."

"I wanted *your* poem."

Her elegant shrug. Whatever.

How to end this? Sarah needed her to leave, needed to check her phone for messages. But she couldn't let her think that this was okay either.

"Candice, do you know what plagiarism is?" But Candice would not be frightened into compliance. She refused to meet Sarah's eyes. Candice knew she was bluffing, so Sarah tried another tactic. "If you're not going to do your assignments, you're not fulfilling the requirements of the program. Just show-ing up is not enough. I'll have to report this to Mr. Chaudhary."

Whatever, still.

"Is that what you want me to do?"

Sarah waited.

"Go fuck yourself," said Candice. Still smiling, displaying the one of her incisors that was capped with gold. "You wanted a poem? I gave you a poem." Then she slung her bag over the shoulder and was gone.

•   •   •

Sarah read the message in the stairwell, the one in the back of the building that no one ever used. Sitting on the top step, scroll-ing down because this message was a long one. Jane Q had gone berserk. Same subject line still: *Who do you think you are?*

Whoever you think you are, she'd written, *the fact is that I could be anyone. I'm realizing there's real power in that. I am nameless and faceless, and it's the closest thing I can think of to justice at this moment when I am so desperate for it. Justice or revenge, or is there any difference between the two? I'll take another trip through your archives, there's probably a post about that, you've covered everything there, it seems.*

But of course, you do actually know me, and I'm probably even closer than you think. Close enough to understand just how you've used the lives of everybody you know, to comprehend the way we've all been exploited. Well, guess what, Sarah, you don't get to be in charge anymore. I'm serious: Game Over. I may be making up this story as I go along, but that's the point, and I am definitely going to be author of the next chapter.

Sarah dialed Andrea in Seattle and was put through to her voice mail. "Not going away," she explained. "There's a new message and it's really wild. I really don't know what to do." She waited on the line for a few seconds, as though there were a chance of Andrea cutting in with some answers. She needed to hear another human voice.

Ending her message, she dialed Chris at work. As usual, it went straight to his voice mail too. She said, "Hey, love, just touching base. I was thinking of you."

She continued sitting there, holding her phone as though it somehow charged her. Running an inventory of everybody she'd ever known, which was pretty much the same as everyone she'd ever written about. Who was Jane Q? There were no obvious suggestions—her writing life as Mitzi Bytes was a secret she'd never let slip once. It was easier that way, instead of picking and choosing whom to trust. And while those closest to her— her husband, her friends—might have been the most obvious candidates for disclosure, the matter was doubly complicated with them—by the time she might have confessed, there were already hundreds of posts on the site in which their lives and circumstances had been exposed. Posts that, it was true, wouldn't tell any of these people anything they didn't already know; her modus operandi was honesty, after all. But while the truth as an abstract concept is one thing, its solid fact is another. Not everyone likes being hit with truth in the face. Not everyone likes it broadcast on the Internet either.

Did honesty still count when you couldn't be honest about being honest? Sarah liked to think that unlike most people, she was honest where it really counted, calling things as she really saw them. She'd justified her work by coming up with a complex equation balancing out with her being more honest about the people she wrote than those people were about themselves, people who'd never recognize themselves in her stories in a million years. But perhaps there was a fault in her logic.

How honest was it anyway to tell it like it was and then not sign your name? Where was the courage in that?

Sarah clenched her fist around her phone, willing it to buzz, craving a connection to somewhere else to stop the ideas ricocheting through her mind. She wanted to talk to Andrea. She needed someone to tell her everything would be okay.

She replied to Jane Q's message. She could no longer avoid engaging. The stakes were too high. She wrote, *What do you want?* Imagining all kinds of possible consequences. If this was blackmail, serious revenge, or just merely psychological torture, what would she have to do to make this problem go away? Would Jane Q even give her that option?

Already, this figure had assumed a persona in Sarah's mind. And she was a "she" for sure. A man would be more direct. Sarah pictured a woman shrouded in black, rubbing gnarled hands above a bubbling cauldron. She tried to reconcile this idea with the people she knew in her life, to see if any witches sprang to mind. But there was nobody. Or else it could have been anyone at all.

The sun was pouring in through windows that stretched the entire three storeys of the stairwell, down on Sarah where she sat and all the way to the bottom of the stairs. Her phone was silent. Sarah stuffed it in her bag and started down the stairs, heading outside to hide in the world for a while.

•   •   •

That evening while Sarah was preparing dinner, Frances arrived at the front door with a bag of brand-name, high-quality hand-me-downs, clothes that had belonged to Charlotte and were ready to be passed along to Gladys.

"I've been driving around with these in my back seat for a week," she said. "I had a minute now and thought I'd finally get rid of them."

Luckily, the shambles had been tidied—the cleaning woman had been. "Do you want to come in?" asked Sarah, once Frances had handed her the bag but remained in the doorway. The clothes were only part of the story. Frances wasn't so charitable, and she rarely did anything without an ulterior motive. Frances didn't usually drop by at all, even with their houses so close. She wasn't one to stand still, instead always a whirlwind, forever late for something urgent to which her presence was essential. She might remember to honk and wave as her car roared by.

But tonight she was ready to stop. "Just for a minute," said Frances, restive, her busy feet sweeping the doormat. She came in to find Chris sitting at the table, helping the girls with their homework. He'd arrived home unexpectedly early—it was rare that he got away from work on time—and Frances was as surprised to see him as Sarah had been when he'd walked through the door.

Except Frances let her puzzlement show. "Don't they pay you for a full day's work?" she asked. "Nobody has any problem with you taking off early?" And when he tried to shrug off her accusations good-naturedly—"I don't know if you'd call it *early*"—she said, "Well, it must be nice."

"Aw, come on, Frances," he said.

And Frances explained that she was heading *back* to the office, having left to attend Charlotte's bass-guitar recital—a terrifying-sounding event, Sarah thought. Frances stood at the counter, started popping the cherry tomatoes that Sarah had just washed for a salad. Clementine was nearly finished with the inane worksheets that constituted her homework for the sake of homework, and Gladys was drawing. Chris had prompted them to greet their aunt, and they'd each flapped an arm in her direction, with barely a glance. It was possible, Sarah considered, that other people thought her children were horrible.

She asked Frances, "What's up?" Now that Frances was finished berating her brother, it was clear that her current business was with Sarah. Frances was standing before her at the counter, making her nervous, though that part was the one thing that wasn't out of the ordinary. It was essential to keep one's guard up around Frances, but guardedness was difficult to come by at the moment. A person could only attend to so many invasions. Plus, the tomatoes. Sarah was concerned for her salad.

"I had to move heaven and earth to get out of there for the recital," Frances was saying to Sarah. "I haven't been home once before midnight for the last two weeks—it's the time of year." The bank's fiscal year-end was just one crazy season among many. Thankfully, Frances had an extensive network of babysitters at her disposal. "And Evan's been so busy with the album. But I just wanted to ask you while I had a chance; what's this about you scoping out my yard yesterday?"

Sarah was slicing an onion, and she set down the blade.

"Chris said you'd been hatching plots. And I just wondered what you thought you'd seen."

"Chris?" He was listening to every word, she knew, but he looked up now as if he had no idea what they had been talking about. "What did you tell her?" She said to Frances, "It was nothing."

"That's what he said."

"So why did you tell her that?" Sarah asked him. "'Nothing.'"

"Because it *was* nothing," he said. "You'd gone over there, and everything was fine. It was a non-story. And no news is good news. So it really doesn't matter. Right?" Nervous laughter, as though anybody was in the mood for a joke.

"But telling her makes it matter," said Sarah. "It makes it into something." She looked back at Frances, still popping tomatoes. "There's really not much to it. I thought I saw somebody there. Something orange. I saw it through the trees."

"But there was no one."

"I don't think so. When I went over, everything was still."

"So it's like *Rear Window* over here, then."

"Not quite as dramatic. I don't know. Eyes play tricks. What if I hadn't checked, and somebody had broken into your garage? I had to do something, don't you think?" There was stereo and band equipment up in the room above it, valuable stuff. Evan used it as a practice space.

"It's peculiar is what I think," said Frances. "I just wonder what you thought you were looking for."

"I didn't know."

"These are good," said Frances, finishing the last of the tomatoes. "Organic? From the farmer's market?" Sarah nodded. "Lucky you to have the time for that," said Frances. "For a lot of things, actually." Eyes back on her absconding brother. "Both of you."

Sarah went back to chopping for her decimated salad.

"Anyway, you're getting dinner on. I'll let you go." Sarah didn't answer. "Oh, come on now, don't be like that. I just wanted to know what you thought you had seen."

"Exactly what Chris told you," said Sarah. "It was nothing. Are you accusing me of something?"

"Don't twist this," said Frances. "I'm not accusing you of anything. If anything, it's the other way around."

"Well, what did you think I might have seen?"

"If I knew," said Frances, "I wouldn't be standing here asking."

• • •

Jane Q had no reply. Maybe she'd scared her off? Sarah kept her phone logged in to the Mitzi email account, and watched comments and messages arrive from the usual suspects. They were suspects still, all these people whose online selves were so familiar to her—long-time readers, other bloggers, her blogger friends, and ever the trolls who kept coming in spite of themselves. Could Jane Q be among them? Anyone armed with the right combination of details and online savvy could possibly find their way along the trail from her blogging persona to her actual self, but she'd always just assumed that nobody cared enough to bother, although one should never underestimate the terrible potential of boredom plus Internet access.

Sarah wondered if Jane Q's life was a mirror of her own, if the silence this evening was because she was putting her own kids to bed. How a person might walk around in their day wielding terror over the head of another but look so ordinary from the outside. The way we're all just figments of one another's imaginations after all.

Chris knew she was angry and stayed out of her way in a delicate dance, hurrying the girls through bath and bedtime preparations while she tidied the kitchen after dinner. She kept meeting his sheepish smiles with a glare, and didn't feel like talking until he came upstairs later when she was reading in bed. She'd heard him in the kitchen, then locking up downstairs, turning out the lights. His footsteps on the stairs were slower than usual. He stopped to check on both the girls before he finally entered their room.

He said, "What?" He looked sideways, a deflection.

"I didn't say anything."

"You didn't have to," he said.

Sarah put down *To the Lighthouse*. "She's crazy, Chris. Why did you tell her anything?" Their general policy with Frances was disengagement. One doesn't hand-feed information to the enemy. Having family over the back fence would have been a good idea if they'd been a different kind of family. When she'd bought the place, Frances had claimed to be excited by the proximity, spinning tales of backyard barbecues, shared nannies, and wide-open doors. While Sarah had known how the whole thing would transpire, Chris had encouraged her to be optimistic, but things turned out exactly as she'd expected. It wasn't just family ties that Frances was after, Sarah could see now, but control over the brother she'd always been able to tell exactly what to do, until he'd had the nerve to fall in love with somebody.

Frances didn't trust her, Sarah knew. Frances loved her brother but couldn't fathom what any woman might see in him. Perpetually single, he would have been forever at her disposal, the opposite of her flaky husband (who needed a reliable spouse when your brother was Chris?). For Chris, none of this awkward puzzle was remarkable—he'd never known a world uncomplicated by his sister. But for Sarah, who hadn't had a sibling, the end of the earth couldn't have been enough distance from Frances. The one saving grace was that Frances was so distant in every way but geography that she considered it a mark of her superiority—both social and professional—that she could not be pinned down.

"She emailed me," he said. "She needed something. When does that ever happen?"

Sarah put down her book. "It always happens," she said.

"I mean, she needed something real," he said. "Assurance. She's worried about Evan." He saw her look. "More than usual."

"I thought these days Evan was riding high," said Sarah. He'd been holding down his job at a guitar store for a few years now, and Frances had been crowing ever since he had successfully crowdfunded the album he'd been talking about making for a decade. He'd even surpassed his target, miraculously, thanks to an anonymous donor who, Sarah had suspected all along, was actually his wife.

"He's riding too high, maybe. She says he's been acting strange, not showing up for work. So I told her you'd been over to her place and everything was fine. Someone in a hat, you said. But there was no one. Which I thought might mean something. Or nothing. Either way."

"It means she came over here tonight and interrogated me."

"Interrogating is a bit of a stretch. She thinks he's using again. That's why I told her. She thinks he's up to something."

"He probably is."

"Not this time. With the album and the money, he's getting pretty serious."

"How do *you* know?"

He was offended by her tone. "I talk to him sometimes."

"Stay out of it, Chris."

"This is different."

"But I didn't see anything," Sarah said. "That's the whole point. It means nothing."

"I know," he said. "But I wanted to give her something. I didn't think it was going to implicate you."

He went into the bathroom to brush his teeth. She called to him, "I don't like it, though, you talking about me. To her especially. You know that."

He came out with the toothbrush in his mouth. "I wasn't talking about you. We were talking about Evan," he told her, his words slurred with a mouthful of foam. "Frances is tricky. You never know how she's going to take things."

"No, *you* never know," she called after him as he went back in the bathroom to spit. "I've never met anyone whose unpredictability is so predictable. This is always how she takes things, so you shouldn't give her anything at all."

"She's my sister," he said.

"Well, what does that mean?" Sarah asked. Chris shrugged. "Anyway, she thinks I'm nuts now."

"She always did," said Chris. "She thinks everybody outside of her brain is unfathomable."

"She's not wrong about that. Except maybe she should have doubts about the inside of her brain too." She crawled up beside him as he got into bed and lay her head on his chest. "All day," said Sarah, "it's like I've been walking around with a target on my back. One of the students told me to go fuck myself."

"And what did you say to her?"

"I was speechless."

"Probably safest."

"Do you think I'm a good person?" Sarah asked him.

"Of course I do."

"No, I mean, like, outside of your love for me. If you didn't know me at all and there I was; would you say I was a person of integrity?"

"No. Probably not. Not if I didn't know you at all."

"I mean, if you only knew me from the outside."

"I only do know you from the outside. Remember? Everybody is unfathomable."

"I didn't mean us," said Sarah. "You make sense to me."

"Well, you don't completely," said Chris. "I think you ask weird questions. And I want to read my book. Please?" He didn't usually do fiction, and he was trying to understand its appeal, how it worked: *Tigana* by Guy Gavriel Kay. An epic fantasy to get lost in, and he had so little time to read. And none of this was his fault, really. So Sarah left him alone and turned out her bedside lamp, and his tablet lit up the room.

From the Archives: Mitzi Bytes
Everybody Is Unfathomable

Have I told you about The Programmer's sister? Who didn't come to our wedding because she was volunteering at a Romanian orphanage? Which sounded impressive until I learned that she was volunteering at the orphanage for precisely three days only, a privilege for which she'd paid thousands of dollars. Because what does an emotionally crippled twenty-seven-year-old banker have to offer Romanian orphans, really? I also learned that The Sister had booked her do-gooding getaway long after our wedding date was set. Instead of flying in from the West Coast for the ceremony as planned, she'd be literally flying over the city as we exchanged our vows, en route to the adventure she'd brilliantly manufactured as an excuse to not have to watch her brother get married.

She's a remarkable woman, The Sister. Their mother died when they were very young, and throughout their childhood, The Sister was the brightest star in The Programmer's universe, the one who helped him navigate social mores, stood up to his bullies, and shared her every confidence. They're only sixteen months apart, nearly twins, and though he's the elder, she's always been the strong one. The Programmer worships her, though I've never seen a love so intermingled with terror, which I never understood until I met her myself. And then it all clicked. The Sister is the scariest woman I've ever known.

She'd never liked the sound of me. She'd said as much to The Programmer as soon as he told her I existed. She thought I was using him, that I would string him along. Which I did for a while, but then it got serious, and she refused to change her mind. When she found out we were getting married, she was furious. Partly out of concern for her brother, but also for selfish reasons—she couldn't stand to lose him. And because our wedding would remind everybody that she was still single, with a kind-of-sort-of boyfriend who was refusing to commit.

I didn't know about any of this for a very long time. Until recently, I knew The Sister only through The Programmer's eyes, this incredible person who was his best friend, who was brilliant. An orphanage volunteer. A persona that practically came with a cape and tights.

So I was surprised he warned me before we finally met last week. He said, "The thing is, she can be a little bit forceful. It's just her, and it's not personal, and if you can see past it, it's for the best."

This was odd. The Programmer has never been one for social nuance, but I suppose that he would know his sister better than he knows anyone. He's well versed in the art of handling her.

But I was still unprepared when we finally met. She walked into our place and looked me up and down. She said, "I thought you'd be prettier—more *conventionally* pretty, I mean." Then she went and had an asthma attack. Apologized, thinking she'd be all cute. "So sorry," she said between manufactured wheezes. "I just can't help it—all this dust."

She left to stay in a hotel, and I'm not sure if dust was the problem, or if it was me, and I was not so secretly glad to see the back of her even though I was also seething with rage at her rudeness.

"It's her asthma," he kept saying. "She's always had a problem with dust— she's really sensitive." He said, "Listen, I just want the two of you to get along." He made her take me out for lunch one day during the week. She picked me up at my office, and we went to a place downstairs that served vegetarian food, which she found annoying, so we were off on the wrong foot again.

Waiting for our food to come, she said, "Listen," and I actually thought perhaps she was going to apologize. That we were going to start over. I wanted to like her. I really wanted a sister, in addition to a husband. And I had admired her for so long, but being in her presence was like traipsing across a minefield. She said, "I know what your game is."

"What?"

She said, "If you're playing my brother, I will make you sorry."

"I don't know what you're talking about."

"He's oblivious," she said, "but I get it. I've seen what you've got hiding in your corners."

"The dusty ones?" I said.

"Dusty what?"

"Dusty corners."

"And then some."

I said, "You've really got the wrong idea."

She said, "My brother's a good guy, the best. Most people don't know that."

"I do."

"You don't," she said. "You don't know the half of it."

Our food arrived. We'd ordered rice bowls, and she explored hers with a fork, with disdain. Called the server back and asked for Caesar dressing.

I said, "I married him."

She said, "That's what I don't understand. Is this about money?"

"I've got money."

She said, "You've been married before."

"But that was different," I said.

She cocked her head and folded her arms. Case closed.

We finished lunch without much more conversation, and the rest of the week went on like that. She infantilized my husband, cooking him vile meals that he was apparently mad for in childhood—pork and beans, and Hamburger Helper—and telling stories that were incomprehensible to me. "You had to be there," they explained. She kept calling him "Sport." I'm sure she was rummaging through my drawers and closets when my back was turned.

And when she was gone, The Programmer was bereft, and kept saying, "I just wish that she lived closer." I thought he was kidding, but he wasn't.

CHAPTER 6

. . . .

Jane Q's response was waiting in the morning. Sarah read it while sitting on the toilet, brushing her teeth, as the children banged on the door, but the door was locked for once. She ignored the noise.

The email said, *What I want is for you to feel sick to your stomach when you read my words. I want you to be afraid, to know your world is under threat. I want you thinking of your little girls and of all the places they go, how often they're outside of arm's reach, and what are you going to do about that? How are you going to control it all? I want you to think about your perfect life, the bright and colourful scenes you paint, and how easily it could all go to pieces—do you even know that? What I want is you to be scared, Sarah Lundy. I want you quaking in your pretty little shoes.*

The girls were still at the door. "Just a minute," she yelled.

She was changing the stakes, Jane Q, bringing the children into all this. If anything could get Sarah quaking, it would certainly be that, but she was also put off by the deliberateness of the tactic. She put her phone on the counter and looked down at her feet on the bathmat, at all her ugly toes. Whoever Jane Q was, she really didn't know Sarah that well. Or her shoes. Sarah hadn't worn pretty shoes in years. She had feet like a sasquatch.

She picked up the phone again. *I'm not quaking,* she replied. *Maybe if I knew who you were, I could understand where you're coming from, but what am I supposed to do with this? Threats and ranting? It's not reasonable. Giving into that would be submitting to tyranny, and I'm stronger than that. I've known plenty of trolls, and you don't scare me. I wrote what I wrote, and I'll own every word, and I'm even willing to engage in discussion about it, but I'm not going to start quaking, and I will not yield.*

Then she rummaged through a drawer for nail polish, jacking one foot and then the other up on the edge of the counter, and slapping the polish on. Shameless Red: a few spots of colour in an otherwise dreary day. She got dressed while the girls cavorted like monkeys on her unmade bed, shutting down their frolic just when things got too ramped up and somebody's injury seemed imminent. As a mother, she had a talent for timing. And also for breakfast, as she conjured spinach omelettes out of a nearly barren fridge, cheese and ketchup being the trick to getting the girls to eat it. Her children were most certainly well protected.

At the table, Clementine was playing on her mother's phone, and Sarah yanked it out of her hands, placing her dish of eggs before her. "Eat," she said to Clementine's protests about wanting to finish her game. She squeezed more ketchup onto Gladys's plate. And then she ate her own breakfast as she loaded the dishwasher, rinsing her own plate and teacup last.

In today's race against the clock, she was winning. Faces wiped, hair tangles unsnarled, backpacks loaded and by the door. She would not yield.

"Let's go, let's go, let's go," she called through the house, and the girls came running. She found that hat of hers and stuck it on her hair. And then out the door and into the car. The wheel was ever turning this life of hers, every day another scramble, but she was on top of it today, sure-footed and fast.

"About the article," said Starry Fiske when Sarah encountered her on the way into school. She was impossible to avoid. Maybe it was the hat that gave Sarah away every time.

"I'm on it," said Sarah. "Olive oil. I'll be giving you a call, okay?" Waving over her shoulder as she left Starry behind, delivering her daughters to their classrooms—a quick conference with Ms. Terry in Grade 2 about overdue books from the school library. Tomorrow, she promised, she would remember. Kissing Clementine goodbye, and then she was alone, finally done. Back to her car, her safest place. If she could just stay here right now in this moment, everything under control. She laid her forehead on the wheel and relished the cool of the leather against her skin.

Was Sarah Lundy Mitzi Bytes? She said she owned her words, but did she really? Once upon a time, Sarah had aspired to be Mitzi. She'd needed a life, so she'd invented one, and for a while, the two led the very same existence, one whose adventures she'd turned into stories because the stories were all that she had. But somewhere along the line, her two selves had diverged. She supposed it had happened when her paramount experiences ceased to be those she could spin into five-hundred-word anecdotes. When she stopped being the clown in all her stories. When she fell in love with Chris.

But Sarah wasn't finished with Mitzi—she might have been ambivalent before, but being pushed into a corner was making her adamant about this. It was for practical reasons, first of all. Mitzi Bytes made more money than Sarah Lundy. Her advertising revenue wasn't what it had been ten years ago, but then again, nobody's was, and it was still something. Her own pot of gold. Easy money too—she earned it by sitting down at her desk and letting her fingers run over the keyboard, tapping words that fell out of her mind like a melody. And it wasn't even about the money—this was becoming clearer. Without that outlet, she wouldn't know how to be herself. Giving up Mitzi Bytes would be like giving up reading, or seeing, or the name she'd been born with. There would be all the pieces she'd taken of the world all around her, but nowhere for any of it to go.

But maybe she didn't have to be finished. She could fess up, come clean. Sarah imagined this. There'd probably be a whole other book in it. She imagined herself on talk-show couches, practised her look of contrition in the vanity mirror. It wasn't very convincing. They'd make her join Twitter. Her mother would kill her. Her friends would never speak to her again, and she couldn't fathom what Chris would say about the whole thing. The media might not be very interested anyway—the talk show would probably be broadcast on somebody's YouTube channel. Bloggers weren't very remarkable these days.

"You can't have it both ways," Andrea had told her so many times, pointing to her awkward balance as an anonymous public figure. One way or another, she was going to lose. Her most vitriolic commenters would just be saying the same. *You can't have it both ways.*

But it was possible that they'd all underestimated the force of Sarah's will. She drummed a roll on the top of the steering wheel, snapped the visor above her shut. One way or another. She was convinced there was a way that she could.

•   •   •

This was the morning she was meeting Leslie (*Poor Leslie*) at a new bakeshop not far from her neighbourhood. Driving over from the school, the radio was on, an interview with a self-proclaimed sociopath who'd written a book about herself, and then more news at the bottom of the clock. About the baby who'd been discovered without vital signs the day before, drowned in a bathtub, pronounced dead. Shocking, but even the shock was kind of familiar. Routine by now. Sarah could picture it—cameras set up outside the house already, a suburban home built as a small-scale castle, a two-car garage. The kind of place a couple would buy imagining it big enough for all their dreams, or at least the starter ones, not figuring on the police tape strung up across the fake Greek columns. Never imagining the irreversible actions of a single moment, the linchpins of an ordinary life disappearing. All those blank-faced suburban houses, not even sidewalks on the street, and nobody around in the daytime. It was so lonely. Sarah wasn't sure why anyone was ever shocked when terrible things happened in places like that.

She found a parking spot not far from the bakery, turned off the engine, the radio with it. In her side mirror she spied Leslie coming down the sidewalk, her look already set for spring. A white trench coat, matching boots, her blonde hair bouncing on her shoulders. Usually the women in Sarah's daytime world were not so glowing, not as coiffed, but Leslie came from someplace else. She worked four days a week as a legal secretary at a big firm downtown, and even off-duty, Sarah noted, removing her own hat and shaking her hair from its ponytail, her friend wore the uniform of someone with a career. And like those houses with their careful driveways and perfect columns, you wouldn't have thought that anything awful could happen in her midst either.

But there had been trouble enough. Sarah and Leslie had met years ago when they were both students, working together in a summer job guiding schoolchildren on tours of the city. Not long after, Leslie married Ian and became pregnant. She was Sarah's first friend to be pregnant, her first friend to move away from downtown, out to the West End, to a pretty semi on a shady street that was lined with others just like it. Another place whose reality hadn't panned out like the dreams. When their son, Jamie, was three and his disabilities were becoming apparent, Ian walked out on them, running away to the West Coast to have a breakdown. Leaving Leslie alone to carry the burden, although she would object to the term, to Jamie being a burden. Leslie was fierce about semantics. If you told her she was brave, she'd say, "What choice do I have?"

She was fierce about a lot of things. Leslie could drive people away, and friends speculated behind her back that it was this force that had ended her marriage as much as Jamie's problems. But this same ferocity had kept her chaotic life in balance for so long, a balance however precarious. Anyone who told her it couldn't be done—single parenthood, having a child with special needs, and a demanding career—only made her more determined to prove them otherwise. As she was doing right now, with her perfect hair and boots, her son safely at school, to which he was delivered each day on a bright yellow bus. He was taught skills that could one day help him lead a more independent life— speech and language therapy; practice taking part in everyday interactions, like waiting in line at a checkout, or taking the bus;

and exercises in gauging social cues. They took care of him there so that now, for a few hours anyway, his harried mother could walk down the sidewalk carefree.

But perhaps she wasn't. There was something about her eye. Sarah noticed this once she'd retreated from their embrace, standing back from her friend—the left side of her face was twitching, as though she were trying but failing to wink. This complicated her expression. Leslie pressed her palm to her troubled spot. "I don't know what it is," she says. "It comes and goes. I think it's that I'm so tired." Jamie was usually up most of the night.

Inside she bought a coffee, Sarah had tea, and they each ordered big fat banana muffins—gluten-free like everything in the place—that crumbled like sand when they pulled off the wrappers. Leslie sat staring at the mess on her plate, her eye only twitching sporadically.

"You heard this place was good?" Sarah whispered.

"A woman at work said it was. She's religious about gluten-free, though. Maybe she shouldn't be trusted. Mostly, I just thought it's pretty close to you." She took a sip of her drink. "The coffee's okay."

Sarah said, "I was listening to the news in the car. The baby and the bathtub."

Leslie said, "Terrible," shaking her head. Her face was contorting again. Sarah decided against telling her the story of her uncle who'd had Bell's palsy, and instead she talked about the story, about the space between this baby and that other one, from Audrey's poem, who'd recently been abandoned in a parking garage stairwell on a bitter cold night.

"It's just strange that I have so much more understanding for one situation than the other," said Sarah. "The most brutal one too. But with the abandoned baby, empathy has to stretch so much further. I mean, I don't know that stairwell, the parking lot on the coldest night, but I've been at home, you know, the safest place in the world, and suddenly even your mind's not safe there anymore and anything can happen. I remember those early days when the babies were new, the world all blurry and sort of askew. I don't know if I can judge anybody for what happens then."

"But empathy isn't a stretch," said Leslie. "It's more like a leap. You just make it. You shut your eyes and go." She shut her own eyes.

"You okay?" Sarah asked her. Leslie nodded. Sarah said, "I just can't imagine myself—"

"All you ever do is imagine yourself," Leslie interrupted.

"What?"

"You're not so singular in that either," said Leslie, backtracking. "I mean, it's a pretty universal trait. You look out the window, and you see your own reflection. And it's true, that mother in the parking garage is a million miles away in terms of geography, race, socio-economic class. It's a huge leap for anybody."

Sarah said, "I don't know if that's the whole of it. Maybe it's a different gap. A complicated thing. The mother in the stairwell put her baby in harm's way, but with the other, it was an act of safety. In a convoluted way. I understand."

"It was about safety for both of them, ultimately—that stairwell was a means to an end. And that baby survived."

"But which action was more selfless?"

Leslie said, "Why would you ask such a thing of anyone?"

It was a good question.

"We live in such a bubble," said Sarah. "All of us in the same city, but we're so far removed." She was thinking of Candice. "These last few days, I've had a lot on my mind. And I really messed things up with one of my students." She told Leslie about the daffodils poem. "I should have handled it better. She'd recited a poem by Wordsworth, for god's sake—it wasn't the assignment, but still. She's not a stupid girl, but that's part of the problem."

"What's going on, then?" Leslie asked. "Other than the daffodils." Then she got up for a refill, giving Sarah time to consider her answer. And what could she say? There was nothing to convey without disclosing everything. She wanted to spill—thoughts unexpressed weren't in keeping with her character—but Sarah was accustomed to holding on to Mitzi and didn't know how to loosen her grip.

When Leslie sat down again, Sarah said, "I've been questioning things. Why I do what I do."

"Do what?" With an edge that made Sarah look up. She'd been avoiding Leslie's face. The twitch was distracting.

"What?"

"You know, it's simple. You spend all day driving your kids around. It gives you too much time to think about why you do what you do. Get out of the car and walk for a while. Problem solved."

"I didn't say I had a problem."

"So what is it?" asked Leslie.

"Stop it." Leslie could be like this. You never knew how you were going to find her. Usually a cup of coffee and snack helped, though. With adults, just like children, the problem was very often the basic things.

Sarah resisted the urge to get up and storm out, to leave behind her crummy muffin, because that wasn't how you conducted a friendship. Part of being a friend was being a punching bag. Decades of experience had taught her this.

"Listen, I don't want to be an asshole," said Leslie. "I mean to be more . . . challenging."

"I don't drive around in my car all day."

"I know you don't. And I'm not a complete jerk. Let's not judge things by their surfaces, okay? We had a rough night. I'm actually really not fit for company."

"But this is what I mean, actually," said Sarah. "It's as though as women, we're always expected to be fit for company. We're never allowed to be more than one thing."

"So you want me to be an asshole."

"No. It's more like I understand it when you are."

Things were easy between them after that. They picked through the pieces of their muffins, which were as much like sand in taste as texture. There was a basket of fruit at the till. Leslie said, "I should have ordered that."

Sarah said, "Some bakery." But for the first time in three days, she really felt okay. She wished she could look Jane Q in the eye and tell her so. She sat back in her chair, took a deep and restorative breath from the bottom of her lungs. Leslie seemed more relaxed too, the twitching ceased. She was talking now, about her job, about her son, her recent visit with Beth-Ellen (whose triplets, she said, behaved like absolute monsters), and Sarah listened, really listened, all the while attempting to strike the pose of a woman without a care in the world.

•   •   •

That afternoon, Sarah emailed Starry Fiske and set up a phone interview, because resistance would be futile. She finished transcribing the tape of Betty and the babysitting co-op, though the tape ran out in the middle of a sentence about frictions in the community, how it hadn't all been as simple as it sounded, but weren't women just—

Betty's story wasn't over yet, and somewhere in that cardboard box jumbled with uncatalogued cassettes, some with the tape unspooled, Sarah hoped, would be the rest of it.

And then she updated her blog, her first post since hearing from Jane Q. She'd never felt so self-conscious at the keyboard before as she gathered the thoughts and ideas that had been occurring to her since her trouble had started. The post would be an attempt to piece them together, though she wasn't sure what the through-line would be, or where the thoughts would take her. She usually didn't know until a post was done. She'd long ago realized that the best posts began from a jumping-off point instead of with a careful route plotted on a map. Every time she posted, it was just a little bit an act of faith.

This post was going to be about women, she knew. She was thinking of the mother of the baby in the bathtub, of Leslie kept awake at night. Of all the men in towers supposing they were conducting the business of the world, imagining themselves to be the foundation civilization was resting upon—financial markets, circuit boards, and machine guns. Systems to which libraries of multi-volume encyclopedias had been devoted—the history of the world—but all of it was theory. Fiction. Theirs were worlds dreamt up, right down to every last detail, while women's real lives, the stuff of life itself—blood, milk, sweat, tears, and the burn of fevered foreheads—was deemed inconsequential, or even worse, these stories weren't acknowledged, weren't even written down, let alone read, reviewed, history continuing on as it had ever been, delivered by the pens of men.

It's not strictly oppositional, though, Mitzi writes. *This is not just men versus women. You can't draw lines on a map for these kinds of fronts. The problem is that we live in a patriarchal system in which war is waged as a biological imperative, and every argument is set up with a counter-argument, two extremes disguised as wholeness, truth—such a bloated, bloated canon. These men and too few women who've made careers of opposition, their own camps carved into sub-camps of sub-camps. These are people who debate for fun, the whole exercise nothing more than a game. And women, whose interests are to theory what earth is to the clouds, only have this template for understanding each other. Contemplating another woman is like staring into a mirror and taking a step back in horror—the same but different. Which is where the impulse comes in to start slinging stones, to break the glass, to play the war games, but there is nothing of the game about it, the stuff of women's lives. Blood, milk, sweat, tears, and the burn of fevered foreheads. The trouble is that we don't know how to disagree with each other without destroying each other. None of us has yet learned a better way.*

It's because I'm a woman is what she was thinking, is what she'd been thinking since Tuesday night, since the moment the email from Jane Q had arrived, a moment that had taken shape in her mind as "the attack." *It's because I'm a woman* was the kind of thought that often occurred to her, the way a knock to the knee resulted in a leg jerk. In spite of itself. There'd been resistance to the idea—Janie in her wannabe bomber days deflecting Sarah's burgeoning undergraduate feminism. "Because I'm a woman, nothing," she'd asserted. She'd refused to have gender be her destiny.

But it was true that a woman who dared to have a voice made herself a target. Which made it not just personal but political, that somebody out there was telling her to shut up. That somebody was trying to shut Mitzi down.

In her post, Sarah made no mention of the problems assailing her the past few days, but instead went along to write a story that went against determined notions that women were set up to fail each other, to betray each other. She wrote about the morning she'd just spent with her friend, about yesterday's lunch with her two best friends of years and years, and the luxury of time so rich in company. Of course, mornings like this were balanced out by the rest of her life—the nights the children kept her up or vomited on her, and the times when they wouldn't stop whining, when she wanted to put them out into the backyard and lock the door forever. But then there would be a few hours like these ones suggesting her life was an embarrassment of wonderful things. That the whole history of the world was wrong.

It was the kind of post that would bring out the trolls, all her rampant smugness made manifest, but she didn't write it to brag. Rather, she wanted to keep it as a record, to preserve the way the sun had filled the bakery, even with its terrible muffins, as she and Leslie talked, its rays flowing as their conversation— she'd snapped a photo of the light on the Formica tabletop. She wanted to address the fact of friendship, these women in her life whom she'd known longer than she'd known her husband, whom she'd seen through love and heartbreak, from youth to middle age. Glancing at Leslie across the table, thinking of Janie and Beth-Ellen yesterday, she'd thought, I've been looking at these faces since we were practically children; these conversations are extensions of ones we've been having for twenty years. History with a capital *H*.

The post went up, and Sarah leaned back in her chair, became conscious of her breath, and tried to relax her shoulders. Mitzi would not be bullied into submission.

She spun around in her chair and looked out the window

framing the familiar view of Frances and Evan's backyard. And this time, she knew she wasn't imagining things. She had an excellent view up here above the trees. Her brother-in-law was standing on his back deck, kissing an orange-haired girl who wasn't his wife.

Sarah pushed off from the desk, and her chair rolled to the window ledge. There was a plot after all. Evan should have been at work, teaching guitar lessons and selling tambourines. He was a bit of a local celebrity, mostly from his days in local bands and DJing at dive bars. Even after everything, Frances still considered landing such a husband an achievement up there with her MBA and six-figure salary, and it's true that she'd had to go out of her way to make the marriage happen, as well as accept several key compromises, including rehab stints, general unreliability, and his flagrant misuse of her money.

As far as Sarah knew, he'd always been faithful, though, at least in the one sense, so the sight of him embracing somebody in the yard was unexpected. Snorting cocaine would have been one thing, but here was a whole other level of schmuck.

What she would have given for binoculars. Sarah leaned close to the glass, but the pattern on the screen before her sent her cross-eyed. She took off her glasses, but the image was further out of focus, so she put them on again. She picked up her phone from the desk and took a picture—for what? Evan and the girl were standing apart now, face to face. Sarah didn't recognize her, but that was Evan, certainly. She wanted to be sure about that. Though to what end, she didn't know. She certainly wasn't going to tell Frances, because then she'd only be implicated.

Sarah spun her chair around. "Not my business," she muttered, though she was unconvinced and ended up spinning

360 degrees. Outside, the girl was gone, and Evan was standing alone. She checked her phone in her hand to find that her
photo was a blur, the window screen itself in focus, nothing else
definitive. So she decided to go over there and find out what was
going on.

· · ·

Her boots were still by the door, and she pulled the green ones
this time, even though the ground was dry now. Tracing her
steps from the other day—so something had been happening
after all. She felt sort of pleased that her suspicions had not been
a bored-housewife fantasy she'd conjured—but what were they?
She didn't know who the woman was, or what Evan was doing
with her. And now here she was and the backyard was empty,
and perhaps she'd imagined it all again.

But no. She would have to have more faith in her vision.
Upstairs in the room over the garage, she could hear Evan playing his guitar. It was a sad song, the kind he always played, the
kind of song that had hooked Frances, a smart woman in so many
other ways, making her think that she might be the solution to all
his yearning, that he was looking for a solution at all.

Over the music, he wouldn't be able to hear her coming up
the stairs. When she got to the top, she knocked loudly on the
door. The music stopped.

"I knew it . . ." he said when he opened the door, but evidently he didn't, because he was surprised to see her there.

"Sazz," he said. The idiotic nickname he insisted on. He
knew she hated it. He was bare from the waist up.

She said, "Uh-huh." She was staring at his nipples. They
were pointy, a bit repulsive, yet fascinating.

"What's up?"

"I wondered," she said. Travelling her eyes up to his face.

"What?"

"Just wasn't expecting you to be around," she said. "In the afternoon."

He leaned in close. "You keeping tabs on me?" He made it sound dirty. Then he stepped back, less assured. "Did Frances send you here?"

"Does Frances know you're here?"

"I live here," he said. "What's with the accusation?"

"I wasn't accusing until you got so defensive."

"Well, good," said Evan. "We're stonewalled. So there's no reason you're standing at my door?"

"I thought I saw something," she said. "Out in the yard."

"Oh yeah?" said Evan, raising an eyebrow. Lying was undoubtedly his most expert skill. His nerves didn't show at all. Or maybe years of sneaking around had rubbed them smooth, and now he would wiggle out of anything.

"I was just surprised," she said. "I wasn't expecting you to be home. And there's been that guy breaking into garages—"

"You think I'm breaking into garages. Woo, boy."

"And the laneway arsonist—"

"Come on."

She would back off. He knew she was onto him after all, diverting the path of their conversation and trying to make himself the victim. Victimhood was his specialty, after lying. It made everybody want to fix him, except the people who knew him well enough. She didn't want to push him over the edge, though. With Evan, the edge was always closer than you thought.

"I was just around," she said, "and you were around, and I thought I'd stop and say hi. That's all." It sounded impossible and stupid. She wasn't sure why she'd even bothered. If Chris and Frances were worlds apart, the people they'd married were separated by galaxies. In-laws were a tricky business, wholly arbitrary. Evan didn't belong to her world.

"So you were just around, yeah?" He rubbed his eyes. He always seemed so innocent, like he was waking up from something. If she hadn't seen it herself, she'd really think he was. He stepped away from her, opening the door wider. The drum kit behind him, guitars on their stands, the futon that was the only piece of furniture he'd owned when he'd married Frances, and even that he'd inherited from a roommate. The futon was wide open, and partially clad in rumpled dark-green sheets.

"You're here alone?" she asked.

"I'm practising. You heard me. Getting ready for the album. It's a pivotal moment. I'm taking some time off work."

"I can see everything that happens back here, you know, from out the upstairs window. Did you know that?"

"So you're just sitting there at the window?"

"I've got a desk," she said.

"A desk," he laughed. "I bet you do." He found the idea as absurd as whoever had written that online "Moms with Desks" feature with the stand mixer. He said, "So what do you see, then?"

She said, "You tell me." She wanted him to take the dare, but he refused to.

He said, "You don't know as much as you think you know."

"No?" Oh. Too many echoes. They sounded like idiots. She wondered what he thought she was talking about. If they could be both talking about the very same thing. "What do *you* know?"

"I *know*," said Evan, "that you're wasting my time. I've got fifteen thousand dollars and an album to make. People are counting on this. I've got to be responsible. I've got to focus."

"I was just stopping by," she said. "Letting you know I'm around. Just over the back fence."

"Oh, but I already know that," he said. "I do." He lowered his voice. "Admit it, though," he said. "You've spent all afternoon gazing out the window, coming up with excuses to see me with my shirt off."

•　•　•

Claudia Kincardine was at the school when Sarah arrived to get the girls, conducting a Skype call on her iPad. Fucking Mary Poppins had the day off. Claudia waggled her fingers in Sarah's direction as a greeting, and Sarah waved back. She had created her own company manufacturing baby wraps made from sustainable organic fibres. Her daughter, Paige, was playing with Gladys and Clementine, the three of them attempting to walk up the slide. One would lose her footing, and then they'd all crash down together, rubber soles squeaking on the plastic, landing in a tangle of limbs. Somebody was going to get hurt. Nearby, Paige's brother was eating sand, employing a fat twig as a utensil. Sarah tried not to look. The boy was evidently outside of his mother's line of vision, just obscured by a giant plastic bumblebee on which somebody's baby was crying. Claudia broke off from her virtual conversation to scream across the playground at Paige to keep her shoes on. For Claudia, motherhood and business went hand in hand. "What I tell people," she always said in her magazine profiles, "is that attachment parenting is what inspired my business in the first place."

Though it helped that she had a nanny as capable as Cherry. Of which Claudia tried to stay cognizant. "You know, we couldn't live without her," she always said. But there was always something, another "All I ask . . ." It was hard to have your life so entwined with that of another adult whom you didn't even love. The Mary Poppins factor wasn't always a benefit either, as it required Claudia to up her game, to be the mom who brought squirrel-shaped cookies to the bake sale, just so no one would ever think that being a working mom meant that she couldn't. Mothers like Sarah had so much less to prove.

There was an edge to Claudia, one that was hard to take. You had to tread carefully, which is why Sarah tensed when Claudia finished her call and came to sit beside her.

"I hear you were privy to a conversation about labour terms at our house the other day," Claudia said.

"It wasn't like that," said Sarah. "Did Cherry tell you?" She would be an advocate for Cherry, but only behind Claudia's back. Face to face, she was a coward who knew the whole thing was none of her concern. Perhaps she really was the asshole Jane Q thought she was. It was easier telling the truth when you could hide in plain sight.

"Katie Burkett overheard the whole thing," said Claudia. This was their conversation in the playground about Cherry's trip to the Philippines. Sarah felt sick again. Surely there was a limit to the number of people who could hate you in a day?

"And I know how she is," said Claudia. "Cherry. She makes herself out to be righteous."

"I just listened," said Sarah.

"But even the listening," said Claudia, "it gives her entitlement. To talk. With no regard as to the connection between what she says and reality. If you get my drift."

"I get it," said Sarah.

"Shoes ON, Paige," called Claudia. "All I ask," she said to Sarah, "is for a bit of discretion. And if she couldn't do that, I'd hope you'd back me up."

"It's got nothing to do with me," said Sarah. The children had made it up to the top of the slide and didn't know what to do with themselves. Her own girls had shed their shoes along the way, and Sarah couldn't be bothered to battle on this front. She too loved the feeling of warm sand on her soles.

"Because you don't judge, right?" said Claudia. "Well, that's not a luxury the rest of us can afford. It's not just about principle, Sarah. It's about day-to-day life. It's about who's going to care for my kids while their caregiver takes off for five weeks out of the blue. It's being practical."

"Truthfully," said Sarah, "it's not so much that I don't judge as that I don't care. I really don't." Her tone was more feeble than threatening. She willed one of the children to start screaming for her to break up a scuffle or rescue somebody from the top of the fireman's pole. But the kids were occupied, pretending the top of the slide was an air-traffic control tower. She could hear Clementine's voice, muffled and amplified by her fist at once— "747, come in. Do you hear me? Coming in for a landing on runway six." Gladys was spinning, her arms were wings, making that "neeeeeow" sound for air traffic that children seem to learn in the womb.

Claudia wasn't done. "Katie Burkett said it seemed like you cared."

"I don't know Katie Burkett," said Sarah.

"Liam's mom. In the yoga pants." Which meant she was everyone. Spies, all around her. All the boys were Liams. Was Katie Burkett Jane Q? Was Jane Q possibly someone Sarah didn't even know?

"Well, I don't know what she said, but it was probably wrong. If she'd been listening right, she'd have known that it wasn't worth reporting."

"I think it made her feel uncomfortable," said Claudia, "to hear my name being driven through the mud."

"It wasn't," said Sarah. "I was just talking to Cherry, and I like Cherry."

"We all like Cherry," said Claudia. "Liking Cherry is not the point."

"The point is solidarity," said Sarah. She always got these things far too late in the game.

"Well, yeah. And respect is a two-way street, you know. All I ask is that she not take advantage of our generosity. You know, she talks to me like I'm two feet tall. A little respect would go a real long way."

"Okay," said Sarah, because Claudia was waiting for something.

"Anyway," said Claudia, "Starry Fiske says you're writing her a column. Do you do that? Like advertorials?"

"It's not exactly made to order," said Sarah.

"We should talk about it," said Claudia. "I've got some ideas you could use." Their conflict seemingly forgotten, Sarah sat back on the bench and let Claudia share those ideas while their children concocted elaborate ways to crash and burn, to leap from high places and endanger their precious lives.

*　　*　　*

Another message from Jane Q. There had been nothing all day. Sarah had stopped obsessively checking the account, so she didn't get to read it until that evening after the kids were in bed. Chris was working late.

"Again?" she said when he called. "It's Friday night."

"We'll have all weekend," he said. "It's just—well, you know how it is."

But she didn't, and she didn't know if he didn't know that, or if he just couldn't be bothered to explain.

The message said, *What part of Game Over don't you understand? Am I being too subtle? I wanted you quaking, but there you go serving up the same old self-serving garbage.*

Well, why do you keep reading it, then? Sarah wondered. It was remarkable how many people went out of their way to visit websites whose content drove them crazy. But there was such an appetite for rage. Though perhaps it was only natural in this age of irony, in which it was shameful to feel anything too deeply. Anger might be the only valid emotion left.

But this was personal. The usual trolls she would dismiss with a press of the trash button. She wasn't real to them, which enabled all their online abuse, and they weren't real to her either. Jane Q, on the other hand, was leaping off the screen, not fading away. She nearly lived in three dimensions, and was starting to inform each of Sarah's. Even with her insistence on video game verbiage, *Game Over, Game Over*, just like a flashing screen.

I can't tell if you think you're being nervy, or if you're just clueless. Either way, I'm not getting through to you at all, so I'm going to have to be clearer.

And Sarah was actually relieved to read this. If Jane Q would just tell her what she wanted, Sarah could wrap it up in a box and send it. The threat to this point had been something different, omnipresent in the generalness. This woman was becoming unhinged.

The message continued. *I want the blog to stop. Enough. Which you'll imagine is censorship, I'm sure, or that this is about feminism and midwives and shit, but I'm not talking archetypes. I want you to stop what you're doing because it's hurting people.*

I also want it to feel disconcerting for you to have your life in somebody else's hands. Because that's how it feels to come across the things you've written, to see people's lives and stories splayed out there for your own purposes. Soon all those people are going to see what you've done, and you're going to have to account for your words. You're going to have to account for you. And what will you have to write about then, Sarah? Because you'd actually have to implicate yourself, and you could never do that.

You are not remotely brave.

From the Archives: Mitzi Bytes
Not My Business

I dated guys like my brother-in-law before The Programmer. The laid-back guys who gave the illusion of being low maintenance, and it's so attractive, this idea that at least one thing in our lives might be simple. But beneath that rumpled, flannel surface lies a mess of feelings, wounds, sensitivities, and unresolved mother issues. The fake low-maintenance guy (FLMG) is the worst kind of betrayer because you kind of imagine he's got it all figured out, and then he turns around and wants you to build him from scratch.

All this is relevant because my brother-in-law has just stolen The Sister's credit card and taken off to New Orleans. But he didn't really steal it because his name is on the card, not that he pays any of their bills. Which we're not allowed to talk about because he's sensitive about failing to live up to the male Ideal of being a provider, which The Sister has to help him through too. Not by making him get a job, of course, which would be much too simple. He has other dreams he wants to pursue between the hours of nine and five.

But FLMG taking off is not even the whole story. The whole thing started two months ago when The Sister got pregnant for the second time, which she told me about straight away. This kind of disclosure isn't typical between us and only came about because I'm pregnant too, and so it was mostly one-upmanship. She told me before she'd even told her husband, and I was happy for her, because she's as good at being a mother as she is at everything, except that I think that this one thing she even derives joy from.

When she told FLMG, though, shit hit the fan, and she ended up over at our place in tears. He was furious. He didn't want another baby. He said he loved her and he loved their daughter, but she hadn't even turned two yet, and having her had so thoroughly rocked their marriage and his life that he was adamant that he couldn't go through it again.

He gave The Sister an ultimatum: she could get rid of the baby, or she'd be getting rid of him. Which wasn't really much of an ultimatum, I thought. If he was "got rid of," where on earth would he go? The guy is a parasite. So I thought he was bluffing, but The Sister said she didn't want to find out if he wasn't. She said she'd known he wasn't crazy about the idea of a baby, but she thought once it happened he'd be on board. She thought he was just scared.

So last week, I took The Sister to get an abortion. FLMG said he couldn't handle being there because he'd been through it two times before with old girl-friends, and he didn't want to stir up memories. And The Sister had nobody else to take her, because she doesn't have a friend in the world, except for her brother, but since abortion is a woman's business, the responsibility fell to me, much to the discomfort of us both.

It was sort of weird showing up at the clinic, because I'm so visibly pregnant, and at first I was concerned that the protesters out front would think I was the patient. And then I decided I didn't care what impressions I made on the kinds of people who picket abortion clinics, so I said, "Fuck it" and walked in defiantly, with my arm around my sister-in-law, who was devastated at having to be there.

I'd never really considered that an abortion could be traumatic. When I had my own a few years ago, it was the most enormous relief, bringing with it the end of a pregnancy that was so wrong and awful, and that I had no desire to continue with.

The Sister, on the other hand, was a sorry pile of nerves and emotions, which annoyed me at first, because surely all of us should be bouncing in for our abortions like a feminist rite of passage. Her trauma seemed to negate the rightness of my own decision years ago, like some kind of an affront. But then I got over myself and realized that women are allowed to process things differently, particularly things that are very *different*. I thought of my own baby turning somersaults inside of me, and of how painful it would be to walk in my sister-in-law's shoes. A single thing can have so many realities, I was thinking. And as I sat there with her in the waiting room, holding her hand—and she let me, even though she hates me—but not saying a word, and after I let go of her hand and watched her disappear behind the door, I realized what's wrong with *choice* being the word the whole abortion debate hinges on. That for some women, it's not choice but rather circumstance that dictates they will have an abortion, which makes things so much more complicated. That these women can "choose" an abortion, but that choice can merely be the lesser of two heartbreaks.

Anyway, she came through it fine, I took her home, and it was then that we found FLMG loading up his knapsack. "I'm taking off for a while," he was saying. "The last few weeks have just been too much." He said he needed some space. That he wasn't sure when he'd be back, but he promised he would be. The Sister had been crying since we'd left the clinic, but she stopped and just got angry. And then he left, and it was just the two of us, and she said all she wanted to do was have a long hot bath, but she couldn't because of the bleeding, and also because her daughter would be coming home from daycare, and she couldn't even go pick her up because she was still woozy, so she had to let me do that for her.

So that's where we're at now. And I have no doubt he'll be back, because there's nowhere else for him to go, but in the meantime, The Sister feels like she's lost everything. And so I'm trying to be there for her, but it's tough, because it's not me she wants anyway. She says that every time the phone rings and it's me, she wants to throw something at the wall.

CHAPTER 7

• • • • • • • • • • • • • • •

There were some days—more than she liked to admit—when Sarah forgot that the things that mattered were things she could hold on to. Not the minutiae of web traffic stats, the fleeting glory of a place on a bestseller list, or the pleasure she got from acknowledgement by a popular blogger's link. The affirmation that even after all these years, Mitzi Bytes was still here, even if "here" was a place that didn't physically exist.

You wouldn't know it to look at her. That external validations were her preoccupations as she went about her daily life. At the back of her mind, or perhaps not all the way back, she was someplace else, above it all. Not worrying about where she fit in the PTA social hierarchy (which was very low), because she mattered in a whole other stratosphere. She was one of *Time*'s "Top 40 Bloggers of the Decade." The previous decade, but still.

But the previous decade. When she thought about that, here was where she quaked. She'd lost her edge, sold her soul, become a mom-blogger, and who cared anymore? The *Bite-Sized Mitzi Bytes 365 Desk Calendar* had been a bust in 2006.

"Next thing," somebody had written on an online forum specifically created to discuss why Mitzi Bytes needed to get off the Internet, the minute details of her life ridiculously dissected by a whole lot of vicious people with a lot of time on their hands, "she's going to be posting photos of her crafting room." She didn't have a crafting room, though. She didn't do crafts. She hadn't lost her edge entirely.

Despite the critics, her following remained substantial. Her life had evolved in much the way her readers' had, so they had come along with her. People still bought her books, although the most recent had had disappointing sales, but most books did these days. She remained a well-known blogger still—as much as anybody ever is. *Well-known blogger* is an oxymoron. These were lines she recited to buoy her spirits, to insist to herself that she still mattered, that she existed after all.

But if her online persona and all its illusory trappings disappeared, she knew she'd still be here, the architecture of her life basically sound. If life itself, though—that which took place within the walls of this house, as conducted by the three other people who made up her universe—if that life went awry, she'd possibly never find her way back to herself, back to anything. It was why she slept the way she did, all those uneasy dreams, as she wrapped her body around her husband's sleeping back, clinging in fear of a day she might not have anything to hold on to anymore.

"Right here, now" was what she knew when she closed her eyes and focused. Saturday morning, and she had no other place to be. She'd had the dreams again last night, but now the night was over, and there would be no alarm until Gladys's jump, and even then there was a chance she might not arrive until after eight. The day wide open before them, which could go either way. Elastic enough to hold all the things they'd fill it with, or gaping wide and bloated—it would depend on the kids' temperaments, and on her own. Everything was still possible from where she was lying now, though, and she relished the moment. The whole house quiet, life as she knew it. *This. This. This.*

Chris stirred, and Sarah stayed still so he wouldn't awaken. She wasn't ready to face him yet, to begin the motions of the day with so much on her mind. He couldn't know, and she couldn't tell him, and her aloneness now was the worst thing. Loving Chris was supposed to have saved her from that.

He'd always supported her endeavours, trusting that she'd do the right thing. Could his faith in her ever waver? She'd often thought never—she was smug about this thing, maybe about this one thing among many—but the blog might be a step too far. Once he'd made up his mind, Chris could be as strong-willed as his sister. Sarah could argue over and over again, but he wasn't a man who was easily swayed. "Just because you didn't know about it didn't mean it wasn't there, and you loved me all the while," she might say, but he would not be moved. This was the fact of loving a steadfast man.

He had empathy, though, or something like it—loving Frances had taught him the way. While he lacked imagination enough to be wholly engaged in someone else's experience, he knew the motions, that the motions were important even, that you were to feel for another person who was broken or sad. He'd learned that other people's lives were about more than just a series of problems requiring a solution. And could he still do that for her—go out on that precarious limb toward understanding—even with the shadow self he'd never glimpsed before? What would he think of the stories she told? Would it matter that she'd always told the truth if she'd been keeping this one single truth from him all along?

She could not deny that she hadn't always been kind to him on her blog, at least not in the beginning. But he knew that too, how she'd felt about him then, and he'd forgiven her—she'd only been finding her way to him, he understood. She was growing up. And it was true that almost every story she'd ever told about him on her blog, she'd also told around some table at a dinner party in his presence. Their tortured early history was their family's origin story. He could stand to be teased, and he could laugh at himself. A man with a thin skin wouldn't have stuck around long anyway.

Since what was between them had become solid, though, she'd made Chris less of a subject. This wasn't an act of conscious restraint; she just really loved him, and if she wrote about that too often or too deeply, her readers would start gagging. It wasn't so much that all happy families were alike, but just that nobody really wanted to read about them. When she tried to articulate just what she meant, it sounded too simple. "Marriage is hard" is what everyone said, but hers wasn't. She had to keep this a secret.

So maybe he wouldn't be too upset if he got to know her alter ego. Maybe he'd still smile the way he was smiling right now, rolled onto his back, greeting her along with the morning sun. He said, "Hi." She was still snuggled close to him, and once upon a time, a moment like this would have certainly led to sex, but they had children now, and a door without a lock. A door that stood wide open all night so she could hear the girls if one called her, and they were due to come barrelling through it any time now.

You are not remotely brave, said the message she'd received the night before. Oh, but I am, she thought, or maybe just stupid. To gamble this. She'd loved him for so long. His lips on hers, and she thought for the ten thousandth time: If these are the only lips I ever kiss again, I will have everything I ever wanted.

Chris was not so preoccupied by the wide-open door, however. He was kissing her neck, her left breast in his hand. She moved over to her side and pushed him away. "Not now."

He didn't have to ask why. He rubbed his eyes. She said, "Good morning." Her voice was low. Once the girls were up, they'd be up all day. Right now, time was stopped, and she wanted it to stay there.

He said, "You didn't wait up for me last night." But she had. She'd just been pretending to be asleep when he finally made it home. He'd worked past ten almost every night that week, which pretty much resembled all the weeks before it. It was too much, and too hard, but not so easy to determine this, because he loved his job. She reasoned that she'd rather have an absent husband who was happy and fulfilled than one who lived by the clock and was miserable. Sometimes she even believed it.

"You were late," she said.

He said, "Not so late."

She said, "I was tired." This was true. It had been one thing after another, and she'd just wanted the day to be over. She didn't want to have to talk to a single other person, but this morning she felt better. After a week racked with stresses, strangeness, and anxiety, today seemed just ordinary, nothing out of place. It was a relief. And the terms were different on Saturdays anyway, when the clock belonged to her, and Chris was home, their family balanced in its symmetry. The house was bigger, the children were quieter, and while the disaster they left in their wake was just as much a hurricane, there was somebody else to help clean it up.

Plus, he got up first, as he always did, and she wasn't even required to get up at all. He pulled on pyjama bottoms and a T-shirt. "Tea?" he asked, although he didn't have to. He'd be bringing it up to her once it had steeped.

He kissed her forehead and went downstairs, quieter footsteps than usual. Saturdays were not for heavy treading. She stole his pillow and propped it under her head, picked up her copy of *To the Lighthouse* from her bedside, the book nearly done in time for Monday's book club meeting. Her conversation with Beth-Ellen had inspired her. This was her fifth encounter with the novel. She'd finally sprung and replaced her university copy, whose inane marginalia had become too embarrassing, as well as its pages and pages of entirely highlighted paragraphs. With every read, she understood the book better, but coming face to face with her previous ignorance left her cringing, sort of like a trip back through her blog's archives, which was one she rarely took. The best thing about a blog, of course, was that it was a record of one's own experiences, but that was the worst thing too. Memory itself did a necessary and most effective job of modifying and dulling life's details, just so you didn't want to die when you thought of it all.

Her new copy of the book was still unmarked, and she intended to keep it this way, for this read at least, to encounter the story for itself and not be distracted by her own past lives or anticipated future selves. This would be the closest she'd ever come again to reading the book for the very first time. Instead of all the obvious symbolism labelled in blue pen in her twenty-year-old hand, suddenly those symbols could mean anything.

But now she put the book down. She was stuck on the passage about the duration of the war. Downstairs, she could hear the kettle starting to boil, the bash and clang of pots and pans. Her phone was downstairs too because they had a strict rule she almost never broke about no Internet in the bedroom. She hadn't replied to Jane Q's message, because how could she engage with a person like that? It didn't matter what she said anyway, because it seemed that Jane Q was going to dictate the terms of their communication. She wondered if another message had arrived, anticipating it with a strange mix of longing and dread.

The girls were up, but Chris diverted them on his way to deliver the tea. "Leave Mommy alone," she heard him tell them, and they weren't about to listen, until he told them he'd make them egg-in-the-hole, which they delighted in because they'd be able to eat it with ketchup.

She sipped her tea slowly, listening to the noise downstairs—the conversation, eruptions of laughter, and then a wail when somebody spilled her juice. Life could go on without her, she knew. As a mother, it was essential to have that affirmed on a regular basis. To know that you could just stay in bed a little longer and things would be just fine. And when the tea was cooled, she downed the whole mugful—the mug was bigger than most teapots. It was her favourite one. Then she got out of bed, put her robe on, and crept upstairs to her office, treading softly, quietly slipping inside. The scene outside the window was entirely still. She sat down at her desk and opened her laptop, logged in to her Mitzi account, and checked the messages there.

Five comments on her latest post, the usual suspects. Nothing from Jane Q. And then she heard something outside. A slam. A door? Spinning around in her chair to see, she spotted the woman from the day before, her electric orange hair behind the trees, a blur on the stairs before she disappeared around the front of the garage. In the morning quiet Sarah heard the click of Frances and Evan's back gate. She knew that sound as well as she knew the sound of her own front door. Her ears were keen.

"Mommy." She spun back again. Not so keen. Those girls crept like cats, and Clementine was there, Gladys peering around her, morning hair like giant nests atop their curly heads. "Mommy, what are you doing in *here*?"

•   •   •

Downstairs, the girls spun around her, white nightgowns like ghosts, and Sarah took their picture. Still no messages on her phone.

"Mommy, pretend you're a superhero, okay?" Gladys dove off the couch and bounded around the room with airplane arms.

"Make her stop," said Clementine, attempting the Tree Pose on the carpet in front of the fireplace. "Watching you is making me dizzy." Clementine yoga'd into Warrior II, and her nightgown rode up, her bum sticking out. She was chronically averse to wearing underwear.

"Here," said Gladys, draping a fleece blanket around Sarah's shoulders as she sat on the couch. "You are Polycystic Ovary Girl."

"What?" Sarah turned around and looked at Chris in the kitchen. He smiled and shrugged.

"Never mind. Change the subject," said Gladys, and she took off again, sending her sister teetering.

"Mom," said Clementine, stretching the word into multiple syllables.

"Gladys, sit down," said Chris. "Or go outside. Or something."

"I haven't got *shoes* on," said Gladys, as though this made the idea even more compelling. She started clamouring at the door, her breath fogging up the window. She stepped back to draw a lopsided heart with her finger.

Clementine collapsed in a heap, and then Gladys fell down beside her. They both stared at the ceiling, contemplating the view from below. And Sarah stared at them as they were unaware, trying to process the abundance of their presence with how unfathomable was their existence still, even after years and years. She couldn't figure out whether it was stranger that they hadn't always been here, or that they were here at all. That she had made them; they had lived in her body. These simple bio-logical facts somehow beyond her ken, even though she'd been there all along, watching the whole thing unfolding.

She sipped her tea, her third cup that morning. When you measure out your days in cups like this, it's impossible that life ever seems scant. The girls got up and left the room, on their way to make mischief elsewhere. And Sarah thought about the woman she'd seen twice now, the blur in the photo on her phone, if she was obligated to tell Frances. She wasn't sure her report would carry much weight, though, after the reputation she was getting for curious hallucinations in her sister-in-law's yard. It would prove as much as the photo did. Perhaps it was here where she should mind her own business; or was this just cowardice, avoidance? She didn't feel like having to deal with other people's problems. She had plenty of her own.

There was a crash somewhere in the house, and she waited to hear if it would be followed by a cry, and when it wasn't, she decided to enjoy the quiet moment she had before her. Taking a deep breath, and realizing her shoulders were tense again. She closed her eyes and tried to relax them. Had she become one of those women, she wondered, spying on the neighbours from behind lace curtains. Hadn't she anything better to do?

She wondered if Jane Q could be Evan, or possibly Frances? It's true, if either of them had discovered the blog, threatening emails would be uncharacteristic—too passive. A brick hurled through the window was more Frances's speed. As for Evan, he was capable of anything, but it seemed like a lot of trouble. Evan had enough trouble—he didn't need to go creating it. Perhaps Sarah should have taken a cue from him a long time ago.

"Have you talked to Frances?" she asked, talking to Chris behind her without turning around. He shook his head. After their conversation the other night, he didn't want to discuss his sister. "Never mind," she said.

The girls came back in wearing winter hats from the basket in the hall, for no reason she could discern. "Mommy," said Gladys, "pretend you're a lightning bolt."

Chris laughed. Saturday mornings, Sarah was anything but.

Clementine sat down on the couch and cuddled up beside her. Sarah wrapped her arm around her shoulder and put her tea down so it wouldn't spill. "I love you," she said to her big girl—someone you'd put your tea down for is the definition of love indeed—and then she yanked Clementine's nightgown over her knees. Brand new and it was too small for her already. Clementine was beginning to burst forth, the way a crocus bud arrives in the spring. Her baby was developing edges. Sarah squeezed her closer.

"Mommy, be a thunderbolt," pleaded Gladys, stretching her arms out before her and glaring, as though a special force was emitting from her fingertips. But there was no effect.

"What's she doing?" whispered Clementine.

Sarah whispered back, "I don't know."

Which made Gladys cry. She hated to be mocked, her fierce dignity a necessary protection as the youngest child.

"Ah, come on," said Sarah, opening up her other arm. There was room for a Gladys there. "I'll be a thunderbolt." Gladys crawled on board. "What does a thunderbolt do?"

"You've got to rumble."

"I'm too old to rumble," said Sarah.

"Oh Mommy, no," said Gladys. "You're never too old to rumble."

"She's right," said Clementine wisely, and the eldest daughter must never be argued with. It was in the constitution.

Sarah hugged them close. "My girls," she said, these people who belonged to her and who also never would. Who would spend their lives trying to shake off the holds on them she supposed she had.

•   •   •

Speaking of thunderbolts, her own mother arrived for lunch. She walked in the door and took over the atmosphere. There was always something. Today it was her sinuses. "Honestly, it's like someone's driving a jackhammer into my skull," she said before she even said hello. She kicked the door shut behind her, dropped to her knees, and shouted, "Where are you, dollies?" and then, "Goddamn, my knees."

Gladys and Clementine rushed into her arms.

"Where's Milton?" asked Sarah, referring to her mother's boyfriend.

"Couldn't make it" was the answer. Milton had tried for a while, but eventually he grew weary of Sarah's unrelenting hostility, which she felt bad about now. It wasn't his fault; she would have disliked anyone her mother dragged along as an adjunct into their family, but also Milton was so boring and passive, and maybe if he'd tried to stand up to her, she might have made things easier on him. Or not.

"Hi, Marilyn," said Chris, coming in from the kitchen. The girls had knocked her to the floor. She barely acknowledged him in response, an arrangement that suited them both. Chris and Sarah's mother lived at opposite ends of the emotional spectrum, and things were easier when that distance was maintained.

"Somebody help me up," Marilyn was commanding, marooned on the tiles, a small mountain of scarves and other draping fabrics. Sarah hauled her to her feet, then she patted her purple hair, reapplied her lipstick. "Traffic was murder," she said, smacking her lips.

"Something smells delicious," she called as the girls pulled her down the hall, clouds of perfume left in her wake. It was going to give Sarah a migraine. When Sarah reminded her mother of her perfume allergy, her mother would accuse her of trying to be difficult.

By the time she left, the whole house would be soaked in scent. Chris and Sarah would have to open all the windows, and the smell would leak into even the most distant corners, where Marilyn hadn't even been. Sarah would lie awake at night still smelling it, or imagining that she was. Every time the girls walked near the perfume counters in a department store, they'd inhale and shout "Nana." Marilyn didn't have a signature scent. Scent was her signature scent, bales of it. "What is it that you're trying to hide?" Sarah had once dared to ask, to which her mother had responded, "I'm hiding nothing. I want to project."

She didn't need perfume to project, though. Her voice carried as far as her scent did. She'd fashioned herself as an actor, and talked the same way both on the stage and off it, which made her particularly commanding in the drama classes she taught and from which she made her living and to those who watched her even from the cheap seats at the community theatre, but she could be a bit much in smaller venues. She never quit, which made her a good match for Milton, who backed down easily, but a formidable foe for everybody else.

Her backbone was particularly remarkable for the decades she hadn't had one. There had been a time her voice hadn't carried at all, when she'd starved herself thin and hung back in the shadow of her husband, Sarah's father, an incredible decades-long performance in the role of lawyer's wife. But after he'd died suddenly at his desk in the office late at night, Marilyn had turned down widow's weeds for a full-scale blossoming at the age of forty-five. A triumph, really, except that Sarah hated it, because this was her mother, who should have been through with blossoming—wasn't it a mother's imperative to always stay the same? Of course, it was possible that Sarah might have hated any project her mother had undertaken. She already saw glimmers of it with her own children ("Stop singing, Mommy"), a daughter's prerogative to find fault with her mother's every move.

Sarah followed everyone into the kitchen, where a goat-cheese kale tart was baking in the oven. Clementine and Gladys were hanging onto their grandmother, who had taken off two of her pendants and placed them around their necks. They were waiting for her to open her bag to reveal what she'd brought them, a bestowing that would be declared void if they dared to ask her "Whadja bring me?" They could do patience, both of them, if they were sure that immediate gratification would be the result.

Marilyn would keep them hanging, though. "And what have you been up to?" she asked her daughter, which was a kind of accusation (although Sarah suspected as much about everything her mother ever said). She too conflated Sarah's days spent behind the wheel of an SUV with a life of leisure, resenting it (so Sarah believed) as the life she should have had herself. In addition to finding herself a widow at forty-five, Marilyn had discovered that her husband's finances were a mess. They'd lost their house, and then she'd scrambled to put herself through school to become a teacher, and then put Sarah through school. She'd done it too, though not without a great deal of complaining. She taught at a private school, so her pay was low, and there was no pension. "I'll be working until I'm eighty," she frequently professed, her arms in grand gestures. Put-upon was her favourite part to play. She could often be found at family gatherings with her dress yanked up, taking an inventory of her varicose veins. "Ooooh," she'd moan. "Who's going to rub her nana's feet?"

So what had she been up to? Sarah tried to take stock. "Oh, the usual things," she said. "School, the literacy class. I'm writing an article on fair-trade olive oil."

"Low cholesterol," said Marilyn, sitting down at the table. "I am famished."

"I've just been keeping up with the girls. The Heritage Project—did I tell you about that?"

"Mmm," answered Marilyn, which was not so much an answer as it was that she was stuffing her face with French bread. She didn't like her daughter's lifestyle. "I was you once," she said on many occasions, "squandering my skills and my best years for something that was never going to give back. I was a *homemaker*," she said, the word voiced with disdain, "which is a synonym for somebody you wipe your feet on." She said, "I thought I learned that lesson so that you would never have to."

Sarah had long ago learned that the reply "But I'm not you, Mom" would not suffice. Her mother was unmoved in her conviction that generations were a series of nesting dolls, that her daughter was simply another version of herself. That she'd once been carried inside her and so would be forevermore. "I know you," her mother always said, though Sarah was adamant that she didn't, and that she never would. That their lives were not the same.

They ate lunch in the kitchen, the tart was delicious, and Sarah had made it from scratch. It was as much for sustenance as it was to mark the distance that lay between her and her mother, who'd never met a pie crust that didn't come from the freezer. Marilyn had thirds. Clementine and Gladys behaved. They all listened as Marilyn told stories about her students, playing how they played their roles. Drama class was an emotional place, and always there was somebody crying. She had a girl who, offstage, was desperately trying to fake an eating disorder, muster concern from her classmates, but she was utterly unconvincing.

"They all want so much to be *seen*," said Marilyn. "Not to be just part of a chorus.

"Whereas in my class," said Sarah, "they're all praying to become invisible." She told them about Candice, and the daffodils poem.

"A little harsh," said Marilyn.

"It's the spirit of the thing."

"What spirit? It's not like it's a real class." She saw Sarah about to pounce. "You know I don't mean that. It's just, you're lucky that she shows up at all."

"I know," said Sarah. "And she knows it too. That's the worst thing."

"How does the poem go?" asked Clementine. "The daffodils one."

"I wandered lonely as a cloud—" said Sarah. Which was as far as she got.

"See?" said her mother. "That girl's got something on you." And Sarah couldn't figure out why her mother so delighted in this. Her glee too when she approached Sarah later, once the dishes were cleared away.

"What is it?" she said. "Something's bothering you." When Sarah denied it, Marilyn shook her head. "You're lying. I can read you like a book."

"I'm not a book."

"No," Marilyn agreed, "you're more like a hieroglyphic."

"What do you mean by that?"

"When you're ready to talk," said Marilyn, "I'm ready to listen."

Sarah suppressed the urge to pitch a fit. Her mother was impossible, but also incredible in her ability to push and push until she'd brought out the child she was so determined to prove was at her daughter's core. Every time it was like this—Marilyn would sweep back the curtain to reveal that it had been her all along pulling all the strings. And she thought it was funny.

· · ·

No messages. No messages. So Sarah read the last one over and over, trying to decipher something new from the same words. *People's lives and stories splayed out there for your own purposes.* Was that what it all looked like? Was it really possible that her story was not her own?

The girls were spinning again, and she watched them from where she sat on the couch. Chris was beside her watching TV, a nature special. She'd been wary of these ever since this one time she'd had to watch a penguin being eaten by a seal. She hadn't seen it coming, the scene switching from adorable to awful in seconds. She'd never imagined a penguin as prey, so she was looking away from the screen now. So she watched Clementine and Gladys, dressed now in colourful gowns from the dress-up box that resembled butterfly wings as they turned around and around, delighting in the dizziness and then the all-fall-down.

From the Archives: Mitzi Bytes
Falling Down

I could have spent the entirety of this week under the duvet—perhaps alone, maybe with my children, because they'd totally be up for it if I called it a fort. This week has been heartbreaking, and I've been hiding from the world in more subtle ways, turning off the radio, throwing out the paper as soon as it arrives. The Internet offering no relief, reflecting the trouble back but so much louder.

All this week, ever since that terrible tragedy in which a gunman massacred an entire kindergarten class, arguments have been raging about gun control. Because apparently it's still up for debate whether the guns whose bullets exploded twenty tiny perfect beautiful bodies had anything to do with the killings. A debate we're not meant to get emotional about or we're exploiting these deaths for political purposes. Purposes whose ends are finding means of preventing the murder of children, but I digress.

The one thing we can all agree on is that Kimberly Richard is a terrible mother. Kimberly Richard, who—among circles with all eyes glued to the blogosphere—is now notorious as the author of the blog post "The Kindergarten Killer Could Have Been My Boy."

As news filtered out about the killings, Richard wrote in her post, she noted parallels between the killer and her own son, a boy she calls Jake. Jake has suffered from mental disturbances from a young age, inflicts physical and emotional violence on his mother and his siblings, and has spent the last decade in and out of psychiatric care. Kimberly Richard is a single mother with limited means, and in her post she despairs at the future for her boy, who is now fifteen. And despairs at her own future too, wondering if she'll one day find herself staring down the barrel of a gun, her son about to pull the trigger.

What she's saying is that this isn't an isolated case. That young people with troubling mental illness are all too common, and even more common is the lack of support.

Terrifying, true, and important, but all that got lost in the hubbub. The post went viral, and instead of readers considering the desperation that would inspire such a post, they slapped a Bad Mother label on her chest and they set her stake on fire.

"Because it's not her story," her critics say. "It belongs to her son." Kimberly Richard has failed as a mother by making herself a subject, violating the sacred tenet of motherhood to be self-effacing, like those 19th-century photos of hovering babies, who were actually held in their mother's arms, the mothers rendered invisible by being draped, like furniture, in black sheets.

It is offensive to assert that once a woman has children, her story is no longer her own. Think of the infinite number of shitty things that can happen to a mother—you have a picture in your mind of what your life is going to be, and so often reality is different. Parenthood is an enormous risk, a risk that's implicit in the experience, but to shrug at a woman whose teenage son, say, has made a habit of being physically threatening to her and her other children and who has exhausted all available mental health resources, to tell her she's made her bed so should lie in it, is to be utterly devoid of compassion.

As mothers, we're expected to be martyrs. Failing to put up and shut up constitutes a sin. But then what about my friend who's raising her autistic son alone, and is allotted three hours a week of respite care, during which she collapses into desperate sleep. She spends her nights sitting up with him, or watching him breathe and waiting for him to awake, and he always does. And when he does wake, he resists any physical overtures—he cannot stand to be touched—but if his mother disappears from his sight, he goes ballistic. So there she stays, every night, and she'll tell you this is nothing. "What choice do I have?" As a mother, she says, you simply do what you have to do, but what if some of the things you have to do are unbearable? Society itself having shifted off the burden, and so many mothers' backs must be breaking under the strain.

For too long, women haven't been permitted to own their lives. We have been somebody's daughter, mother, wife, but so rarely a person in her own right, a person with a voice, with a story to tell. It seems archaic to me that anyone would fault Kimberly Richard, a woman whose existence has been subsumed by the demands of her son, for demanding a piece of the story for herself. For speaking out against a social system that has not only failed her but also failed the boy to whose defence so many of you now purport to rally.

CHAPTER 8

. . . .

On Sunday the sky was blue and as cloudless as it was endless, and the girls ran outside without coats on. Sarah went out on the deck after them and sat down on a patio chair, its cushion in basement storage for the winter. She was still wearing her pyjamas, a hoodie thrown on top, and her feet were bare, cold too, so she sat cross-legged and tucked them beneath her. She sipped her tea. In the trees above her, birds sang—the sparrows they'd been hearing all winter long, somewhere a cardinal. Down on the lawn, Gladys and Clementine were gathering broken branches that had fallen after the winter's ice storms. They were building a house for Eeyore, they explained, calling back over their shoulders when she asked them. She'd left the patio door open wide so that springtime air could drift indoors. The house had been shut up for so long.

Chris came outside once he'd finished clearing up from breakfast. Sensibly, he'd put on shoes, a coat. He was holding the teapot, having guessed correctly that she would have finished her first mug already. She thanked him, and he sat down with her on the end of her chair.

He reached for her hand. And there they were, right on the cusp of springtime, the morning of a brand new day. Usually this was her favourite kind of moment, the moment before, on the edge of possibility. She squeezed his hand, and he squeezed back, and she felt bad because he thought he knew what she was thinking about. She smiled at him, felt even worse.

He said, "It could all come crashing down, you know." The broken branches, Eeyore's house. He meant the silver maple that hovered over their house like a mother.

She said, "Surely it's not as bad as that."

"I don't know," he said. They'd had the tree trimmed back the spring before, though the arborist had advised that it was only a short-term measure. The trees in their neighbourhood had been planted more than a hundred years ago, when these streets had still been farmland. Scattered in gardens up and down their streets were bedraggled, outsized apple trees, from somebody's ancient orchard. The apples were too high to pick before the worms got them. And trees like their maple loomed so large that their limbs were unstable. The trees were the reason Maplewood Village had been so hard hit by the ice storm last December—cars crushed by fallen trunks, their rot exposed now; heavy branches breaking, falling power lines, and the electricity out for days. Lying in bed on those dark December nights, before they gave in to the elements and fled to a hotel to celebrate New Year's over canned pop and lukewarm pizza, Sarah had been kept awake by the sound of breaking branches, like somebody outside stalking the ice-slick streets, cracking the night with a whip.

The damage was only becoming apparent now that the snow and ice had melted. They were lucky that the damage in their own backyard hadn't been worse. No matter what happened, this was the sort of thing people told themselves: at least the tree didn't hit the house, or if it did, at least nobody was hurt. Who really needs a house anyway?

She said, "I wouldn't want to lose it." She couldn't imagine their house without that tree, or at least without its shade. The tree itself she rarely looked at—really couldn't bear to since the arborist had cut it back so far.

"It's all in the risk," Chris said. Owning a home was so perilous—nobody had ever told them that. Not just financially. All the danger, the acts of god, items quantified on their insurance forms. Water and wind and fire and trees. And blocked sewage pipes, and broken water mains. *Safe as houses* was an expression that meant nothing at all.

She said, "I think it's going to be okay." She really did have faith in their tree—its nature was benevolent. Still holding Chris's hand, her other hand warmed by the mug of tea. They were feeling especially connected that morning, the distance and tensions of the previous days somehow lessened. Just after seven thirty, Gladys had leaped onto the bed, Clementine not far behind her. And Sarah hadn't even peeked from beneath the covers before Chris was up and had taken them both downstairs, supplying them with orange juice, two bowls of cereal, and, crucially, the television tuned to streaming cartoons. And then he'd come back up, peeling off his pyjama bottoms, slipping back into place, and they'd moved together, her arms around him. Relishing the luxury of dozing, being allowed a half start. There was no urgency as the inane tinny sound of children's programming echoed from downstairs, so far away. The lull was heavy, until something inside had stirred them both and then the urgency took hold—the slow, heavy, unspoken kind. One thing leading to another, although their eyes were barely open, while they hadn't said a word.

It was the way his finger drew a circle on her thigh, light and easy, yet deliberate. She pressed close to him, her breasts against his back, skin on skin. She licked his shoulder—he tasted different in the morning, as though he'd been marinating in himself. He reached for her hand and held it against his chest, something fervent in his grip that she held for a moment, but then she pulled her hand away and made its way down his body where she knew exactly what she'd find, aroused and waiting. There were no surprises here in this slow and easy Sunday-morning under-the-covers love. As easy to fall into as sleep was—he moved on top of her, and with her arms around him, she led him inside her. Moving together like wave over wave, hard and soft, push and pull, ebb and flow, come and go, until the waves were building inside her, in both of them, she knew—she could tell by how he shuddered and by how he clutched her shoulders as he came, and she was coming too, this perfect union. It could be like this, absolute satiation, even after all these years.

Even when it was over, it wasn't, and he fell down on her chest. They lay there together, and he fluttered his fingers across her nipples, took one in his mouth. No urgency now—a kind of savouring of the moment. They'd only had a handful of moments like this since the girls were born, of mornings with four walls to themselves. Chris's mouth on her breast—she looked down at him, his eyes closed. A dull tingling as the pulses in her body were retreating. She loved how it felt, what she saw—this image she held in her mind when she got herself off on work breaks during weekday afternoons while she waited for the kettle to boil.

He looked asleep, the way her babies used to pass out with

her nipple in their mouths. Pacified. Though it wasn't the same thing, of course, and neither he nor she had ever suffered any confusion about this, even when their children had been small and her nipples would erupt with milk at his touch. He would lick and suck them when they made love, and she'd experience the same letdown, his mouth filling with the sweet taste. He said he liked it, and she found this vaguely erotic in a way she wasn't comfortable admitting—rare for her. That her body could be for nourishment and pleasure—her own—all at once; she was like an anatomical GoBot. It was empowering, really, to be earth mother and temptress, giving and receiving, to be both. Making her feel like she still belonged to herself during that time in which she'd been pulled in all directions.

But there was no such tension now as they lay together, a mess of arms and legs, sticky and sweaty, and so they disentangled, got out of bed, and it was nearly nine.

"I do believe in the tree," she said now, where they were in the backyard just an hour or so later, still holding on.

He said, "I know you do." He took her beliefs as seriously as he did the arborist's advisements. He could put his faith in things far less rooted than trees.

Down below, the girls started shouting: Clementine hadn't authorized her sister's extension of the east wing, but Gladys was gunning for it anyway, bulldozing an entire wall made of branches and bramble.

"Daddy, Gladys is wrecking it all," Clem shouted, but he was nearly there already. "Sort it out yourselves," Sarah called down, over the sound of Chris's calm voice trying to find some reason between their points of view. "Why does Eeyore need another door?" she heard him asking, a question that garnered a considered answer that had something to do with Rabbit's house, the need for a second exit. "It's precautions," Clementine was explaining, and without seeing, Sarah knew Chris was listening to this, nodding, his full attention given to his daughters, to the matter of Eeyore's house, taking it all as seriously as he did everything.

Which freed her for a moment to drift away from all of that, to sink back in her chair—comfortable even without the plush— and feel the sun on her face, warmth for the first time in months.

•   •   •

The peace of Sunday was always going to be temporary. Jane Q was in touch again on Monday morning as Sarah was at her desk trying to find the focus to work. She'd been spinning around in her chair, staring out the window, waiting for something to happen, for another glimpse of the girl with orange hair, when the message arrived, the other shoe dropping. She'd been waiting for it. There were so many shoes. The sky was raining with them.

Reading your archives, the message went, *I find myself alternating between rage and despair. And I've been thinking of desperate measures—suing for libel, blackmail, forcing you to just shut the whole thing down, or just sending the URL to a few key folks so I could destroy you. If I'm honest, though, I'm nearly enjoying this act of haunting you, of causing you something close to the discomfort you've brought my way. Of hijacking your life just the way you did mine.*

It broke off there. More shoes to come. Sarah reread the list of possible consequences, and considered which would be the worst. She wasn't sure the libel suit could work; wondered who the few key folks might be. Blackmail didn't sound so bad.

Jane Q could be anyone. This was the point—who didn't have it in them to destroy someone when given cause and half a chance? Opening a new post on her blog, she set out to write toward the answer. About bullies—that provocative buzzword—and about her children, and whether it was preferable for one's child to be the bullied or the bully. A moot point, since every child was usually a bit of both. *What's the unfortunate phone call you'd rather receive from your child's school?* The bully, at least, she supposed, would have some agency to change the situation. The bullied, on the other hand, the hapless victim of falling shoes, stolen sneakers. Acts of god. Life is like that.

People are jerks, she wrote. *It's as it's ever been. You can't outlaw human behaviour, though we can try to teach our kids some compassion. But it's a project that's not always going to have immediate results.*

Anti-bullying was a movement. It had its own school club. The bullies even joined, never imagining themselves as the targets, those in need of changing. The very idea of targeting bullies was absurd anyway. It was the modern elementary-school version of the McCarthy witch hunts. Clementine had wanted to join, but Sarah advised her against it. Persuaded her to sign up for lunchtime choir instead, even though she was tone-deaf.

She pressed Publish. She was tired of the sanctimony of someone occupying moral high ground while threatening blackmail.

She'd written, *Everybody's really got to calm the fuck down. Speaking of targets, we're actually missing it here. Most of what everyone is so up in arms about is simple child's play. Play that teaches kids lessons when they're left alone to figure things out for themselves.* When she'd been a kid, they'd called her Bigfoot, mocked her for wearing store-brand jeans, and the one time she'd had a decent pair of running shoes, someone had stolen them. Did she wish that none of that had ever happened? Of course she did. But did she see any way that it could have been prevented? Absolutely not.

She'd been on both sides, though. That was the worst thing, and what compounded her parental anxiety. Having always been a bit rotten herself, she had no faith in human goodness, particularly among children who hadn't learned yet how to be—it was a dirty world out there. Each morning, she dropped off her daughters at school, leaving them to fend for themselves, and when she really thought about it, life itself was terrifying, the whole wide world.

To the Lighthouse sitting before her on the desk, and the book's centre, Mrs. Ramsay, was trying to reconcile having had eight children with her acute sense of dread. "There were the eternal problems: suffering; death; the poor. There was always a woman dying of cancer even here. And yet she had said to all these children, You shall go through it all."

It was irreconcilable, but so were most things. Sarah assured herself by reasoning that she herself was glad to have been born, grateful for the life she'd lived so far, never mind Bigfoot and the stolen shoes. Even Jane Q couldn't change her mind about that. And hopefully the life she'd brought her children wouldn't only be a burden. But were the girls her distraction from the suffering and death, she wondered? A futile attempt to counter it?

The distraction only worked so far. That very morning her eldest distraction had hurled a rain boot at her head, having failed in her feeble attempts to locate its mate. "I would like to pound you into pieces," Clementine screeched, such a peculiar utterance that Sarah had smiled, which only heightened the fury.

"She has a vicious streak" was something Sarah had said about her daughter often, usually with a bit of pride. She was glad to be raising a strong-willed girl, no shrinking violet. But how far was too far? And how much cruelty was a mask for social clumsiness? What if Clementine was merely as socially inept as Sarah herself had been for so long (forever) and Sarah was just dressing the whole thing up in respectability?

She'd learn, though. She'd be okay, Clementine, notwithstanding her chances of being hit by a bus, or a pedophile ring among the leaders of the Brownie pack. See, all these things parents and well-meaning clubs can't possibly control, no matter how they try. *They shall go through it all.*

•   •   •

The Book Club, a histrionic gathering of perimenopausal middle-class white women, had come very close to being a cliché unto itself, but Sarah's book club was another story. Her book club was wonderful. She loved it, these monthly gatherings with women who were all so smart and who gathered in order to challenge and learn from one another. It was a local affair, a tightly woven social web, with Janie, Beth-Ellen, Leslie, a few women from the others' circles, some from the school. Membership capped—they didn't want the numbers to get unruly. Paige's mom, Claudia, was still annoyed that they'd refused her, but she was proof of why the cap was necessary.

The meetings were set on the calendar weeks in advance, and those nights Chris was home in time to fix dinner for the girls as she slipped out the door for the evening. Their host that night was Michelle, whom Sarah knew through Leslie: Michelle was Leslie's ex-husband's cousin, the one thing of Ian's she'd kept after the divorce, Leslie liked to explain. Her place was an immaculate townhouse built as infill off a laneway. Not only did Michelle live alone, which kept her home in order, but she was a producer for a home decor television channel, and therefore she knew her stuff. Hospitality was her forte, the table decked with expensive cheese and fancy organic seed crackers. She had lit candles and turned the lights down. The room was inviting and warm. Every place to sit was comfortable. Sarah curled up on a corner of the chesterfield. Beth-Ellen sat beside her.

Leslie wasn't coming. She'd called a few hours before, Michelle said. "She's going through some stuff right now." Sarah remembered the twitching eye. Leslie's absence wasn't unexpected—she cancelled more often than she actually came. She'd get her mother-in-law to babysit, but if Jamie was having a bad day, the arrangement didn't work.

The rest of the women assembled, setting down their plates heaped with hors d'oeuvre. Each of them was bearing a different edition of the book—battered Penguin paperbacks, stiff library hardbacks, one with a silhouette of Woolf on the cover, others with images of actual lighthouses.

"Phallic," said Janie, who saw penises everywhere.

"This book, this book . . . " said Allison Choi, who was Janie's next-door neighbour. "Do you know how many times I've tried to read it? I've never managed to penetrate it." ("Ha!" said Janie.) "Halfway through, and they're only having dinner. The world's longest soup course."

"But that's what I love about it," said Sarah. "The depth of a single moment. It's not that time stands still, but she bores so much inside it. The perspective of every single person, and even within each perspective, there's all the sides."

"But Lily Briscoe," said Beth-Ellen. "Her Chinese eyes. What Mrs. Ramsay said . . ." She thumbed through her book for the page she'd marked with a bright yellow Post-it. "'What we call "knowing" people, "thinking" of them, "being fond" of them! Not a word of it was true; she had made it up . . . She went on tunnelling her way into her picture.'"

"It's not true, though," said Michelle, coming in from the kitchen with a new bottle of wine. They were just getting started, but she was already topping up their glasses. "That the idea of knowledge of others is all made up. I don't buy that. We can know things. Some people really are transparent."

"Which is what they want you to think," said Naomi Lloyd, a mischievous glint in her eyes.

"Nobody ever surprises me," said Michelle. She was never one to relinquish a point.

"I don't think it's true that we're all so isolated as the book says," said Janie. "You know, standing on a tiny slip between land and sea. I mean, I know people. I love people."

"But the 'you' and the 'people,'" said Sarah. "That's the point, I think. They're always changing. Nobody is ever just one thing."

Beth-Ellen said, "Multiplicity."

Michelle was shaking her head. "You're just not looking properly. People are not that complicated."

Though Sarah wondered how Michelle could be so confident. Personally, people surprised her all the time. When she wrote about them on her blog, she supposed, it was a way to try to pin them down, like biologists' specimens, nineteenth-century butterflies. And almost every time, they managed to peel their wings from the pages, to return to life and surprise her again.

"Her vision is all so hopeless," continued Michelle. "I don't think that anybody is really as alone as that."

"Because of love," said Allison. "She keeps seizing on that, Mrs. Ramsay. The way she wants to pair everybody off, end with a wedding. But real life doesn't work like that."

"Of course not," said Michelle. "She says not being married is like standing alone on the edge of the cliff. I reject that."

"But even when you *are* married, it can be," said Sarah. "Says Woolf," she added. It wasn't quite her experience. Chris was nowhere near as remote as Mr. Ramsay in *To the Lighthouse*. What he'd done is give her the space to be whomever she wanted, but she wondered now what it might be like to be *known*.

"What about friendship, though?" said Naomi. "That's what missing."

"Mrs. Ramsay had eight children," said Janie. "There wasn't time."

"But it wasn't just her," Beth-Ellen said. "Lily Briscoe too. She's alone. They all are."

"Friendship was rarer then," said Michelle. "Or at least stories about it were—between women, I mean. Remember the line from *A Room of One's Own*? 'Chloe liked Olivia.' The idea was groundbreaking. Nobody was writing about this part of women's experience. Not even Woolf, I guess. In her novels at least."

"Do you think women know each other in a way that men and women can't?" asked Allison.

"Or is it that men are unknowable?" said Janie.

"But that's not it at all," said Sarah. "I mean, Mr. Ramsay is there with his head in the clouds, fixated on tables, but he's still *there*. Even his theoretical kitchen table is something solid. Whereas Mrs. Ramsay is at a remove, in the picture but never quite in focus."

"Or is it that she's something so different to everyone that she's ceased to exist?"

"Yes!" Beth-Ellen flipped to another yellow note. "'So boasting of her capacity to surround and protect, there was scarcely a shell of herself left for her to know herself by.'"

"That," said Sarah. "That's the tyranny you've got to fight against." And did she know herself, Sarah wondered? Though no one had ever boasted about her capacity to surround and protect. Just showing up sometimes took it all out of her. Sarah wasn't Mrs. Ramsay. Nobody was.

"She was writing about her mother, you know," said Naomi. "Virginia Woolf. She died when she was thirteen."

Though it wasn't specific to mothers. "My dad died when I was eleven," said Sarah. "And she gets it exactly right, the boat ride at the end. How the whole family is unmoored without its centre."

"The structure is frustrating," said Allison. "Everything happens in parentheses. And then we spend pages and pages watching a scarf hanging from a skull on the wall, blowing in the breeze."

"Once you've got to the end of the soup course," said Janie.

Allison said, "Exactly."

"What about the blurriness of the mother, Mrs. Ramsay?" said Naomi. "I mean, with another writer, we'd be calling her out on that. Shouldn't she be striving for clarity?"

"I think she tried," said Sarah. "Maybe. And then she realized that there was no such thing."

"It's like an impressionist painting," said Michelle. "When you look too close, you're overwhelmed by the atoms." Exactly.

They got up then to replenish their plates, pleased with themselves for having sustained literary conversation so far before lapsing into the far less demanding subjects they returned to all the time—their children, workplace politics, and phalluses, which were either too much with them, or not at all. This time the former: Allison's son had been exposing himself at daycare. There'd been complaints from the other children. They were threatening to bring in a psychologist.

"I'm raising a social menace," she screeched.

"What is it about boys and their lighthouses?" said Michelle.

"He'll grow out of it," said Janie. "They grow out of every-thing." Her stepchildren were raised, and she said she no longer worried about anything, though she also speculated it was only because her will had been broken.

"Some don't, though," said Naomi. There was a man in a John Deere cap who'd been going around grocery stores down-town and getting his bits out in the frozen meats.

Beth-Ellen said, "I just thank god I'm a vegetarian."

"You could write about it," said Michelle to Sarah. "Isn't it something, how it's everywhere?" She took a survey. "Who among you hasn't encountered a dirty man hiding in the bushes, with his penis in his hands."

"Sometimes not even dirty," said Naomi, and there was not a single one of them whose hand wasn't raised. "Some of those men were decidedly clean."

"The things we have to contend with," said Allison.

They shall go through it all, thought Sarah. She said, "Might be a bit racy for the *Sentinel*."

Conversation was going on around them, and Michelle low-ered her voice a tone. "Okay, then," she said. "What about the other thing? The online one? Your covert operation? Seems like your gig—provocative, a little bit naughty."

The shoe smacked. Sarah felt it lodged in her guts. "What other thing?" she asked.

"Oh," said Michelle, smiling even with her eyes, and Sarah wasn't sure if this was kindness or if something more malicious lay beneath her expression. "I've been hearing you had some-thing else going on, a sideline."

"No," said Sarah, but she hung on too long to the word, made it sound like a question. She spoke louder, "I don't know what you mean."

"Okay," said Michelle, raising her hand as though to silence her, her tone making clear that she was not convinced. When Sarah spoke again, Michelle said, "Never mind" and started gathering plates and glasses.

Sarah followed her into the kitchen. "Who told you about that?"

Michelle was loading the dishwasher. "I said never mind," she said. "I made a mistake."

"But where did you hear about it?" Sarah asked.

Michelle set down a glass on the counter. "Did I make a mistake?" she asked. Sarah nodded. "Then why does it matter?" She resumed her work, stacking the dishwasher like a puzzle.

Sarah looked behind her—the other women were still busy talking, and periodically exploding into raucous laughter. She turned back. "Is it you?" she asked.

"What?" said Michelle, who had her hands full, a bowl of olive pits teetering on top of a stack of dishes she was bringing over from the table. Sarah took it and set it on the counter. "Thanks," said Michelle. "Is what me?"

"Jane Q," said Sarah, her voice a whisper.

"I don't know what you're talking about," Michelle whispered back. Then speaking at a normal volume: "Sarah, you're acting bizarre."

Sarah tried to regain her composure. "It's a weird thing, actually, what you said," she said.

"I made a mistake," Michelle said. "We established that. I thought I heard it somewhere. I guess I was wrong."

"Somewhere?"

"Sarah, seriously," said Michelle. Then, "Jane Q?" *Jank you.* It really sounded like she didn't know.

Naomi and Janie tramped in. Naomi had brought the cake, which was still in its box in the fridge. They needed a plate to put it on, a knife, and a server. Sarah hung back, watching Michelle, who moved from point to point in her perfect kitchen that she'd designed and built herself. It was all about the details. She'd built drawers deep enough to store her appliances in. Apparently toasters were unsightly. Sarah had never realized.

When the cake was ready, Sarah and Michelle were meant to follow it back to the group. And after that, Sarah didn't get a chance to speak to Michelle, because whenever she got close, Michelle moved again, or struck up a conversation with someone across the room.

Were the brush-offs deliberate? Sarah sat quietly eating her cake, a piece of the lighthouse, a nice slab with red and white stripes like a barbershop pole, now reduced to crumbs on a napkin. No one seemed to notice she was quiet.

Allison said, "He's infatuated. And now the only song he wants to listen to is 'My Ding-a-Ling.'"

Somebody else was asking, "Who's Anthony? Who's Anthony?"

Sarah caught Michelle looking at her, quickly looking away, or maybe she was just going out of her mind. She'd been looking for any piece of the puzzle, but this new one didn't fit any place she could think of.

How long did you think you'd get away with this?

Michelle hugged her goodbye at the door, but she hugged everybody. Her voice betraying nothing as she called for them all to drive safely, the cheery message ringing into the night.

From the Archives: Mitzi Bytes
The Trouble

I met M's new boyfriend, G, a few weeks ago at her Christmas party. She knows him through work, I've heard all about him, and so it was exciting to finally see him in the flesh, to find out if he was everything she'd said he was. And he was everything, upon first glance. Dashingly handsome, and actually employed, which are the two main hurdles when you're looking for love in your forties.

The new guy was really charming and funny, and he kept putting his hand on the small of her back in a way that wasn't possessive, but instead just seemed like he wanted to be touching her always. I listened to him talking about her with another friend. "She's phenomenal," he was saying, so obviously besotted, and I thought, *She really deserves that.*

"Finally," I thought as I drove home that night. A happy ending. There is something so comforting, so tidy, about the idea of people in pairs. They would get married, and it wasn't even too late for kids.

But I got it all wrong. This week I ran into M at the mall. The school had sprung a Pyjama Day on us, and all the ones we had were obscenely small and ratty, so I was buying new pairs. M was out shopping for a shoe rack. So we sat down together in the food court for a quick cup of caffeine, and she appeared still to be glowing with something—happiness? The way she said his name was with such relish, as though it were the smoothest thing in the world.

I said, "So things are really happening."

She said, "It's pretty serious."

I said, "You think there might be a ring on the horizon?"

She looked at me like I was crazy. "Well, no," she said. "On account of his wife."

"I thought I told you," she said when she saw my expression. "And it's not like that. They're not really married. She has cancer."

Even once M explained, it still didn't make sense. The cancer was terminal, but the prognosis was good. She'd been living with it for six years already. The marriage had been over for even longer than she'd had cancer, but they stayed married because she needed his medical benefits. And because they had three kids. They still lived together. They were on vacation in Florida together, with the kids, for spring break.

"It sounds like they're really married," I told her.

She rolled her eyes. "You just don't understand."

"I wouldn't take my ex on vacation."

"Well, not everybody is as *conventional* as you are," she told me, spitting out the word as though it were the worst kind of slur.

I had to defend myself. "I'm not," I said.

She shrugged. "I call it as I see it, Mitzi," she said.

"Well, so do I," I told her, "and this guy is married."

"G," she said, "has an arrangement."

"He certainly does," I said, "and you're going to get fucked over."

"Couldn't you just be supportive?" she asked.

I said, "I just want to be happy for you."

She said, "Well, then be happy. I'm happy. Nothing's been this good in forever."

By now, our paper cups were empty. I'd taken off the sleeve, and I was ripping it to pieces, and I'd been hoping for some kind of an evolution in her thinking by the time it was shredded, but here we were, right where we had started.

I told her, "I'm appealing to you, not just as a friend but as a wife. Somebody who knows what that woman's got to lose, and if she's really got cancer, M," I said, "she's going to lose anyway. How could you do this?"

She said, "Oh, for fuck's sake, you're really serious, aren't you? You're honestly trying to appeal to me from some moral high ground because you're a *wife*." She said *wife* the same way she'd said *conventional*. "As though that means anything."

"But it does."

She said, "You have no idea what you're talking about."

"It's immoral," I said. "Another woman's husband. A betrayal."

She said, "Not my betrayal. I don't even know the woman."

"Then you're dating an asshole," I told her, as hysterical as one could sound when talking in a *sotto voce*. I couldn't help but take it personally. M had no idea of the stakes she was playing for, the weight of an entire family collapsed upon her shoulders. She didn't know how hard you had to work to make a family happen, to hold the whole thing together. A cancer diagnosis, the allure of a sexy co-worker; calamity could happen any time, and we did it anyway—lived in these houses, created these lives. But to M, the whole thing was just another encounter. It was infuriating.

She'd been staring into her empty cup, trying to read something in the dregs of her coffee, and now she set the cup on the table. "I missed my cue a minute ago," she said. "The part where I was supposed to storm off in a fury, but it's not my style, Mitzi. I really don't do dramatics."

She'd reduced me to a fool. As a manoeuvre, it was impressive.

"So what are we going to do?" I asked.

"The trouble with you," she said, "is that you stick your nose into things that you don't understand."

"I guess I don't," I said. "Understand, I mean."

She shrugged. "That part's not my problem."

I waited a moment. So we were done, then. I got up from the table, started gathering my shopping bags.

She said, "You're not even going to apologize."

"I've got nothing to be sorry for."

"But neither do I," she said, getting up too. "So I'll be generous for friendship's sake, and let's just call it even."

CHAPTER 9

. . . .

Frances called in the morning, after the kids were at school. Sarah was in her office transcribing a tape by a woman called Verna Foxworth, who'd spent the war working as a nurse in Halifax, at a psychiatric hospital that cared for soldiers home from the front. "For some reason, I'd thought this would be a great way to find a husband," she was saying, and Sarah was on a roll when she had to stop the tape, answer the phone.

Frances said, "I hear you're still snooping around."

"Seriously?" said Sarah. "It was days ago."

"I suppose you're wondering about the girl."

"Well . . ." Sarah saved her file. "Yes. I am."

"She's the backup singer," said Frances. "She's living over the garage for a while, while she's working some stuff out in her personal life." It sounded as though she were reading lines off a page.

"Okay," said Sarah, not sure what Frances expected her to make of this information. Though it was good to hear that

the orange-haired girl she'd seen with Evan was real and not a
mirage, and that she had a reason for being there. One thing in
the world made sense. Never mind the kissing, which made its
own kind of sense. Or else the trees along the lot line misconstrued things. An obscuring curtain between here and reality.
You couldn't see the forest for them.

Sarah asked, "Why hasn't Evan been working?" He'd had the
job for a few years, perfectly tailored for his lifestyle. They didn't
mind when he showed up late, or when he showed up stoned.

"He's taken a sabbatical."

"A sabbatical?"

"Don't be sarcastic. He needs what he needs. This money is
the biggest thing that's ever happened to him. He wants the time
to focus."

"On the album."

"On everything. The album's just part of a larger strategy."

"And the girl?"

"She's playing on the album. He's helping her. It's a
mentorship."

"Right," said Sarah.

"I know what you think."

"I don't think anything," said Sarah, who found the whole
arrangement exhausting. She wasn't sure how much trauma
Evan would have to inflict upon his wife before she finally conceded that he was hurting her. Sarah was also unnerved by her
own feelings, by how desperate she was for Frances to stop
defending him and finally break. A few times Frances had come
close, but the hard shell was always restored by the next time
Sarah saw her, and if anything, Frances was harsher than usual
for having betrayed herself. It was all too much. Sarah would
have liked just to detach from the whole thing. Why did she

care? Why were they still having this conversation? Surely Frances had work to do too?

"So she's living there," said Sarah. That part didn't really make sense. "The girl."

"It's temporary. And it's easier for rehearsals. Anyway, she's married, but she's having trouble with the husband. Evan's doing her a favour." Sarah tried to interrupt, but Frances kept talking. "And you've got to leave them to it. This is about art. He needs his focus. You're not helping by going over there and getting in the middle of things."

"Once, Frances," said Sarah. "I went over there once. I was there less than two minutes. I'm sure his focus is safe."

"Just leave him alone. You're ganging up on him."

Sarah said, "I'm not a gang."

"You might as well be," said Frances. "Just leave things alone." Their call suddenly cut off, no accident. The touch-tone version of a slammed receiver. Sarah stood listening to the silence for a moment before the busy signal kicked in.

Then she dialed Chris, who actually answered. She said, "It's a miracle!"

He said, "It's you."

"Who else?"

"No, I'm just—I'm expecting a call."

"Very twentieth century of you. From who?"

"It's complicated," he said. "About work. But what's up? What's a miracle?"

"Your sister's being aggressive."

"And that's a miracle."

She said, "No, the miracle is that you answered your phone. Your sister's the same as ever."

"Well, that's good to know."

She said, "Has Frances said anything to you? About me, I mean."

He said, "You told me not to talk about you."

"So she hasn't?"

He said, "I've barely talked to her at all."

"Really?"

"Really."

"You seem preoccupied," she said.

He said, "I'm at work."

"I should have known," she said.

"See?" he said, but not unkindly. "This is why I don't answer the phone."

·   ·   ·

That afternoon, she was teaching. She supposed she'd have to report what happened with Candice and her daffodils, that she'd driven one of her students to tell her to go fuck herself. Apart from Candice having memorized Wordsworth, none of this was so remarkable, but it was still best to keep her supervisor informed of what was going on.

His door was open. Sarah hung back and knocked on the frame.

Ashwin looked up and saw her there. "What's the damage?" he asked.

She never stopped by unless there was some. "I behaved out of line last week," she said. "I let one of them get to me, Candice, and then she told me to go fuck myself. I accused her of plagiarism."

"Plagiarism," he said. He leaned back in his chair. "Now that's not a crime we often see reported around these parts. Kind of refreshing," he smiled. "Like it's a school or something. How did she manage to pull that off?"

"No idea," said Sarah. "She was supposed to write a poem, but she recited one instead. By Wordsworth. Does it count as plagiarism if you don't write it down?" Ashwin shrugged. "Anyway, the point is that I went about it all wrong. I'm sorry, Ashwin." And she was. But it was also good to be here facing him now, admitting to her mistake. To a problem that had nothing to do with Mitzi Bytes and Jane Q. She didn't refer to her job or students on the blog—her patchy sense of ethics stretched that far at least. They'd made her sign a confidentiality form. So in this one instance, at least, she was innocent. Innocent enough.

Ashwin said, "Or maybe you haven't? Gone about it wrong. That's really something, you know. The poem. She must have wanted to impress you."

"Or to outwit me."

"Which means she thinks you have wits. Don't disregard that."

"I didn't handle it well."

He nodded. "Maybe."

"She doesn't read," said Sarah. "Not even a little bit. She's incredibly smart, so she gets away with a lot, but the signs are there. It's not hard to tell."

"See if she shows today," said Ashwin. "It won't be the first time she's surprised you."

And Candice did show, even on time, settling down in her usual seat when Sarah came into the library. Every week she looked like she couldn't possibly get any bigger, and then the next week, there she was. Lolo and Audrey were coming in behind her, and Tasvir was already seated. Another full house. All the girls, except Tasvir, were busy on their phones. Sarah noted this, and decided to go off-script for the day. She'd been planning on reading the next chapter of their discussion book together—a short novel for adults with low literacy, about a young woman who unwittingly gets involved in a jewel heist—but that lesson could wait.

She sat down on the edge of the table and faced the group, their mad moving thumbs sending messages out into the ether. Who was she kidding that any of them lacked literacy skills?

She said, "Right now, what are you doing there?" They all looked up, even Candice, as though Sarah had just accused them of something. Lolo and Audrey went to put their phones away. Sarah said, "No, it's a real question. I want to know. What are you doing on your phone? What apps are open at the moment?"

They answered by reciting the names of all kind of social-media platforms, the usual and also ones she'd never heard of, plus about eight different messengers and a parenting forum.

They each had at least three apps opened at once. It was not surprising, Sarah thought, that so often it seemed like the girls' minds were elsewhere, because they probably were, spread thin across cyberspace.

She said, "I've been thinking a lot about what it means for us to live our lives online. You've all heard about cyberbullying, about how the same laws that apply in the real world have to be enforced on the Internet too. And that's kind of straightforward, but what about the rest of it? What are the connections between who you are online and who you are in the world? Is it seamless? Does it even matter?"

"Online," said Lolo, without missing a beat, "I can make myself up. From scratch."

"What do you mean?" asked Sarah.

"When I talk to guys online, it's not about how I look but

about what I say. They listen to me. They answer me. It's never like that in real life, but online I get to decide who I am. I'm a person instead of a body. I used to have a cartoon avatar, but now I have a picture of Divine."

"See, that's dangerous," said Audrey, shaking her head. "I don't post pictures of Lester. I just couldn't."

"Why not?" asked Lolo.

"Pedophiles, obviously," she said, "or some other crazy person who'd come and take him away."

Sarah was tempted to promise her that nobody would ever take Lester away, or if anybody did, they'd return him in a hurry.

"What about you, Candice?" she asked. "Do you post pictures of Joey?"

Candice didn't answer, her expression revealing her calculations, the wheels spinning in her brain. She was trying to fashion the correct response, the answer Sarah was looking for, not realizing that there wasn't just one. Sarah was actually interested in the girls' points of view. There didn't always have to be an agenda.

"Would you post picture of your kids on a blog?" she asked the group.

"A blog?" said Tasvir.

"Like Tumblr," explained Lolo. Blogs were for old people. "If the pictures were cute, I would."

"You wouldn't worry about the impact?"

Lolo shrugged. "The Internet is full of kids. And cats."

"Without the Internet," said Tasvir, "I'd have nothing. It's how I talk to my sisters, my cousins. In the world, it's like I'm totally alone sometimes, but I'm not, really."

"Because online," said Audrey, "the rules don't apply.

She's not supposed to be allowed to talk to her family, but the Internet lets her get away with it. It lets Lolo talk to boys. Everybody's on the same level. It's like justice. It all makes more sense."

"So the rules aren't justice," said Sarah.

"A lot of them aren't," said Tasvir.

"But *I've* got a body online," said Candice, interrupting. "And a face. Portfolios." She said, "For modelling. And people see it, my photos, all the time."

"And you get jobs?" asked Sarah.

Candice pointed to her belly. "Not now," she said, "but I have. I will. It's a chance, you know. You can make yourself be anything. Like she said," pointing to Lolo. "But not only a cartoon."

"But what about who you really are?"

"But that's it," said Lolo. "Online you can *be* who you really are."

"And why can't you be it here and now?"

"It's the rules," said Tasvir. "We've got to pretend to abide by them. But online, you get to pretend better things."

"I wonder about the consequences, though," said Sarah, "of these divided selves. If we don't all get a little scrambled by the whole thing. Can it be healthy?"

"I don't know, miss," said Lolo. "It's like I have a hundred parts of me anyway, never mind on the Internet. Sometimes I want to sit down and make a list to sort the whole motherfucker out. Has there ever been a person really who is only just one thing?"

"If anything," said Audrey, "isn't it healthier that we don't have to pretend we're not pretending?"

"About the daffodils," said Sarah at the end of the class. Candice tilted back in her chair. "Listen, I was thinking," she said, starting again, "about memorization, recitation. Your assignment for this week is to find a poem and learn it. Learn to say it, to make the words start and stop in all the right places."

"Where do we find a poem?" asked Lolo, who was already back on her phone, the class nearly over.

"How about a book?" suggested Sarah. "Or you could try the library?" She gestured to the shelves all around them. "Or if all else fails," she smiled, "though you already know, you can always turn to the *Internet*."

Candice lingered, packing up her bag, or maybe it wasn't deliberate—she was so close to the end of her pregnancy, and even in all her loveliness, she lumbered like an elephant. Which Sarah didn't mention. Instead, she said, "You know, I don't like being made a fool of."

Candice provided something between a smirk and a smile. "Neither do I."

"I can help you, you know," said Sarah. "With your reading. It's why you're here. And I know it can be a struggle. But you're not the only one."

Candice pointed to the clock on the wall. "Class is over, miss," she said. "I don't have to be here anymore." She hauled her bag onto her shoulder and rubbed her back. "No offence," she said as she made her way out the door.

• • •

Sarah got stuck in traffic and was late to pick up the kids, who were still in their classrooms being minded by their grim-faced teachers, who had to listen to apologies and excuses by late parents like Sarah every single day. As least she wasn't the very last, Sarah told herself—as she'd arrived, there had been other parents pulling up to the curb behind her.

But it wasn't good enough for Gladys, who said, "I thought

you'd never come." Her eyes were teary. "I thought I'd have to live at the school forever, and I'd never go home ever again."

It was the trouble with being generally reliable. It so raised expectations that when things slipped up, the effect was devastating.

"I always come," said Sarah. "You know I do." But Gladys hadn't been around long enough to count on what she knew. Her mother had been late once, and now anything was possible.

They encountered Starry Fiske on their way back to the car, as imperceptive as ever, or maybe just didn't very much care that Sarah was in a hurry. She was walking with another woman, each of them carrying a stack of cardboard boxes. The boxes looked heavy, but Starry was not deterred.

"Thanks for getting in touch about the interview, Sarah," Starry sang to her as they all jumped to dodge a family of scooters zipping down the pathway. "We're expecting big things from you." She said to the woman she was with, "You know Sarah, don't you, Sheila? Our journalist?" She said the word in a pair of her invisible quotations.

"Oh yeah," said Sheila, a funny-looking woman whose features were all crowded in the centre of her face. She was like the man in the moon, if he'd had glasses. She was straining under the weight of the boxes. She said, "I've heard about you."

Nobody saying anything else. Gladys was still crying, and Sarah had her keys in her hand. Clementine was pulling on her arm. She wondered what Starry Fiske was waiting for. She said, "Listen, Starry, I've got to get going. Nice to meet you, Sheila." Sarah moved to shake her hand, but as Sheila's arms were full, she ended up waving instead. Idiotic jazz hands.

"About the article?" called Starry as Sarah went on her way.

"I'm working on it," Sarah called back over her shoulder.

"You know, the *Sentinel* reaches twenty-five thousand households. You've got a voice," yelled Starry.

"I'm using it," Sarah yelled back, unlocking the door, hustling the kids into their booster seats. She saluted Starry across the asphalt, got into her own seat. "Olive oil," she said.

I've heard about you. What had the moon-faced woman heard, and from whom did she hear it? Sarah had no idea, which concerned her as she drove the familiar streets toward home. Had she been talking to Claudia Kincardine? Michelle? Did she have a direct line to Jane Q herself?

Gladys and Clementine were chattering in the back seat, singing to the radio. Disturbingly, they both knew every lyric to "Gypsys, Tramps and Thieves." Really getting into it at the part about how Papa would have shot him if he'd knew what he'd done. How every night all the men would come around.

The problem with the multiplicity of the self—an idea that appealed to minds as wide-ranging as Virginia Woolf's and Lolo's, not to mention Cher's—was that you never knew which part of you anybody was talking about. The problem with the multiplicity of the self was that there could be enough of you to get spread all over town.

From the Archives: Mitzi Bites
Escape

It's occurred to me lately how much of my recklessness is pure cowardice instead of any kind of gutsiness. That it would take a person braver than I am to stay in on a Friday night contemplating the weight of their aloneness. And so instead, I escape. I go out into the night, raised up on stilettos and a push-up bra. Because it's so much easier to get completely schnozzled and fall into somebody's arms than to stay upright on my own accord.

So here is the story of my latest amazing feat of escape, which led to the necessity of another much more desperate one. Basically, I'm Houdini. And I just got off with a ventriloquist. The whole wide world is a circus, you know.

My friend P had a ticket for a fringe play, because his girlfriend had been called in for an extra shift, and I said I'd go, even though I didn't know what the play was. I didn't care. It was a Friday evening, and now I had something to do. End of story, I thought, but it wasn't. Fortunately for you. Unfortunately for me.

It wasn't until we got there that I realized that the play was a puppet show, the puppets being grotesque papier mâché creatures with bulging eyes, gaping mouths, and what appeared to be festering wounds. They were supposed to be animals that lived inside the Chernobyl nuclear reactor, suffering the effects of radiation and extreme isolation in a comedic fashion. And it really was kind of funny, though it took the audience a while to feel okay about laughing at Chernobyl.

Understandably, it wasn't a long play, and it was also closing night. When the show was finished, the stage turned into a party, and members of the audience were welcome to stay. There were free drinks, and pizza, with music playing over the PA. I'd overdressed for a fringe show, but in the end, I was glad I had, because then there was dancing, and everybody was a bit drunk. When P had to go, I just waved goodbye from across the room, waggling fingers. And P waved back, an expression I'd seen before, exasperated, bored, and amused all at once. He'd left me behind in a lot of places.

This time it was with Jonathan, who'd been in the show. But the Chernobyl puppets weren't his main gig, no. Offstage, he carried on his shoulder a marionette, who was called Eric, and Eric was the one who talked to me.

Jonathan, Eric told me confidentially, was a little bit shy. Jonathan's lips didn't even quiver or twitch, his face perfectly still. Flattering me, the puppet continued: Jonathan could never have found the nerve to talk to a girl like me. Then he leaned in close and asked if I wouldn't mind a kiss.

Not from the puppet, thank goodness, but from Jonathan himself, who wasn't bad looking, and could kiss as well as he threw his voice. I'd had worse. And as Jonathan wrapped his long arms around me, Eric was perched on my shoulder, kind of nuzzling my neck, and I tried my best to ignore him.

At two, they shut the music down, and the party was moving elsewhere. Eric got down off my shoulder and asked me if I wanted to come with him. Which all sounds a bit absurd now that I've got it down on paper, but I'd had too much to drink already, and Eric spoke in a voice that sounded almost human. Plus, I'd been watching the Chernobyl puppet play, so absurdity itself had lost its meaning hours ago.

So I didn't flinch when the puppet leaned in closer and asked me if I wanted to ditch the party and come back to his place instead.

Reader, I went. I wanted to know what would happen next, and I wanted to see where the puppet lived. I imagined he had a home on a stand, like a hat or a bird. I was curious to know just how far the bond with the puppet extended: Would Jonathan take it off when we had sex?

He was not an altogether normal guy, Jonathan, I could see that fast. None of the other players in the show went around with a puppet on their shoulders. There was definitely something creepy about that shiny face, the sharp mechanical jaw, and his funny little dangling legs. Jonathan's own face was so still, inert, the puppet's wooden features more expressive. I wondered if Jonathan was some kind of crazy puppet savant, or else like the kind of person who rode a unicycle around the city as though it were a perfectly ordinary occupation.

That puppet was polite, though—I had to give him that. He made small talk with the taxi driver, and tipped him generously, even though I know that the takings from the fringe show had not been huge.

Jonathan had to have a day job, I decided, but then I re-evaluated that theory when I saw his apartment, which was smaller than mine and shared with three other actors.

"I'll give you the tour," said Eric. It took sixty seconds. We ended up in

Jonathan's room, which was the end of a hallway, divided by a curtain. With his puppet's hand, Jonathan traced the length of my body, and this was the point at which I finally had to draw the line. Even I have never been so desperate for escape that I'd accept cunnilingus from a wooden mouth.

"Take the puppet off," I told Jonathan, meeting his eyes for the first time that night. And suddenly, Eric was disembodied, a pile of limbs empty and tangled on the floor. His eyes were looking off into the middle distance, and I followed them, up to the ceiling, where a series of glow-in-the-dark stickers had been affixed.

I watched the stars as Jonathan worked away on top of me, grunting and panting. It was like he thought of me too as a puppet, an object he had to inhabit, perhaps to animate, and so I wasn't altogether present, or maybe I was, but too much so entirely. Reaching down to the floor, I fumbled for Eric's hand, held it tight. The sex wasn't terrible, but I was drunk, and it was all so weird, warped, and doubled, like scenes projected onto funhouse mirrors. On the ceiling, the stickers weren't arranged in any order that I could discern, a chaotic constellation of stars and moons and circles and rings. It wasn't a low ceiling. You would have had to stand on a ladder to get them there. I wondered how the whole thing had transpired, the celestial journey taken by whoever placed them there.

When he was finished, Jonathan rolled off me and kissed my shoulder. "What can I do for you?" he asked me, but in Eric's voice, the puppet voice. And it was unnerving to watch his lips move. He kissed my shoulder again.

I swatted him on the back and said, "Stop it."

"What?" He thought I meant the kissing, but I didn't.

"Enough with the puppet voice," I said, but it dawned on me as the words were leaving my mouth that it hadn't been the puppet's voice. That the voice was Jonathan's, and Eric was only borrowing it. The puppet voice had not in fact been an affectation after all.

Jonathan looked crestfallen. All night long, he'd had a face like stone, but now he actually could have been a mime for all the pain and emotion he expressed as his eyes were cast downward, a trajectory I could trace, as though the barely discernible life in his expression had all been drained away. From where he was, heaped on the floor, even Eric looked much more lively, though of course his smile was painted on. Which helps.

I said, "Oh, come on." I kissed his bony shoulder. I was feeling charitable now. "I was kidding."

"No, you weren't," he said. I still couldn't believe it was really his voice. That a person couldn't help but sound like that. Because couldn't he have found a way to make it stop? Resorting to even hypnosis, acupuncture, aromatherapy in the end? It was nothing a session with a champion elocutionist couldn't have fixed.

He'd rolled as far away from me as he possibly could, which wasn't very far because the bed was a twin. And even as he was obviously in so much despair, I started laughing. I was inappropriately drunk, and the whole thing was so insane.

He sat up again, though still facing the wall. "Everybody likes Jonathan," he said, arms waving for faux enthusiasm. Then he stopped, his weird voice deadly serious: "Until the puppet comes off."

"No," I said. "I like you." Unconvincing. I patted his arm but he shook me off. Which was fine. I said, "I really do, but it's late, and I've got plans in the morning." I chucked him on the shoulder in a friendly way, and then began to retrieve my clothes from the floor, stepping carefully over Eric.

"So can I call you?" he asked me, perched on the edge of the bed. You had to give him points for not giving up, even with his head in his hands so the words were barely audible, although the voice was the voice regardless. I had to ask him to repeat himself so I could listen to it again.

I scrawled my number on a scrap of paper on his desk. My mind was too frazzled to think to write down the wrong one—I just wanted to get out of there, before he said another word and I became hysterical.

He called the next day and left a voice mail apologizing for any misunderstanding. He said he thought we had some chemistry. As he didn't say his name, just "Hey, it's me," I wasn't sure if it was Eric or Jonathan, and perhaps it didn't matter.

I never called him back. I saved the message and will replay it again and again for my own amusement until the joke gets old, which it never ever will.

CHAPTER 10

· · · · · · · · · · · · · · · · ·

Wednesday mid-morning brought another call from Frances. Because she needed something, she had conveniently forgotten that during their last conversation she'd ordered Sarah to leave her family alone.

"Sarah?" said Frances, who was calling from work. "Any chance you could help me out here?"

Charlotte had forgotten her inhaler. Could Sarah go over there and get it and deliver it to the school as soon as she could? Sarah knew not to mention that Frances had basically forbidden her from trespassing on their property. She knew too not to suggest that she might have anything better to do with her time, because nobody was busier than Frances. As ever, she wondered if this might be her chance to finally get on her sister-in-law's good side and stay there. Chris would want her to say yes; Frances was the only family (except her) that he had in the world.

So, "Of course," said Sarah, because what was she here for if not to perform last-minute favours for Frances. Sarah's schedule, in her eyes, she knew, was ever flexible, almost negligible.

The inhaler was on the kitchen counter. Frances couldn't get hold of Evan on the phone. "He's been so busy," said Frances. "All that rehearsing." Sarah could hear in Frances's voice that she wanted to believe this was perfectly reasonable. "But she needs it, you know she does." Sarah could hear too that Frances was worried for Charlotte.

"I'll do it," said Sarah. "I'll go over right now."

"Thank you," said Frances, who never sounded like herself when she expressed a thing like gratitude. "It means." She stopped. "It means a lot. I mean, I don't know what I'd do otherwise."

"It's no problem," said Sarah. "No problem at all."

*   *   *

So once again, Sarah wound a path through the fence, the back-and-forth journey she'd been taking all week. Her senses were heightened—for days she'd been anticipating bad news and surprises around every corner, usually these very corners she was taking now. The messages from Jane Q seemed connected to this route, to Frances and Evan, the sight of their house from her office window. She couldn't shake the idea that somehow all the pieces fit.

She stopped when she got to the bottom of the stairs beside the garage. She couldn't hear anything, no music, but she wasn't going to take the chance of going up to check. It wasn't part of her mission, and she'd only get called out again for interrupting Evan's focus. So she kept walking, down the driveway and around to the front of the house. She'd brought the spare key to their bright red front door.

Sarah climbed the steps to the porch, the big wide veranda with the hanging swing upon whose super-plush floral cushion seat no one ever sat. While just a block away geographically, the house Frances had bought in their neighbourhood was from a different world, one whose great mansions loomed over the narrow terraces and worker's cottages on recently gentrified streets like Sarah's. The mansions had fallen into decline, long ago divided up into rooming houses, as they'd remained for decades, but in recent years they were being bought up and fixed up by single families as downtown life once again became desirable. Frances and Evan got their place for a steal, and they'd spent just as much restoring it, removing the dropped ceiling panels and linoleum floors, mouldy carpets and fire doors. The woodwork in the vestibule was gleaming, polished, dusted, and rich with grain. You would have thought the wood was one of the house's original fixtures, if you didn't know the whole story. Sarah, however, was aware of every single detail. The precise cost of the leaded glass doors that led her into the hallway, for example—a ridiculous fortune.

She paused at the bottom of the stairs, considering the echoing silence of the place. It was hard to fill a house like this; it was more like a museum than a home. Perhaps if Frances and Evan had had another child? But that was another story, and they would have had to have at least fifteen of them, considering the house's size. Particularly if the children had been anything like Charlotte, who was pale and small and scarcely there, overwhelmed by the frill and flounce of the fussy dresses her mother made her wear. Only in her asthma did she ever make a stir, imperilled and gasping for air—a legacy from her mother, who curiously didn't seem to suffer the affliction any longer. Charlotte's attacks were the only thing Sarah had ever known to derail Frances's fervent planning, or to for once snap Evan's easy eyelids wide, making him appear to be completely awake.

The kitchen was perfectly tidy, not a dirty dish in sight, and even the clean pots and dish rack were stored away. The dishwasher itself was hidden, like the fridge was, behind what appeared to be a cupboard door, so you had to look for appliances in a place like this, opening random cupboard doors, never sure of what you might find.

An artful ceramic bowl was the only item on the countertop, and the inhaler was resting inside it, along with a tube of medicated lip balm and two nickels. Just where Frances had said it would be, for she was not the type to lose track of things. The nickels must have been some kind of rare lapse. And no doubt, they were someone else's error, just as it was that the inhaler was not now at school with Charlotte as it should have been. Being Frances must be exasperating, actually, Sarah thought, because all her problems were other people's screw-ups. All of mine, at least, she thought, are my own.

Charlotte Katherine Bennett-Grayson, written on the prescription. The middle name for Chris and Frances's mother, the woman whose ability to produce such disparate offspring Sarah so often wondered about.

Sarah went to the window and looked outside at her own house through the trees, though their own small backyard was only one of four that backed onto Frances and Evan's grand one. Her little house over there was just like all the others. There were buds on some of the trees now, the world on the cusp of spring, but for the moment, everything was still.

The back staircase creaked as she climbed to the second floor—she might as well take advantage of the situation, Sarah thought, and do a little reconnaissance. She ran her hand along the oak wainscotting down the corridor. Not a spot of dust there either, though that was down to Charlotte's breathing troubles as much as to her mother's meticulousness—Frances had paid a fortune to have an air filtration system installed for her daughter's benefit.

Sarah passed Charlotte's room, with no toys and clothes on the floor, her bed neatly made. She had a playroom next door, and Evan's study was next door to that, a room that annoyed Sarah whenever she considered it, but because he was a man and not a mother, nobody ever wondered why he might require a room of his own. And had there ever been a house more inappropriate for just three people to live in? They had so many rooms, they had to dream up uses for them. If Hitler had lived here, he would have been provided a room for transcendental meditation.

"Hellooooo," called Sarah, just to hear her voice come back. "Coo-eee." Evan's study was untidy, books and papers scattered throughout, which was to be expected, except that it meant that he actually went in there—surprising. Just what did Evan study in his study? Frances used to claim that he was writing a musical, but that was years ago, back when Evan played guitar in a second-tier Grateful Dead cover band and Frances was trying to make him into something more than that.

She went inside and tried to scope things out without disturbing the chaos. The desk was heaped with economics tomes, and philosophy textbooks that Sarah suspected had been Frances's in university—a quick flip to the inside cover confirmed this. There were also comic books, graphic novels, and several raw-food cookbooks. Yellow notepaper was scattered through the mess, covered in illegible scrawl. Notation paper too, and sheet music. There was a couch in the corner, with a pillow and a blanket, where Evan spent more time sleeping, Sarah suspected, than in the room he shared with his wife.

What was his project? Sarah wondered. Perhaps Evan was full of surprises. But not entirely. Sarah tripped over a coffee table book of lesbian erotica, and kicked it across the floor.

And then she heard something downstairs, somebody coming in the side door. Two people talking. The floor creaked under her footsteps, and she cringed in response, tiptoeing out of Evan's study into the hall toward the front stairs. It was two men, their voices raised in argument. She made her way down—she'd say she'd been looking for the inhaler up there, she decided. Maybe Evan could even deliver it to the school, and then she could get home and back to work.

They were talking in the music room. A grand piano that no one ever played, and an upright bass in the corner. No music now, though. Evan was shouting at somebody, whose responses were muted, an antagonist seemingly much less prone to passion.

Sarah crept down the hall, the tricky floor blessedly silent for once.

"If she knew I'd done it, she would kill me," the quiet voice was saying. It was Chris.

"She's going to kill me anyway," Evan was saying.

"So then what was the point?" It really was Chris. Chris in the middle of the day, when he should have been high up in the sky doing something with apps and banking systems. The only time she'd ever managed to get him out of work, she'd had to come down with appendicitis. And even then, he went back that afternoon.

"It's the principle. That kind of shit cannot be tolerated. I thought you of all people would understand."

"I don't know about the principle that makes it okay to break a guy's face."

"What happened to chivalry?"

"You can explain that to your wife, then."

Evan said, "I thought you were on my side."

Chris said, "I don't even know," and then the side door opened, somebody coming in.

Evan called out, "Hello?"

And Sarah was stuck—whoever was at the door would find her eavesdropping, or else Chris and Evan would catch her creeping past the music room, skulking along the corridor like the meddling snoop they'd accused her of being.

"It's me," called out a woman's voice, not Frances.

Sarah had a split second in which to make her decision, partly inspired by the novel she'd been reading with her children. Behind her was the dumbwaiter, the sole original feature in that whole gleaming house that had been so ravaged by the twentieth century. The dumbwaiter no longer worked, left over from the days in which servants had prepared meals in the basement, but was a charming anachronism, not to mention only slightly too small to accommodate a grown woman.

As footsteps bounded up the short flight of steps from the side door, Sarah hauled herself up into the nook in the wall and pulled the door shut. It groaned slightly, the noise masked by the sound of that orange-haired girl, the backup singer, who was calling out, "Where are you?" as she came around the corner. Sarah watched the scene through a small round window that was discoloured and made everything appear sepia toned. She breathed in; the air was already close.

"In here," Evan called out.

"You motherfucker," the girl started screeching, and Sarah envisioned her leaping onto Evan's back, scratching at his eyes.

"Hey, hey, cool it," came the other voice, Chris's voice. Sarah could not fathom how he'd found his way into what appeared to be a scene from *Cops*.

"Listen, I've got to get out here," said Chris.

"No way, man," said Evan. "You're a part of this."

And now Chris was talking, but too quietly for Sarah to hear. It was hard to hear much, actually, except for screeching, because she was curled up so tight, her ear plastered against her shoulder, and also because the enclosed space amplified her breathing, the sound of her heart. Sarah pushed against the side of the dumbwaiter to create a millimetre or two of extra space to move in. She clearly hadn't thought this through, she realized, as her spine began to ache, her knees. Charlotte's inhaler in her pants pocket was stabbing against her thigh. This place would prove a very poor sanctuary in a minute or two.

The girl was talking. The backup singer. And then some, Sarah supposed, and Chris being here was more incongruous than all the rest of it. He would be there for Frances, no matter what, but now he and Evan were colluding about something, and had Chris known about the backup singer all along?

She hadn't been in a situation this ridiculous for years. It was such a Mitzi Bytes scenario, stuffed inside a dumbwaiter for the sake of a story to tell, except that she couldn't follow the story.

Sarah pulled the doors open a crack to let some air in. Dumbwaiters clearly hadn't been constructed with human occupancy in mind. And with the crack, she could hear better, Evan saying, "Take it easy, Jen," and the girl, Jen, explaining, "He'll drop the charges, but only if I go back home to him."

"But you can't do that," said Chris. And Sarah wondered how he could be so sure.

"So you're just going to throw me under the bus," said Evan.

"What about the principle?" said Chris. He was being sarcastic. He said, "I posted the bail. Surely that's enough. Now you're on your own. The buck stops here." What was he talking about? Who was feeding him these lines?

"I could tell her everything," said Evan.

"But you won't," said Chris. "Not now. The whole thing looks so much worse on you. So the threats aren't going to work anymore. It's all over."

Jen was saying, "You've really fucked up this time."

"I was trying to help," said Evan.

"You were drunk out of your mind," said Jen. "Not helpful."

"There is such a thing as good intentions," said Evan.

"Tell me about it," said Chris. "It's what got me into this mess in the first place."

"Oh, take off your self-righteous hero sweater," said Evan. "Get over yourself. You had your own motivations. I know you did."

"I wanted to help."

"See? Then we're not so far apart, you and me. Which is how I know how it really was. You didn't want to help. You wanted to be a saviour."

"There's no saving you."

"Well, now you know," said Evan. "So you can't even lord it over me."

"You're both idiots," said Jen. "And I've got to get my stuff."

"I really have to get back," said Chris.

"You didn't seem to think I was an idiot when you were taking my money," said Evan.

"My money," said Chris.

"Which is the fucking problem with you," said Evan. "How it all comes down to this every time."

"You're both missing the point," said Jen. "Which is that I'm done. I'm leaving."

"Not without me, you're not," said Evan.

"But I am," she said. "You're the reason."

The three of them came into the hall, walked right past the dumbwaiter, oblivious to Sarah's presence, and down the steps to the side door. Chris in yellow, in this context, was like somebody she'd never seen before, though Evan was as slippery as ever. Sarah couldn't get a good look at the girl, who had been and gone before she'd even registered.

Every bit of Sarah's body was pressed against the sides of this unfathomably tiny space. Her head was tucked into her chest, and her neck was strained in a way that didn't seem anatomically possible. If she'd had to hide there any longer, she may have expired, or else opened the door and sheepishly tumbled from its height to the floor.

"Hey, guys," she would have said, the threesome staring down at her incredulously. Or not so incredulously, come to think about it. She was glad to feel the unit shake as the outside door slammed, the house now empty so she was free to go.

She fumbled to get a grip and slide the door open all the way, for one terrible moment fearing it was stuck. But then it budged, and she poked her head out to take a real breath, and to check for silence—nothing. She set about unfolding, unfurling, climbing out of the dumbwaiter without plummeting to the hardwood. There was nothing graceful about it, but she made it, shaking out her jammed-up joints as she made for the front door.

Sarah looked outside in time to see Chris's car pulling away from the sidewalk, hearing the sound of Evan and the girl's feet pounding up the garage stairs once again. She was home free, just barely, and she was also covered with dust. The one place in the house that Frances had forgotten to touch with her frightening perfection, and in spite of everything, Sarah was the smallest bit gratified for having found it.

She locked the front door behind her, and took the long way back around the block toward home.

From the Archives: Mitzi Bytes
Snoop's Monkey Trial

When my first husband was cheating on me, there were many clues, bread crumb trails leading deep into the woods. He began keeping strange hours, deleting messages from his phone, and once I found a condom in his coat pocket, which was weird because I was on the pill. But I never confronted him. There would be suitable explanations for everything, I told myself, and besides, I thought this was what trust was: obliviousness in the face of the blatantly obvious. What else can I say, except that I was very young. And I think he was actually desperate for me to find out, just so he wouldn't have to go to the trouble of telling me. But I refused to see what was in front of my face, preferring my own delusions.

So how does a person learn to trust again after that? There is a short line between having that experience and becoming the kind of person who no longer believes in anything, which is really not such a different kind of delusion—seeing what's in front of one's face but refusing to acknowledge what's there.

It's been a persistent struggle ever since The Programmer and I really got together for me to believe that what he's saying is true. Which is not his fault, but it has meant he's had to get better at saying things, at clarity and avoiding awkwardness, and I've had to work on my end in believing. But this weekend I suffered a lapse.

He's still moving in with me, slowly, slowly. Too slowly, I often protest, but then he'll come over with a lamp or a toaster oven and I'll start freaking out at the sight of his stuff in my space—what if I'm just setting myself up for the same thing all over again? To which he'll respond that this is why we're moving slow, taking things at their natural pace. He'll turn on the lamp and show me the softness of the light that it casts in my den, or else we'll melt cheese on bread in the toaster—delicious. Once he brought up a bedside table, but I decided that was a step way too far, and he said he understood, taking it back home again.

We're really happy. Does it sound that way? I don't intend for it to sound any other way. But it's a real negotiation, made more complicated by everything I went through before. All this is new to him, but it's a bit déjà vu to me—unsettlingly so.

On Saturday I found a note in his pants. He was in the shower, and his pants were on the floor where he'd left them the night before, and I saw the piece of paper poking out of the pocket. I was curious about what it was, so that is what I mean when I say "I found a note in his pants." I mean that I was snooping, but I wasn't considering the connotations or the possible ramifications as I plucked out the paper, folded multiple times. I unfolded it, the folds making squares that were a perfect grid, and it was an email he'd printed, one sent to his work account. It was from the girl he'd been seeing before me, the dumpy one with the tapered jeans. And now I'm being malicious—she's the only girl he'd been seeing before me, at least the only girl for a long time. The message was something about an electric toothbrush that she wanted back. It seemed overly familiar. The girl had signed it "xo." I was unaware that he ever heard from her at all.

I was still holding that paper when he came out of the bathroom, my peach bath towel wrapped around his waist. I was sitting on the edge of the bed, trying to decode all the possible meanings in the message, and he saw me there. He said, "What are you doing?"

I waved the paper at him. "What's this?"

It took a few seconds for him to realize, and I watched his face. It's true there was no panic in his eyes, but that in itself could be a bad sign. For some people, lying comes too easily. He said, "It's what it looks like."

"You still hear from her?"

"Almost never," he said.

"And you didn't tell me?"

"It wasn't important."

"It was important enough for you to print it all out," and he explained that he'd done so in order that he'd remember. He had her electric toothbrush in his bathroom cabinet, and he needed to get it to her. She was moving to Turkey.

"They don't even have the same voltages in Turkey," I protested. The holes in his story were miles wide.

But he just shrugged and said he didn't know. She wanted it. They were going to meet up for coffee one day so he could give it to her, but maybe I'd prefer it if he put it in the post.

"It didn't cross your mind to mention this?" I asked him.

He said it honestly hadn't. There was nothing to mention. And I started spouting off about secret emails, which pissed him off.

"It's not a secret," he said. "I printed it. Who prints out a secret email?"

I said, "Someone who wants to be found out?"

At which a lesser man would have put up his hands and said, "I give up," and gone away for good, but not this man. Instead, he sat down beside me, pulled me around to face him, and took my hands in his. He said, "I love you." He said, "And the only way I can prove that is just to love you and love you and love you, and I do, and you're going to have to decide if that's enough. Because, honestly, it's all I can give."

He said, "I promise you, I'm not the kind of person you have to squint to read. You know that, right? I'll always be where I say I am." He had his eyes locked on mine—it was almost unnerving. "Always. Always."

And what else can a person do with that kind of assurance but calm down and keep going forward? He makes it almost easy.

CHAPTER 11

. . . .

Charlotte attended the same school Sarah's daughters did but was part of its elite alternative program (admissions by lottery, but Sarah suspected Frances had it rigged), which had a different start time from the rest of the school's, so her cousins never came across her in the playground. She was in before-and-after-school care anyway, her school day structured around her mother's busy schedule, so in spite of the close proximity, Sarah's family and Frances's ran in very different circles. But still, Sarah was able to drop the puffer off at the main office, and then on her way out she ran into Cherry in the foyer, who had been delivering Paige to school after a dentist appointment.

"Claudia's been talking about you," she reported. "She gets confused because she's talking about you talking about me, and she forgets that it's me she's talking to."

"I wasn't talking about you," said Sarah. "Talking to you, you mean."

"That too," said Cherry. "She's pretty pissed, you know. I'd say, watch out for the dragon lady."

"Oh, come on, Cherry," Sarah said, and Cherry threw her hands up.

"Don't shoot the fucking messenger." She was back to her phone, its dangling plastic charms clacking. Then she raced away down the sidewalk, free at last, blowing kisses over her shoulder.

• • •

At home, everything seemed ominous. The dappled pattern of sunlight on the carpet, unwashed glasses by the sink, objects on the hall table—a few coins, balled-up receipts, business cards, a gum wrapper. The contents of her husband's pockets—she examined these, but nothing was surprising. She wondered if they'd been picked over. A navy ball-cap was discarded on the hall floor at the foot of the stairs; she'd never seen it in her life.

She couldn't call Janie or Beth-Ellen because it was possible they hated her now. What if she did call and their voices were voices she didn't know anymore? She didn't know if Jane Q had gotten to them yet. It was possible neither of them would answer her call. But she had to talk to someone. Not Chris, obviously. She might not know *his* voice either, and she needed something certain. Not simply someone who was going to tell her that everything would be okay, but someone she'd actually believe when they did so. She needed to talk to the one person who knew her in a way she didn't like to be known under ordinary circumstances, and so she called her mother.

"I'm in trouble, Mom." The call her mother was perpetually on alert for. It was probably a relief that it had finally come.

Marilyn said, "Well, baby, what is it?" She was on her lunch break.

Sarah said, "I don't even know where to start." This was tough. If she told her mother about Chris, she was going to say, "I told you so." Loyalty was a hard habit to break. Sarah said, "What would you do if you found out someone you loved was keeping something from you? That a person you thought you knew has a whole other side of themselves you'd never suspected?"

Her mother said, "This is hypothetical?"

"It's practical," she said. "I mean, how would you broach that? Particularly, maybe, when the way you found out in the first place is a little bit shameful in itself. And when you can't let it go, but you know that it might be the beginning of a discussion that could rip everything apart."

"This is about the Mitzi Bytes?" Marilyn asked.

"What?" How many times in a day can the bottom fall out? Sarah felt like she was falling. She couldn't feel her head.

"A mother knows," Marilyn was saying. "Gloria Platt gave me *Looking for Love in All the Wrong Places* for my birthday ten years ago. She thought I might find it useful. I connected the dots."

"How?" This was another thing altogether. Sarah couldn't possibly connect the dots at all.

Marilyn said, "My dear, you weren't really subtle."

Sarah said, "How can you sound so blasé about this?" She herself sounded furious, her shrillness ringing back in her ears.

"I've had a decade to get used to the idea," said Marilyn.

"But you never said a thing."

Marilyn said, "How could I? That book was completely unreadable." There was a moment of silence. Sarah could breathe. "It's a weight off my shoulders to tell you that."

"So you knew?" said Sarah, calming down. But that wasn't the end of it. "But Jane Q isn't you?"

"Jane Q isn't who?"

"That's the trouble," said Sarah. "Someone found out. They've been sending emails, threatening ones. And I don't even know who's who anymore. Everybody seems like a double-crosser, and then I caught Chris with Evan—"

"Caught him how?"

"Not like that. But that's why I'm calling. The real trouble. And now people are talking about me at school, other mothers. I've getting into trouble everywhere, and I don't know where to start in trying to unravel the whole bloody knot. But you—"

"Me?"

"I don't know. You. It changes things. You know about it, the blog. And *you* still love me."

"Oh, but honey," said Marilyn. "I'm your mother. Everybody else, it's going to be another story."

"But what about Chris?"

Her mother thought about it. "Talk to him," she said. "It might be nothing. And you might be surprised by how far forgiveness can stretch. That's what it takes to love anybody, you know." She paused. "Does he know about Mitzi?"

"No. Or at least, I don't think so." The realization dawned on her. "But maybe he does. He could. Oh Mom," she said. "What am I going to do about all this?"

For a moment Sarah thought her mother wasn't going to answer. Then she said, "You're going to have to come up with your own solution, I think. But a bit of advice in the meantime— there are two things you're going to have to do, Sarah, and you don't like doing either of them. You have to apologize. And you're going to have to lie."

"Lie?"

"Just to wiggle your way out of the corners," said Marilyn. "Tell them what they want to hear. For once in your precious life."

•   •   •

When Sarah hung up the phone, it took a few moments for everything to sink in. If her mother knew about Mitzi Bytes already, who else did?

How long did you think you'd get away with this?

Her agent, Andrea, had warned her that it wouldn't last. "It's too much," she'd told her years ago. "This whole thing is bigger than you."

But Sarah had shrugged off her warnings, partly due to humility—let's not overstate my own importance, she was thinking—but also because shrugging off was just convenient. What would she write about if she had to put her own name on her blog posts? How would the parameters change?

You are not remotely brave.

She had a point, Jane Q. Sarah Lundy was a coward. How easy it was to stay on the sidelines—you never got stuck in a dumbwaiter that way. She hadn't had sex with a ventriloquist for years now. For a while, she'd been the heroine of her own story, galumphing her way to triumph after triumph, but the story got boring around the same time the story got happy, and ever since, she'd been earning a crust by ransacking the skeletons in other people's closets. And no matter how honest she'd been in her writing, there was nothing honest about doing it. When people found out, they were going to hate her.

She went upstairs and opened her laptop. *I'm ready to be done with this,* she wrote to Jane Q. *You could say that I am finally quaking. I am tired of wondering, of wandering, my mind taking me, and this story, to all the wildest places. I would like to feel the ground beneath my feet.*

Her mother was right. She was going to have to apologize, and she was going to have to lie, but now she'd come just short of that. While it might have been easier to grovel, grovelling was disingenuous. Grovelling would leave her with nothing, not even morally solvent, which wasn't worth it. She wasn't that desperate yet.

She waited a few minutes before refreshing her screen, hoping for a fast response to her sort-of surrender. It had been two days now since she'd last heard from Jane Q, and Sarah didn't know whether to be worried or relieved.

But there was nothing, and then her phone buzzed—a text from Leslie. *R U around?* it said. *Need to talk. Something's up.*

Which was weird for a Wednesday, but everything was weird about this Wednesday, and Leslie's whole life tended to leap from crisis to crisis. Poor Leslie. Sarah was used to being her shoulder to cry on—Leslie had nobody else. Sarah had been planning on writing her *Sentinel* column this afternoon, however difficult it would have been to focus. So many tasks were being pushed aside this week, when she was usually so on top of things, and she would have to be more careful. But she could be there for Leslie, and it would be good to see a human face, actually, to hear a voice that had a body attached to it. Perhaps Leslie would have some insight to offer about it all.

While she waited for Leslie to arrive, she dialed Chris—what would he say to her? Would his voice sound the same? Did he actually exist outside the strange sepia twisted vision she had glimpsed of him that morning?—but he didn't answer. And any other time, she would have thought nothing of his lack of response, but now she wondered at the silence. There was nobody more tuned in to communications technology than her husband was. He updated his phone every quarter. So why was he so impossible to get hold of?

Though he'd given her an advantage this way. She called him back again and left a voice mail, the kind of message she wouldn't have had the courage to deliver with him on the other end of the line, if she'd had to anticipate his response. She said, "If there is any possibility that you could be home at a reasonable hour, I'd appreciate it. You and I have a few things to discuss." She took a deep breath: "I'd particularly like to know what was going on this morning. And don't tell me 'nothing,' because I'm not an idiot. Okay, Chris? We really need to talk." Because there was no reason she shouldn't leave him squirming. He was lying to her. She'd seen it with her own eyes.

Unlike most people these days who flaunted their multi-tasking skills as a sign of evolutionary prowess (treadmill desks, work lunches, and educational podcasts consumed while scrubbing pots), Chris claimed he couldn't concentrate on more than one thing at a time. He'd told her how he preferred the way that time passed when he was focused, how it stayed firmly in his grasp. "That way, at the end of the day, I know where the hours went," he'd told her, and once upon a time she'd admired that. She thought it made him better than she was. Because she had a mind like a magpie's, flit-flit-flitting all over the place in search of the next shiny thing. But that wasn't the whole story, she considered now, it having been revealed that if he didn't multi-task, Chris had certain hidden compartments of his own. His focus wasn't as narrow as she'd given him credit for.

And maybe a narrow focus, she considered now, was not so much a skill as a luxury. She thought about what she might have done with eight hours a day to be immersed in a single occupation—her magnum opus might have been less patchy than fifteen years of blog archives. She would have read whole books cover to cover in a single sitting. Even when she'd had her own quite respectable career as a journalist, she'd been paid such a pittance that huge blocks of immersion weren't viable. And now there were always the children, always somewhere to go in her SUV, pickups and drop-offs. She was ever reliable, the person you call when your kid needs her asthma medication delivered pronto. Or at least semi-pronto.

She was the first one Leslie called when something came up,

Sarah was thinking, brushing any remaining dumbwaiter dust out of her hair. Being holed up in the box had left her rattled, never mind everything she'd seen.

What did Chris have to do with whatever Evan was up to, she wondered. Who was Evan threatening to tell, and what was he telling? What about the bail too? What had he done now? And all that talk of money—"my money," Evan had said, but it was also Chris's, which seemed like faulty economics. Nobody should ever pool money with Evan, Sarah was certain.

Downstairs in the kitchen, she put the kettle on, preparing a pot of tea for Leslie's arrival. She had had a loaf of strawberry bread in the freezer and was defrosting it in the microwave. A person who didn't multi-task would never have such provisions on hand, she knew. She was an improviser. Somebody had to be one. Her freezer was always fully stocked, and perhaps a narrow focus was not such evidence of superior intelligence after all. If everybody maintained Chris's singular attention to detail, the universe in a circuit board, the whole world would go to (very tiny) pieces.

She let the bread cool on a cutting board, spooned loose-leaf tea into the pot. She had never doubted him, her husband, that he wasn't where he said he'd be. That he wasn't who he said he'd be. His singular attention was part of her faith in him. She'd supposed his mind was navigable, like a grid. Lines she could cruise down with her eyes shut, like the city streets. Chris and Evan were opposite ends of a spectrum, she'd always imagined. She'd been downright smug about that in her dealings with Frances, and she should have known better. Smugness was always going to end up biting you in the ass.

Anybody else, she might have worried if they never answered their phone. Going whole days without speaking. Chris's reliability had always been implicit, Sarah assumed, but what if everything she knew was wrong?

The doorbell rang. Sarah had been standing at the sink wringing a tea towel, but she put it down and went to greet her friend. At least her face wasn't twitching. Leslie looked terrible, but Sarah wasn't sure she looked much better herself.

"I can't stay long," said Leslie. "I have to get back to work, but it couldn't wait. I needed to talk."

"No, that's fine," said Sarah, closing the door behind Leslie, following her friend down the hall.

The tea and bread were waiting on the coffee table. Leslie gestured toward it. "I didn't mean you had to—"

Sarah cut in. "No, it's okay. It's from the freezer anyway, and I'm glad to see you. I mean, I think I need to talk to you too."

"What is it?" said Leslie.

Sarah said, "No, you go first."

But Leslie had a slice of bread already, was taking a bite. She waved away Sarah and said, with her mouth full, "No, I'm starving. You start."

Sarah said, "I've had the week from hell."

Leslie nodded. She knew exactly what Sarah was talking about.

"And now there's something weird going on between Chris and Evan, and I don't know what to do." She told the story of the puffer and dumbwaiter, of the conversation she'd overheard. "They were talking about pressing charges, posting bail, something about money, and I don't even know the whole story on the orange-haired girl. I swear I saw her kissing Evan, and she's trouble. It's obvious. And all of that is fairly predictable, actually, knowing Evan, but with Chris, it's something different. He's lying, keeping things from me. And I only found out because I was sneaking around, so how can I say anything to him about it? But I can't face him and say nothing. It's like a charade I can't go along with. I'm just not capable of that."

Leslie was listening intently at the other end of the couch. She'd set her food down, hadn't even poured a cup of tea.

"Anyway, here I go, on about myself. That's not the point. Do you want coffee instead? And you don't have long. What's going on here? You've left work? Is it Jamie? Are you okay?" Sarah could hear her voice, shrill and prattling, but Leslie did nothing to stop it. Leslie was just watching her, as though seeing her for the first time, so carefully, as though she were utterly unfamiliar. Her friend of so many years. "You're making me nervous," said Sarah.

Leslie said, "Sorry." She looked down at her lap. She said, "I thought you knew," and looked up again.

"Knew what?"

Leslie said, "I had this idea that you were giving me a segue."

"To what?"

Leslie said, "Fuck, Sarah. You've turned me into a lunatic."

"Like how?"

"Like. . . " She was searching for an example. "Like letters-cut-out-of-a-magazine-and-glued-to-a-ransom-note crazy. The kind of person who breathes on the phone. I don't know—the old lady wearing a parka in summer pushing a doll in a baby carriage down the street. That's how."

"Oh," said Sarah slowly, the sense now dawning on her that her friend was a bit unhinged. "Me?"

"Yes, you," said Leslie, "and I am so angry, this rage rushing through me and I just don't know what to do with it. Like, if there were only some kind of acceptable outlet, but there's not one, and I'm just terrified that I'm going to snap. I'm going to hurt someone."

"Jamie."

"Not fucking Jamie," Leslie shouted. She picked up her tea-cup and crashed it down onto its saucer. "Oh shit," she said. "Oh Sarah, I'm sorry." The cup had broken into pieces. It must have had a crack already. Leslie said, "No, I'm sorry, I'm *not* sorry. I didn't come here to apologize to you. Not even about the cup. Though I am sorry about the cup. But."

Sarah said, "You're scaring me, Leslie."

"Are you 'quaking'?" Leslie asked.

Sarah said, "What do you mean?" Though she knew full well now. And Leslie was scaring her a little less, because now it was starting to make sense. Some. "So this is about me, then, you being here."

Leslie's lips pulled tight, her whole body tense, and she might have smashed something else if not for decorum's sake. "Oh yeah," she said. "It's all about you, Sarah. Mitzi Bytes. But isn't everything?"

Sarah said, "That's not fair."

Leslie exploded again. "Fair?" It was like Sarah was feeding her pellets of rage. These were potent words. "How do I even begin unpacking that?"

Sarah thought of her mother's advice. She said to Leslie, "I'm sorry." Words could work wonders.

"For what?"

"For whatever I did?"

"You. Are. The. Worst," said Leslie, each word laid down one at a time. Leslie started collecting the glass shards, which had shattered so neatly. You could resurrect a teacup from the pieces in her hand, but the sense of wholeness was unnerving, because the teacup was gone. A drinking vessel should not be a puzzle. Leslie let the pieces drop, then picked up the one whose edge was sharpest. She held it tight in her fist, knuckles white. She was finally looking at Sarah and not at the floor, or her lap, or the broken cup. She said, "It's almost like you don't even exist, you know. There you are slinking off to the corner, taking notes, hiding in everybody's fucking dumbwaiter. 'For whatever I did,' you say, like this is nothing. Like it's a fill-in-the-blank. Fucking Mad Libs. You have no idea of the consequences of your actions. What you did is not a 'whatever.' You've stolen my life—that's what it is. You've humiliated me. So are you sorry for that?" She said, "Well?"

Sarah said, "Do you want me to answer?"

That shard, the fist; they were swinging just above her. Sarah inched back, but Leslie was only punching the air. Leslie said, "That is exactly what I am talking about. This feigning of regard, like you give a shit what I want. Like you ever think about anyone else."

"Stop yelling at me," said Sarah limply. A blanket was slung over the back of the couch, and she wanted to pull it over her head. She didn't know what Leslie wanted. Her position was impossible. She said, "Who else knows?"

"Everyone," said Leslie. "I couldn't help it. I kept it to myself for ages—for as long as I could. Last Friday, I was going to confront you, but I couldn't, and then I started telling everybody and now I just can't stop. It feels like a compulsion. Which is why I'm here—it was starting to spiral. I need to see you face to face and talk this out before I do something I really regret."

Sarah said, "Who do mean by everyone?"

Leslie said, "You're missing the point."

"Okay," Sarah said quietly.

Leslie continued, "Do you know how I found it, your site? Someone on one of my message boards sent me a link. That one about your friend and her terrible life. I read it and thought, 'That poor, poor woman.' And then I kept reading, and it all clicked. It was too perfect to be a coincidence, that this was anyone but you. Which meant that she was me, that poor, poor woman. Is that really what you think of me? Think of my life?"

Sarah started to answer, but Leslie interrupted. "Because if it is, do you have any idea how wrong you are? How you're so far off the mark if it's truth you're trying to tell. Or is it?"

"What?"

"Truth," said Leslie. "What is the point of what you're doing?"

Sarah thought about this. She'd asked herself the same question many times, and she'd never been able to come to a satisfying answer. And whenever she got close, it was always different from what she'd answered before. Her blog was a record, a place where she worked out what she thought of things, where she reflected on the world around her, which was not the same as being a reflection of it.

She said, "I wrote it for myself, really."

"But then published it for the whole wide world to see?"

"Not the world," said Sarah. "Traffic's really fallen off. And I took care of things so nobody would know it was you—"

"Because the me you wrote about wasn't even me!" said Leslie. "And not because you 'took care,' but because you're so totally wrong about everything. You don't actually care at all—I know that. You take what you need from the people around you, and then spin it all into some tale that's all about you."

"You told *everyone*?" asked Sarah.

Leslie said, "You know how word gets around."

"They're going to be pissed," said Sarah.

Leslie nodded. "They are." She set down the broken china.

"It was never really about any of you personally, though,"

said Sarah. "Can't you see that? It was more like a tribute, you as a jumping-off point. Inspiration."

"We were fodder."

"Exactly."

Leslie's lips grew tight again. "That's bullshit."

Sarah thought about it. "No, that really doesn't sound good, does it?"

"You know the worst thing?" said Leslie. "Me I can handle. I'm a big girl. I can take care of myself. But you brought my kid into this. My kid, who can't even tie his own shoes, for Christ's sake. He's so bloody vulnerable to everyone and everything. Like this gaping wound I've got walking out into the world, and it's my job to protect him. To keep him safe. And you'd think the one place where I could count on that was with my friends—you know him, you know me. We've been friends for years, Sarah. But here you go, fucking *exploiting* him. That's the word for it, don't you think? When you're using somebody as *fodder*. Don't you see that's what I'm going to be fighting against every day for the rest of my life? And I can't even think of what comes after that. A fucking *tribute*? Well, you can fuck off." She picked up a piece of the cup, a different one this time. Clutched it more like a talisman than a weapon in her hand. Sarah resisted the urge to ask her to be careful.

Instead: "All I meant," she said quietly, "is that you're a good mom. An amazing mom. I think I show that. Didn't you see that?"

"But I know I'm a good mom," said Leslie. She was clutching the shard, her hand shaking, and Sarah couldn't take her eyes off the cutting edge. "And not just because of patronizing comments like yours. I get those all the time. I'm a great mom, but part of that is because I have to be. You can't have lapses with a kid like Jamie. There just isn't the space to fall apart."

"I just—" started Sarah, but Leslie wasn't finished.

"But it's not just me, Sarah. It's not just Jamie. It's everybody. All our friends. The entire book club? Is there anybody whose life you haven't dissected?"

"Well," said Sarah. "There are probably some people who weren't very interesting."

"So some were spared."

"Some."

Sarah said, "What did they say, everybody else? When they saw it. What do I have to do," she said, "to make this okay?"

Leslie shook her head. "Are you serious?"

"I could delete the blog." As she said the words, though, she knew she wouldn't.

"It doesn't matter," said Leslie. "It's that you wrote it in the first place. All those things about us."

"But it's not like that," said Sarah. "Didn't you see it? The nuance?"

"*Nuance?*"

"So you didn't see the nuance."

"None."

The two friends sat, miles apart, the broken cup between them.

"I don't even know where to start," said Sarah. Hiding in the dumbwaiter felt like another lifetime ago now, whatever was happening with Chris and Evan inconsequential. There would be consequences elsewhere.

Chris. Sarah said, "You told him, didn't you. Chris. Did you tell him? He isn't everyone. Tell me you didn't."

"Of course I did," said Leslie. "I told him first." Her grip on the shard was limp now. She was looking at her lap. "Although I don't know that I managed to disturb his oblivion. He keeps his consciousness locked up behind a fortified wall, that one."

"I wrote that."

"Maybe the one thing you got right," said Leslie. "He never answered my email."

"When?" Her world was already skewed and now it was spinning. "I mean, how long has he known?"

"I started emailing him when I emailed you. I had to. It was all about him too. And I was so angry. I still am."

Sarah ran her memory backwards, adding this new layer of understanding to the events of the past week. So Chris had also been receiving messages from Jane Q, although he'd said nothing to her. Which meant the possibility he'd never read them—anonymous emails were just the kind of thing he'd never take seriously anyway. Maybe he'd deleted them unopened, or the messages had gone into junk mail. But if he had read them, it was chilling context for his distance. Perhaps. But then what about Sunday morning? And she'd been sensing distance for longer than since last week. There had to be a different explanation. Whatever had been happening with Evan this morning. What did any of it mean? How can you tell with somebody like Chris? Her mind whirring like a reel once the film strip was over, the loose end going around and around in a flap.

Leslie said, "I have to go."

Sarah said nothing. Leslie didn't have the answers to any questions she was asking now. And Sarah wanted this confrontation to be over anyway, the china shards unhanded, even though this might mean a decade of shared history turfed to the dustbin along with the remains of the cup.

Leslie said, "But I'm so glad I told you. Because it's now your problem. I'm unburdened." She stood up, smoothing her skirt. Sarah saw the weariness beneath her anger—she'd only compounded her friend's troubles. Leslie had misconstrued things, it's true, but the crux of the matter was undeniable. It was her life up there, and Sarah had used it, profited from it. Never mind that the ad revenue was paltry—Sarah could have shown her receipts that proved as much and then some—but it was the principle of the thing.

Sarah said, "I'm sorry. For all of it." She didn't like to apologize, it was true, but this she meant. She knew when she was really wrong—it was one thing she was sure of. She'd never let herself think through the consequences of her actions to their ends. But here they were now, a friend smashing a china cup and shouting her down in angry confrontation. "I'm sorry for using you and your story, but mostly that you didn't like how I portrayed you. I would never have intended that. I really did mean it as a tribute. I am sorry that you read it and thought I'd meant it any other way."

Leslie set down the broken china. "But most of all, you're sorry you've been caught."

This was true.

Leslie said, "Well, you would be, wouldn't you. You're sorry now when it's too late for all that." This was true too. And all Sarah could think of now was Chris. Why hadn't he told her about the messages? All this week, he might have known about everything after all.

But this wasn't only about her marriage. She'd never considered how many bit players were engaged in this scenario. She said, "I hope you see, if you read it all again, that I didn't mean to hurt you. That you maybe could discern my intentions—they were good ones."

But Leslie was shaking her head. "Read it again? I'd die first." She was calmer now. This was the tone of voice she used to talk about things that weren't ultimate betrayals. "I am so angry at you," she said, "but even so, I hope you never have to feel what I feel when I read what you wrote about me. I wouldn't wish that on anybody."

"Because it was so wrong?" said Sarah. This was cutting. She prided herself and her writing on emotional acuity, but it was called into question now that she'd failed to anticipate so many things.

"Because it wasn't yours to use. Don't you see that? Get your own life, Sarah Lundy. Stay the hell out of mine." Her last line delivered with particular passion, and then she was gone, disappeared down the hall. The front door slammed behind her, and the whole house shook.

From the Archives: Mitzi Bytes
On Being on the Outs

The democratic nature of motherhood is a problem. Suddenly we have a world in common with people we would never have otherwise associated with, and somehow it's supposed to be enough as we assemble in circles on carpets, bouncing babies on our knees. Grown women intent on "Itsy Bitsy Spider," and we're all trying to prove ourselves in this mother gig, itsy-bitsying so seriously. This is what passes for my social life these days, because the alternative is being holed up at home going crazy.

This spring, I've enrolled the baby in music lessons, movement classes, and tactility sessions. When my mother found out, she laughed. "Why don't you just hire a babysitter a couple of mornings a week? Go out and do something for you." As though it were that easy, when the baby is still breastfeeding and refuses to take the bottle; she cries if I leave the room, let alone the house; and daytime babysitters aren't easy to come by anyway.

I asked her if she wouldn't mind stepping in herself once in a while, but she reminded me that she's working. "Grandmothers have their own lives now," she told me smugly.

So it's going to have to be tactility sessions for us.

And what are tactility sessions? They're early introductions to art and creation, those of us in the circle passing from hand to hand a variety of textiles—feathers, silk scarves, corduroy, velour—with which to touch our babies, tickle their toes, their tummies, their faces. Stimulating and inspiring them to start engaging with the world.

It's stupid and boring, but at the end of day, I have something to show for the hours I've spent. An answer when The Programmer asks me: "So, what have you been up to?"

Apart from awakening our babies' sense of their selves (crucial, apparently; the poor babies without access to such programs are surely growing up in an existential void), tactility sessions are for mothers too. "Meet other mums! Make new friends!" the brochure had promised, the one I'd spied on the community board at the pediatrician's. The British spelling of *mum* an affectation. Cozy like a tea cozy. All of us are still trying this new life on.

It is possible that the problems with the mothers at tactility session, none of whom have turned out to be friends, is that we all signed up for tactility sessions. What can you say about people like that?

Every Thursday morning, I sit in our circle and contemplate how I arrived here. Sitting among these women whose names I can never keep straight, though I know their babies' names, but mostly because they're Titania, Rupert, Wexler, Amaryllis.

Surrounded by company, I'm so lonely. I don't want to be friends with any of these people. Certainly not Wexler's mother, whose nipples sprout these straggly hairs that drive me crazy. I want to pluck them. She's always got her tits out. I've got tweezers in my bag. I just can't look away. Those hairs are irresistible, so long and black, thick and wiry. Or Rupert's mother, who side-lie breastfeeds on the carpet like a sow. Who does that in public? The mothers who formula-feed are all as awful, but just less gross.

We make polite conversation over the textiles, the session's facilitator leading the discussion. We talk about the things we have in common, which seem to be the ins and outs of breastfeeding, and how little or well our babies sleep. And sometimes I do catch a spark of something, a line that gestures toward humour, a word or two with bite, and I look a bit closer at these women. I wonder, "Who are you?" Or "Who *were* you? Before."

But instead we talk about baby-wearing like it's an actual verb, arguing over the ethics of sleep training, and debating the virtues of the organic store-bought baby food we pay extra for to assuage our guilt at not puréeing the string beans ourselves.

And the thing is that if you walked into our tactility session, you wouldn't be able to pick me out of the crowd. "I don't fit in at all in my moms' group" is what everyone says, so I don't know why we don't all stop going. Why are there moms' groups at all? Or why don't we talk about that instead, how we all feel so far away from the people we were before we were mothers, and yet not far enough for the distance not to matter.

I brought this up once actually at a tactility session, when we were taking turns feeling up a piece of leather. It took courage to deviate from the usual topics of conversation, but I was tired of discussing the colour and consistency of baby shit.

I said, "Do you ever think of what our former selves would say if they could see us now? Sitting cross-legged on a carpet, talking about poo? Don't you just want to tell that self to turn around and run the other way, to just keep on going and never stop taking the pill?"

I scanned the circle, making eye contact with everyone, hoping for someone's glance to register, but came up with nothing. Some of the other mothers actually looked horrified. I was only trying to be funny. Kind of. But nobody seemed amused.

And so ends my foray into reaching out to my peers. There are seven tactility sessions left, for which I've prepaid, and they don't have a money-back escape clause for those of us who've ostracized ourselves from the group. I know, because I've already called to check. They have a no-refunds policy in place, they told me, specifically because they get calls like mine all the time.

Which is vindicating. Somewhat.

CHAPTER 12

. . . .

Nothing like this ever happened to Mrs. Ramsay, sitting pretty in her window, perfect as a picture, albeit a blurry one. An impressionist painting. Whereas Sarah Lundy was more likely to be captured by Picasso, hideous and exaggerated features. Garish. Fractured. Blue. That is, if anyone wanted to paint her at all, and as of yet, no one ever had. Which is why it felt so unreal and uncomfortable now that the attention was all on her. That she truly was the centre of this entire sorry mess.

It was uncomfortable and something else, though. Perhaps this too was fodder. She had nothing left to lose. She'd received a call back from Andrea in Seattle, and filled her in on the details, skipping over the extraneous bits about the dumbwaiter. It had really been the most extraordinary day. She still hadn't heard back from Chris. She didn't know what she'd say to him when she finally did. Because what do you say when you learn that the person you love has a closetful of secrets? When you learn that the person you love might not be that person after all?

Speaking to Andrea now, she said, "It doesn't matter anymore, the anonymity. Everybody who knows me knows already, or they're going to, and they were the only people who mattered anyway."

Andrea said, "So what are you going to do?"

"It's all fallen apart," said Sarah. "The sky's the limit."

"Truth is," said Andrea, "I'm not sure it matters much."

"What?"

"Ten years ago," said Andrea, "when blooks were blooks, and you were top of the game, this would have been a big deal. Your big coming out. But having waited this long, it's not really going to make waves, Sarah."

"I'm saying we could go big with this thing," said Sarah. She was imagining how fame might catapult her right out of her own life. That something could be made with these shattered pieces of her quiet universe after all. "Mitzi Bytes revealed. TV, magazines."

Andrea was quiet for a moment. "I don't think *they're* going to bite, Sarah," she said.

"They did before. The woman who wrote that article 'Still Byting after All These Years.' That wasn't so long ago."

"Listen, I'm giving it to you straight," said Andrea. "I'm not saying you don't have your fans, but outside of those circles, you just don't have the name recognition. Blogs aren't big news anymore. Unless they're dying. Every six months, someone writes an obit. Maybe you could do something like that? 'Why I'm Quitting My Blog,' by Mitzi Bytes."

"I'm not going to quit."

"Then I don't know."

"So I'm a relic."

"You're not. But you're not really on the ascent, are you? It would look like a stunt. Something desperate. Calculating, and I'm not sure it would bring up the result you are looking for."

"You said I could make a book out of this."

"Maybe," said Andrea. "But it would have to be a different book. Something deliberate. Not the kind of book that gets shelved beside *Chicken Soup for the Soul*."

"I really don't need somebody else kicking me today," said Sarah.

"Not a kick," said Andrea. "It's my job to be honest. But I think you could do it, if you wanted to. What do you want to do?"

"I want to turn the page," said Sarah. "I feel like they've got me cornered like an animal, and I'm not sure how I'm going to get out of it."

•   •   •

Chris finally called her back, in a panic, she suspected, but she had no way of knowing. She didn't answer, and he didn't leave a message. The conversation they needed to have couldn't happen over the phone, and she wasn't sure she wanted it to happen anywhere. There was something to be said for limbo in this particular instance, for leaving her marriage perfectly preserved, if only for the moment. She wasn't ready to grapple with that disaster. There wasn't enough time anyway before she had to go pick up the girls.

She left the house and got back behind the wheel, imagining her SUV as an artillery tank she could hole up inside as she drove into battle. For the school would certainly be a war zone. Leslie had said that she'd told everyone, but what did that mean exactly? It wasn't as though she'd hired a skywriter, or taken out a billboard. No, this was the twenty-first century, so she'd probably posted it on Facebook, or sent a message out on the

PTA listserv. Oh, she was doomed, Sarah knew. When Leslie was angry, she was ruthless, and Sarah couldn't even blame her.

She wished she didn't have to go out into the world. She might have asked someone else to pick up the kids, if she could think of anybody who definitely probably wouldn't start seething in fury at seeing her number show up on their phone. She wasn't thinking clearly enough at the moment to be able to sort through her mental Rolodex to make the distinction. It was true that very few people had escaped her gaze online. Everyone who mattered to her had become part of the story.

Although, to her credit, the excellent Mrs. Ramsay had done exactly the same thing. Sitting there at her perch at the window, casting her eye upon the people around her. The young couple in love, how she hears them say *we*: "They'll say that all their lives, she thought." Her assessment of funny Lily Briscoe, with her eyes and her easel. All the desperate bachelor men. Her own children, eight of them. Mrs. Ramsay imagining all the details of their lives as she sits there in the window, knitting that brown stocking for the lighthouse keeper's son. The story was never about her.

But of course it was, Sarah allows, turning left onto Acorn Avenue, the school just up ahead. Mrs. Ramsay had been wrong about everything. That couple, the Rayleys, turn out unhappy. The eldest Ramsay daughter dies. The war. Never mind her own death, which happens in parentheses, in the night. For all her vision, Mrs. Ramsay doesn't see very far. *She* never gets to the lighthouse.

Are Woolf's readers supposed to like Mrs. Ramsay or not? Discussion at the book club had hinged on this point for a while, and then Beth-Ellen had flipped through her copy for another quote she'd marked:

How then did it work out, all this? How did one judge people, think of them? How did one add up this and that and conclude that it was liking one felt, or disliking? And to those words, what meaning attached, after all?

Although the answers seemed more straightforward now, as Sarah eased her car into the last space available on the street outside the school. To "like" someone was to find them not thoroughly detestable or their behaviour reprehensible, Sarah supposed. You most likely would not implore someone you liked to stay the hell out of your life.

Maybe Michelle was right: Woolf simply liked to complicate things. It really could be as easy as that.

Sarah got out of the car and walked around to find Claudia Kincardine waiting on the sidewalk.

"You're late," she told Sarah.

"Yep," Sarah answering, avoiding eye contact, hoping to skirt by her, collect the kids, and get back home fast. "Gotta get my girls." But Claudia followed along as she walked up the path.

"You must have thought you were pretty clever, eh?" said Claudia.

"Never once," said Sarah. Unfortunately, she wasn't late enough. She'd still have to stand outside the door with everyone and wait for the bell to ring.

"Well, you pulled off the act of vacant-headed dodo mom spectacularly, I thought," said Claudia. "You certainly had me fooled."

She was speaking just low enough that nobody could overhear her. From a small distance, they looked like two women having a friendly conversation, never mind the way that Sarah was edging her body away, trying to make space between them.

"You're a snake," Claudia whispered, looming so close that Sarah could feel the breath of her sibilance, a sound that hung in the air. Sarah wanted to grab Claudia by her skinny neck and hoist it high, shouting "Bully!" Which, in this day and age, was even worse than a snake.

Instead Sarah told her firmly, "This has nothing to do with you."

"It does," said Claudia, indignant. Her voice got quiet again. "I went through your archives. I read everything you wrote."

But none of it was about Claudia. On this point, Sarah was quite adamant. She'd never written about Claudia Kincardine, not once. Claudia was not a person of consequence. Sarah told her so.

"You can't lie to me," said Claudia. "All I ask is that you admit the truth. The evidence is right here," and she pulled out her handy iPad, shaking the screen in Sarah's face, Mitzi Bytes wide open on her browser. She said, "You have to take the site down."

"I don't have to do anything," said Sarah. This was exhausting.

"But you do. I've started an online petition. Change.org. Forty-five signatures in an hour." She checked her phone again. "Forty-seven now."

"But why?" said Sarah. "And you're not even there. I never wrote about you."

Claudia said, "You'll say that to everyone."

"No," said Sarah. "Definitely not everyone."

"I know what I read," said Claudia.

But Sarah was shaking her head. Actually, this part wasn't so bad, probably the one enjoyable experience she'd had all day. It was nice to be sure. If only all battles could be this easy. "You're not in the subtext," she said. "Not even once."

"Well, this is bigger than me," said Claudia ominously, as the bell rang and the children started to file outside. Sarah left her and went to get her daughters.

• • •

What's wrong with Mommy?"

"Leave her alone," Clementine told Gladys. "She's lost in a reverie." A new word for daydream. They'd learned it from *Anne of Green Gables*, which they'd read together two novels ago, and Sarah wasn't so far gone that she wasn't paying attention to their conversation.

Home now, she was sitting at one end of the kitchen counter, and it felt strange to no longer be waiting on the phone for her next move. Now she was avoiding the phone, which was switched off, and she'd left it on the other side of the counter by the sink, out of reach. It was too much of a habit. Chris had resorted to calling her on the landline over and over, so she'd taken the receiver off the hook and left it in the hall, the operator's recording imploring her to please hang up and try her call again, before changing to a busy signal and eventually fading away to quiet. A quiet she needed. A tiny pocket to ponder the nature of her various crimes, and whatever those were of Chris and Evan, crimes in which she was, at least, not implicated. As far as she knew. So that she could be a victim too, wounded as well as wrongdoer. But this only made her feel more tangled up in everything, irrevocably entwined. And what she would have given to wiggle free of it all, to shake it off and float away unencumbered. If it weren't for all of the things that kept her tethered to this life. The two small girls playing on the carpet before her, flitting about and fancying the sound of themselves uttering the word *reverie*.

They'd opened a pack of disposable pie plates, which they'd scattered around the room, and were walking about them now, tiptoe-leaping from one glimmering aluminum disc to another. Any step off course would lead to death by alligators or crocodiles—the girls could not decide which. The couch was safety, of course, but one could only linger there so long before being tempted back out on the shining path.

"Rever-eeee!" exclaimed Gladys, leaping from the couch, its cushions tumbling off behind her. Both girls looked up for their mother's reaction, but Sarah gave them nothing.

If she couldn't wiggle free of the matter, she was thinking, how might she begin to unfurl the tangled knot. *There are two things you're going to have to do, Sarah, and you don't like either of them. You have to apologize. And you're going to have to lie.* But it was no longer as simple as that. Because now she was waiting for some kind of apology too. And how would she know if the apology was genuine? Would it really make any difference if it was?

The phone rang, startling her out of the reverie. The land-line. One of the girls must have hung up the receiver in the hall. They both had a real aversion to anything out of place, an unanswered ring being another such thing, which was why Clementine had brought the phone to her, dropping it into her lap. "It's Daddy," she whispered, his name on the caller display. And Sarah couldn't answer. This conversation was a thread on which her entire life was hanging, she thought. Whatever he had to say to her would determine everything, all the king's horses and all the king's men. So she let it keep ringing. Until it stopped.

"Mommy?" Clementine asked. "Why didn't you get it?"

Sarah rubbed her eyes and shook her head. "Because," she

told her daughter, "I've decided I can only focus on one thing at a time right now." The idea amusing her. It might be useful, she thought, for Chris to learn how it felt to come last in terms of priorities. She turned the phone on again to keep the line engaged. Leaving it up on the counter and out of reach. She said, "And there's something I have to do right now. Something very important."

She put on a DVD and fixed the girls up with a bowl of veggie sticks. Made them promise not to bother her unless it was absolutely necessary, and not to touch the phone again, and then she retreated upstairs to her office. The sounds of the movie fading as she made her way to the third floor, though she left the door open just in case. She had responsibilities. The singular focus she dreamt of was not something she could afford.

She flipped open her laptop to find a series of messages from Chris. *I'm getting concerned now* was the latest. *Why aren't you answering your phone?* Previously, *About this morning*, he'd written. *You mean with Evan? I can sort it all out. I just need to talk to you.*

She opened a new window. Create New Post. Title: *An Apology and Explanations.*

New Post: Mitzi Bytes

An Apology and Explanations

Life has always struck me as a many-sided shape, no single moment experienced by any person ever existing in just one way. Because there is the way that I saw it, and how I see it now, and how I think *you* saw it, which will never be exactly like how you actually did. And that's just the two of us, never mind the billions of other humans in the world, and then there's how I'm going to see things tomorrow when something new comes soaring out of the sky, knocking me down on my ass and changing my mind about everything I ever thought was true.

And to me, this has always been the attraction of the blog, that it's a place to record impressions of the innumerable atoms as they fall, to decipher the universe, assembling the chaos into a pattern of days, weeks, and years. A record that This All Happened, even as I read back through my archives and no longer recognize the writer of most of these posts or even what she is describing, let alone what it felt to live the moments she committed to Internet eternity.

Archives are one of the best parts of a blog, these amazing posts that are a window into the mind of the person you used to be. But they are also one of the worst parts of having a blog, evidence that you used to be so stupid, naive, pathetic, bad at grammar, and trying way too hard. I promise: give anyone a window into the mind of the person who they used to be, and they're probably going to be embarrassed.

But, of course, as everybody keeps reminding me, not everything is about me. And it turns out that even more agonizing than how it feels for me to find myself in these posts is how it might feel for others to do so, to encounter their own selves and stories, my angles and my judgments—all those things that all of us think but usually never say . . . I suppose for good reason. And I had never fully appreciated what that might be like. I'd always been so comfortable writing in this space and never thinking through to the real-world ramifications—this suggesting that my stupidity and naivety are not altogether in the past tense, yes. But it has been made clear to me that this blog has hurt people, and all I can do now is apologize.

Not apologize for the things I said, necessarily, because I only ever said what I meant, but I apologize for any dishonesty I implied. And for having used the experiences of people who'd trusted me with the details of their personal lives, assuming a certain measure of privacy. I know that I've let these people down.

I can make no excuses. That I tried to disguise details and did my best to tell the truth doesn't change the fact that friends and family have been betrayed by what they found here. That the firm delineations I tried to make between my "real life" and this online identity were really for my convenience only. And the delineations weren't even all that firm because (and here's one that threw me for a loop) it turns out that my mother has known about Mitzi Bytes for a decade. Though my mother does know everything. BUT . . . I wonder who else knew. So it seems that my real life has in fact been quite recognizable in the stories Mitzi tells here, by which I mean the stories that I tell here, because her pronoun is mine. Mitzi is me. I am her.

And yet . . .

This bringing me back to the beginning, to my point about the many-sidedness of things. Mitzi is me, but so are so many other people, and there are certain perspectives from which Mitzi Bytes is just an abject falsehood. And while the stories I tell here are simply life the way I see it—or at least how it was at the time of telling—these stories were never meant to be anybody's definitive, authoritative truth. They only ever stood for a single side, a tiny sliver of a single side of that many-sided thing: The Entire Story. Life Itself.

My hope is that anybody who can is going to understand that this is where I'm coming from. And while I know this explanation is going to come much too late for other people in my life, regardless of apologies, I hope that eventually these others too will come to understand that I only ever wrote here with the best of intentions and with love in my heart. Except when there wasn't love in my heart. In which case then there's probably not much lost between us. I'm okay with that.

Regardless of what may be decreed by higher powers—whether they be God, my mother, or earnest petitioners at Change.org—I'm not going to be giving up Mitzi Bytes. What this whole experience has taught me is that we two are irrevocably bound. To have one without the other would be its own kind of dishonesty, and I really do remain committed to the truth. So I'm going to keep telling it, just with a fuller kind of disclosure. And while I don't anticipate that you will be noticing many changes around here, do not take this to mean that I've not thought deeply about what it is I'm doing, reflecting on the ethics and responsibilities of my role, and the implications for the people in my stories. I just don't think that any of that reflection will change the way I operate. I've always stood by my words. So I really do intend to keep on doing what I've been doing, but only just out in the open.

CHAPTER 13

· · · · · · · · · · · · · · · ·

Chris's final email said, *I'm leaving now. I told them there's a family crisis. But I'm concerned there actually is a family crisis. Can you call me?* But she didn't. Because there was dinner to make: an avocado pasta sauce, she decided, a simple recipe, with basil from her plant on the windowsill. And she resisted the impulse to look out the window into the backyard, to try to decipher the scene behind the trees. "One thing at a time," she murmured to herself as the scissors clicked and the plant became nearly naked. A quarter cup of basil leaves thrown into the food processor with the avocado and some lemon juice. Flicking the switch, and the house was filled with its whir.

The girls had disappeared somewhere, the pie plates still scattered across the floor. She would have to pick them up herself—they were dented now, probably rendered useless. The pasta on the stove was cooking—four minutes left to al dente. The counters wiped, no dishes in the sink. And here she was, absolutely present in this perfect tidy moment that she'd carved out of the mess of her life right now, and she imagined the moment as a creation, like an origami swan, or an artfully folded napkin. Resisting the impulse to take a photo, to capture the rich green of the avocado sauce as offset by the late-afternoon sun that was pouring through the window, to preserve that light, which shone like something out of a painting by Mary Pratt. Resisting because thoughts of preservation would suggest she wasn't really present at all— *one thing at a time*—but mostly because her phone was out of reach. She shook her hand, as though she were shaking away the yearning to clutch the phone in her fist. It could be possible to live her life and not make the whole thing into a performance.

Which was a thought she was examining when she felt a hand grab her shoulder: she screamed. He yelped in response. Chris, of course, and now her senses were packed with all the noise, her heart pounding in her head. The girls came running up the basement stairs to find out what was happening. And it took a few seconds to decipher where the roar was coming from on top of everything else, before she remembered and turned off the food processor.

He said, "I told you I was coming home."

For a split second she'd been relieved at the sight of him, but that feeling was a vestige of a different life. She told him, "You scared me."

"I was calling," he said. The girls were dancing around him. Their dad was home for dinner, and they were delighted. ("Is it your book club again, Mommy?" Gladys asked.) "You had me so worried," he said. "Why didn't you answer the phone?"

"Why do you *never* answer the phone?" she asked.

"No, not like this," he said. "Please. I don't want to fight."

She said, "Well maybe you don't get to decide." The girls weren't dancing now. Both of them looking up, examining their parents with critical eyes.

"I'm sorry?" he offered. And then she understood why Leslie had been so furious that morning, how an empty apology was like a deflated balloon. Words had to mean something, or else what was the point? Which was what she'd been saying all along, and it felt good to be consistent for once.

But Chris could only see that he'd just upset her further. "How do you know?" he said. "*What* do you know?" Rephrased. Gladys and Clementine waiting for her answer.

"Not now," she said. Glancing at the stove. The linguini was probably mush. She hustled to get down the colander and drain it. "And can somebody please pick up the pie plates?" Turning her back on the whole mess as she dumped the pasta back into the pot and spooned out the avocado sauce. A few moments ago, she'd had everything contained, but now it was all gone.

• • •

There is no such thing as a dinner in awkward silence in the presence of children aged seven and five, for whom words are like oxygen, filling the room. Sitting at the table, linguini looped around their kid-sized forks, the girls told tales without context and went off on elaborate tangents, and nobody stopped them, for once. The pasta was okay, at least, so there was that, and Sarah ate two servings even though her stomach hurt. Her attention to her daughters was much more focused than it usually was, because she was avoiding eye contact with her husband. But if no one ever interrupted the girls, she wondered, might the inane chatter only go on forever? An experiment she'd never attempted, and even now in desperate times she wasn't brave enough to try.

She said, "So," and the girls stopped talking. Chris looked up, hopeful. "How was *your* day?" she asked. Gladys and Clementine buoyed by this semblance of normalcy; she could see relief on their faces. They'd been sensing the tension between their parents. And here an ordinary question—now they were waiting for his ordinary answer.

But it was not forthcoming. Chris was examining her with a puzzled expression. The person before him now was a stranger, she realized, and the strangeness was mutual.

When he finally answered her, he chose his words like somebody walking on ice, each syllable tenuous and careful. "It. Was." He stopped. "Okay?" He didn't know where he stood. Squinting to see her more clearly, he ran his hands through his hair. She didn't say a word about the gesture.

"Well, that's nice," she said. "For you." Everyone had finished eating by now. They could all just get up from the table, probably, the charade of this meal finally over. She thought about all the days she longed to have Chris home for dinner. But the terms were different now. She was thinking about his secrets, how he had layers after all, and that one of his secrets was actually her own. Which meant, gallingly, that not even her secrets properly belonged to her. And why hadn't he told her what he knew about Jane Q? Were her life and experiences really of so little consequence to him?

Chris said, "Girls, go and play." He hadn't taken his eyes off her. The girls didn't move. "Go," he said.

Gladys said, "Mommy?"

"Upstairs," she said. "Daddy and I want to talk."

Clementine had intuited the seriousness of this moment,

and she was already leading Gladys away, tugging her reluctant arm. "Come on, we'll go get out the Lego," she said. "You can be Princess Unikitty."

Chris said, "I don't know what to do."

"About what?"

He said, "At all." He really didn't. She wondered how much longer she'd be able to hold on to the upper hand. "So, tell me. I mean, do I stay or go? Do you want me to talk or listen? I don't even know what's happening. About any of this. This is about Evan? How do you know?"

"Know what?" she said.

"I don't *know*," he said. He sounded desperate. "Can you help me? Please?"

"What's going on with Evan?"

He had his head in his hands, raking his hair.

She said, "Stop it, stop it." He looked up. "Your hair." He put his arms down on the table. He looked at her straight on, and he looked very small. "It's all a big, huge, fucking mess," he said. He usually didn't swear so much. Everything was out of character.

"And you know about Jane Q."

"Jane Q?"

"The emails. The blog. You didn't read them?"

"Oh," he said.

"You saw it."

"I just don't understand," he said. "What one thing has to do with the other."

"I don't know that it does," she said. "I'm really scared."

"Yeah."

She said, "I don't know what's going on, and I don't know if I want whatever you've done to be less bad or worse than what I did."

"Well," he said, "I don't know that it's a contest. But, I mean, I didn't do anything completely immoral."

"And I'm not sure that I can say the same," she said. The look on his face. She said, "No, not cheating. God, no. Not immoral like that. Not immoral in a way that has anything to do with you, or has for a very long time."

"Quit talking around things."

She said, "No. You tell me first. What happened with Evan."

He said, "But how do you know? Did Frances tell you? Does she know too? And, I mean, none of this really has to do with you. Not at all."

She wanted to move around the table so they were sitting side by side, so she could touch him and be sure it was all going to be okay, but the way they were sitting now, at least she could see his face. She needed to be able to look into his eyes. If he stretched out his arms, she could hold his hands in hers, but that would be weird.

She said, "I was there."

"At the club?"

"What club?" He shook his head. She continued, "At the house. I was hiding. Frances asked me to go get Charlotte's puffer, then I heard you come in. This morning."

"You were hiding."

"In the dumbwaiter."

"What's a dumbwaiter?"

"The elevator thing. In the hall."

"The hole in the wall."

"I was in there."

"I didn't see you."

"Exactly."

Chris sighed in a way that said "You're unbelievable," which he didn't necessarily mean as synonym for amazing. And then he gave her the whole story, which had started a few months ago and had been bad from the start.

"I gave him the money," Chris said.

"For the album? Not all of it." But Chris was nodding. "That was fifteen thousand dollars. For Evan?" This was unbelievable too. "Are you insane?"

Chris said, "Maybe."

"Of your money. *Our* money. But why?"

Because if he hadn't done it, Frances would have. She'd told him so. That Evan's crowdfunding campaign was going to be make-or-break not just for his career but for his entire self, and if it failed he would be utterly defeated. Frances said that Evan needed to know that the world had faith in him, never mind that it didn't. Evan would be sustained by the illusion. She wasn't yet ruling out the possibility of a miracle, though—that there was actually going to emerge a crowd to really fund the thing—because she did have faith in Evan after all, and in his talent. She believed in him. A single person who did and he had no idea how fortunate he was to have her.

"But I couldn't let her do it," said Chris. He loved his sister as much as she loved her hapless husband, and he wanted her to be sustained by the illusion too. "I thought I was helping."

"I can't believe it."

"I really didn't think it would go so wrong."

"But of course it would. This is Evan."

"I don't know," he said. "Maybe I had faith too. I wanted it to work. I thought I could arrange things. Anyway, he found out it was me, and I don't know how he did. Probably he was the only one who didn't have faith. And he was furious. I think it was mostly pride, you know? The whole thing outed him as kind of a loser. It was embarrassing."

"So why didn't you just call it off?"

"Because he still wanted the money," said Chris. "Never mind how he'd got it, which was a different matter altogether. He wanted to make the album. But then he started spending the money on other things—he's never going to get around to making the album ever. I don't know how either of us ever thought it was going to be different."

"You'd imagined you weren't throwing fifteen thousand dollars down a hole? That's a huge amount of money." At least she thought so. "Isn't it?"

"But it got worse," said Chris. "He's spending money on this girl, sending her on trips, buying her clothes. And so I tried to talk to him about it, explain that I didn't think it was right. And he said that my donation had been a fraud in itself that negated the terms of the arrangement."

"What?"

"I don't know. But he said that he could spend the funds however he wanted now, and that if I had a problem with it, he'd tell Frances that I'd paid him the money."

"So?"

Chris shrugged. "I didn't want her to find out."

"Sustaining the illusion . . ." said Sarah. She was thinking about Evan, all that talk about his focus.

"That, and mostly that she'd just be really, really pissed at me. She'd think it was all about pity, and I guess it was, which is the worst thing. And she'd hate that."

"So he blackmailed you."

"Kind of. I was an easy target," said Chris. "He had the money already. Oh, I don't know. I thought I could resolve things, but it just got more and more tangled. Mostly, I felt like an idiot. Embarrassed."

"The girl—was that the girl from this morning? The backup singer?"

"Yeah. You saw her last week, I guess. He'd been promising me it was all over, but then he goes and moves her in over the garage."

"What about this morning? What was all that?"

He told her all about the call he'd received from the police station where Evan had been stuck all night in a holding cell.

"Frances didn't say anything," said Sarah. "I talked to her this morning. Surely the fact that he hadn't come home all night—"

"Isn't terribly unusual," said Chris. "And Frances's not really the type who's going to tell you when something's gone wrong. She didn't know where he was. Still doesn't."

"He was in jail?"

"A holding cell," he clarified.

The night before, he'd been out with Jen, the backup singer, whose abusive husband—or ex-husband, it wasn't clear—had shown up at the bar where they were drinking. The husband said something provocative, and Evan beat the crap out of him. He claimed this was chivalry.

"Evan won a fight?" This was remarkable. That he was in a fight at all. Sarah had never known him to show such initiative.

"Apparently the other guy was a Buddhist."

"An abusive Buddhist?"

"He's inconsistent."

"Wow," said Sarah.

"So I don't know what to think," said Chris. "I mean on the one hand, it's noble. It's what was right. From what the girl said, the Buddhist guy had it coming. But then if Evan is cheating on my sister—"

"Is he?"

"He says he isn't. But he says a lot of things."

He'd called Chris because he needed somebody to post bail. They were hoping the guy would drop charges and Frances would never have to know, but then it turned out that Evan had broken the guy's nose, and the Buddhist was pissed. The backup singer was feeling ambivalent about everything.

"I guess they have a child together. But he won't let her sing. He's really controlling. She says it's complicated. Anyway, I showed up, bailed him out, drove him home. And you were there?"

"I was helping," said Sarah. "Charlotte's puffer."

"Right."

"So that's all of it."

"Yep."

"And you were never going to tell me about any of it? Don't you think that maybe I could have helped?"

"The whole situation was supposed to be a whole lot simpler. I didn't think any of it would matter."

"Fifteen thousand dollars isn't simple, though. You know that, right?"

"We could afford it."

"That's not the point. I hope you don't make a habit out of this either. Spending money like that." She was responsible for their day-to-day finances, and Chris took care of the long-term arrangements, their investments and savings plans. She realized that really she had no idea what any of it was all about. He could be financing a seventy-two-piece band for all she knew.

"I didn't want to have to tell you," he said. "Anyway, you would have only told me I had to tell Frances."

"She's going to be so angry," said Sarah.

"You would have told me that too."

"It all makes me uneasy, though," said Sarah. "I really can't believe this, about the money. I never suspected. This whole secret side of you."

"Well, surely this doesn't constitute—"

"I just thought that I knew you completely. Simple. Summed up. And I mean, that doesn't even make sense. You're an actual human being. I should know that. But now it makes me nervous too, you know, the way we just have to believe people. Believe in people."

"But we do. That's the point."

"Frances trusts Evan."

"No, she doesn't. She just can't stand to look closely anymore. It's easier that way. And then that gets to be a habit, and there's even a kind of trust in that. A faith. It's like not looking down when you're teetering on the edge. A decision you make."

"Wilful ignorance."

"I guess."

"Why didn't you tell me?" she said. "About the message. Jane Q." And now their arms were stretched across the table, the way she'd envisioned, not holding hands, but fingers touching. But the girls were coming back downstairs. She said, "You know, I'm in trouble too." Clementine and Gladys clomping into the room, inexplicably wearing winter boots and displaying their Lego creations.

Clementine said, "I kept her barricaded as long as I could." Her parents looked confused, so she clarified. "You were busy and I was in charge, so I made sure she stayed upstairs. But she escaped." She shrugged.

"I wanted to show you my plane," said Gladys.

"Actually, *I* made it," said Clementine. "So, you're done now?"

Chris said, "Get the tablet from my bag. You can go into the living room and play some games."

"Really?" This was a bonanza. Chris's tablet was more coveted than Sarah's phone.

He said, "I need to talk to Mommy." The girls went stomping away. "Take turns," he called. He looked back at Sarah. "So."

She said, "You said nothing."

"About those emails." She nodded. "I don't know. I thought it was spam, a hoax. It's hard to take something seriously from someone who doesn't even use their real name."

"But you read them?" He had. "And you saw the blog?" He nodded. "And?"

A pained expression came over his face. "I don't know," he said. "I just didn't really see the point. Of blogs at all, basically. And I guess, like I said, it was coming from somebody who doesn't have a name."

"So you just disregarded it? It was that easy?"

He shrugged. "I didn't think about it that much. I figured if it was important, you would tell me. I didn't even know for sure if that was about you." He said, "It was you?" She nodded. "I've had a lot on my mind," he said. "And I guess, I'm on your side, you know? Someone turns up in my inbox talking trash about you—I'm not going to spend any time on that."

"It was kind of a big deal, though, you know," she said. "The blog, I mean. You should probably know that." She felt small, having to insist on it, but then she told him everything. About Mitzi Bytes, and the books, and the money that wasn't from transcribing and freelance assignments after all. Money she'd been saving for what, she didn't know, but it was something of her own, what it all signified. She'd kept it hidden away in the account she'd had before they were married. It came down to the fish shop and the life she'd built out of that, and then everything got beyond her.

She said, "There were things I wrote about you, a long time ago. And I put them on the Internet for everybody to read, and they weren't always nice things, what I said. Because you remember what it was like back at the beginning when I didn't know you, or how things would get to be."

"And people read this stuff?"

She said, "They loved it. And they loved it so much, they made it into a book. Three books. Bestsellers." Surely he could see it was really not so unfathomable as that, although she'd always known he wouldn't get it. That he'd see it as silly and frivolous, but even so, he had to know she hadn't dreamt the whole thing. Her actual career. "Well, two of them were bestsellers, at least. And I was on *Time* magazine's list of top bloggers." She wanted him to know that this mattered; she wanted him to be proud of her.

He said, "I must have missed that issue."

She said, "And anyway, it's all got out now. The whole thing crashing down. And it turns out that Jane Q is Leslie, because I wrote about Jamie."

"What about him?"

Sarah paused. "That it's a burden being his mother. Because it's true. A burden and a heartache, but she's not allowed to say it. And then I said it, but I shouldn't have. Because she's right—how could I think I have any idea what it's like? What it's like to be anyone?"

"So you got caught." She nodded. "And otherwise, you probably would have just gone on doing this forever."

She said, "Do you hate me now?"

He said, "Because you've just revealed that you have a vicious streak, no compunction, are socially clumsy, and talk far too much about everybody else's business?"

She said, "I guess so." She got out from under his arm and moved away so she could see his face.

He said, "None of this is news to me. Do you think it would be? Do you think that I pay no attention at all?"

"You didn't know."

"I didn't know about the blog," he said. "But I know you. I mean, it's all kind of keeping with the general framework, no?"

He always had a much easier time accepting reality, its elasticity, than she did.

"I have a general framework?"

He said, "It's not that you never surprise me. It's just that your capacity for being surprising is a built-in feature."

"And for doing ridiculous things."

"That too," he said. "So what are you going to do now?"

"About what?"

He said, "Your tendency to alienate people is also in keeping. But it seems like this time, you've nailed everybody at once."

"The whole book club," she whispered.

"Ah, shit," he whispered back.

"I've got a lot of apologizing to do," she said. "And then I may have to go into some kind of witness protection program if all else fails."

"But you weren't a witness," he said.

"I'll be a witness to something if I can't get a new identity."

"Another one?"

"Maybe two's enough."

"So, Mitzi Bites. Like a rabid dog?"

"Bytes with a y."

"It's supposed to be funny," he supposed.

She praised him: "Very good."

He said, "I've never heard of it."

"I was sort of counting on that." He smiled. And she smiled back. The tension between them dissipated. And right now, she could be swept away on a feel-good tide of free and easy.

But no. There was still the fact of Evan. In spite of herself and her best interests, Sarah knew she wasn't finished yet. She could not simply accept the things her husband had told her, details that may have shifted everything she'd ever thought she knew about him. Her reality was not elastic. Her framework only stretched so far, and he couldn't fault her for that. Never mind the problem of Evan himself, all the blanks that still required filling in.

She told him, "You know, I saw them kissing in the yard. Evan and the girl. And when I was over there, the futon looked, like, *sexed in*."

Chris groaned. "So gross." He got up and went around to the kitchen, got the wineglasses down. He really was free and easy now. "She knows, you know. Frances does. About the girl. She thought he was drinking again, and she doesn't know if it's better or worse that he actually isn't. That it's the girl after all." There was a bottle of wine already open in the fridge. He poured them each a glass.

"She told me to leave him alone," Sarah said. "She said I was disturbing his focus, turning up over there."

"I think she wants you to mind your own business," Chris said, handing Sarah her glass, taking a sip from his own as he sat down beside her. "A message you've been hearing a lot lately."

"The problem is that everybody's business *is* my business. Or at least I've made it that way. Literally."

Chris was thinking. "So you've made money." She nodded. "How much?"

"A lot. You never really paid much attention to what I made."

"Books?"

"The ad revenue, mostly. But yeah, books, though the third one kind of tanked. There were even film options, twice. They kept falling through."

"Because how do you make a movie about a blog?"

"Something like that. It made a lot of things difficult." She put down her glass. "None of that matters anymore," she said. "I'm Web 2.0, and that was a long time ago. But the whole thing is still such a big mess. Chris, I wrote some pretty nasty things about you."

"Years and years ago."

"Yeah."

"And you didn't use my name."

"No, you're The Programmer. Beloved by fans, actually." He looked surprised. "Really. There was even a campaign once, *Team Programmer*. With T-shirts. They thought I didn't deserve you."

"And when was that?"

"Before we got married. I was complaining about how you always left your dirty clothes on the floor."

"Why do people read this stuff?"

"I got hate mail," Sarah said. "Anyway, these days it's pretty tame, you and me. I don't think I've written about your laundry for ages. But you know how things were, before I really knew you."

"When you made fun of my khaki pants and thought I was a savant."

"Pretty much," she said. There was more, though. "I wrote about your underwear. It went viral."

He said, "So in order to really get a sense of what all this means, I've got to go twelve years back in the archive of what is basically your diary."

"My online diary."

"To find something you'd written about jockey shorts?" She'd never seen his eyebrows go so high. "Why would anyone ever do that?"

"Maybe you'd like it," Sarah said. She moved close beside him, into his lap, and wrapped her arms around his neck. "Maybe you should?" She kissed him on the cheek.

And he said, "No, I don't think so. I mean, you need to keep at least one person on your side in the world."

•   •   •

In spite of her apprehensions, it did make a difference to have one person on her side in the world. And this one person in particular, who really was the only person she cared about mattering to. Though it wasn't quite as simple as that. She was still angry with him for giving Evan the money, for not telling her about it. And he didn't seem to understand either why it mattered, Mitzi Bytes. She needed to explain. He had to realize this wasn't nothing.

"Hear me out." They were lying in bed. They'd put the girls to bed together, treading carefully, extending storytime to book after book because it was so much easier to read words that were written on a page, rather than script the whole thing for themselves, these necessary awkward conversations. But now it was time. Chris had turned off his tablet, and everything was dark, and she'd been waiting for this moment, the two of them cocooned in the world, no one else for miles.

He said, "What choice do I have?" But he was kidding. Or at least she thought he was.

She said, "What's the point of a blog?" She'd been thinking about this a lot. It's a question she'd been asking for years. "I wrote it for me, to figure out what I think of things. It was like therapy at first, and I guess I could have written it all down in a notebook and then shut it away in a drawer, but it wouldn't have done any good for me, then." The good wasn't just finding her voice but actually using it, being heard. She was at the lowest she'd ever been, having lost everything she'd thought she had, but all of a sudden, she had stories to tell, and she was funny. That was huge.

It wasn't that the blog mattered simply because people read it, but when people read it, the blog mattered more. It was looking outward—a letter, not a diary. Though she would have written even if nobody was reading, but because people were, she forged connections with them, was challenged by their feedback, pushed herself to be sharper, funnier. She'd tapped into a whole other world of friends and readers, and she could be honest there, when she couldn't be at home.

"It saved my life," she told Chris. Her fortunes had turned around off the page, but Mitzi Bytes was where everything had started. "It gave me licence not to be ashamed of the things that had happened to me, of all the ways I'd gone wrong. I could use them. And it touched people too. Nobody is ever alone. Really, that's what the blog taught me."

"You weren't alone, though," said Chris. "You could have told me."

"But when?" said Sarah. "You liked me. I wanted you to keep liking me, even before I liked you back. It was important to me."

"Your readers liked you."

"Virtual friends are very accepting. It's why they're not really real ones. And once you and I were close enough that it would make sense to tell you, it was too late. I also knew you wouldn't want to read a lot of it." He could live without the details of the life she'd lived before him. "It's not your thing.

"The blog was my place," she told him, "to write about what I thought about the world. It still is." It had changed as her life did. Once the kids were born and she'd left her job, that platform was more important than it ever had been. "My whole universe," she said, "felt as though it had shrunk to the size of a walnut, but I still had Mitzi Bytes. I could send out transmissions to the farthest reaches. I'd lost my purpose, my identity, but I still had a voice. Something that was just mine and had nothing to do with the rest of you."

Chris missed a beat.

"You know what I mean," she said, speaking again before he could. "You have a whole world to yourself, but everything that I own is yours."

"Ours."

"But it's not. That you just went and spent that money for Evan only proves it."

"It does not."

"Of course it does. I would never spend that kind of money without consulting you first."

"But what about the money you earned without consulting me first?"

"I have to consult you about earning money?"

"You know what I mean," he said.

She said, "Come on, it's not the same thing."

"Exact same principle."

"No, it isn't. And this is beside the point anyway. What I mean is that it's not enough, just belonging to you. That I am unwilling to be subsumed. So this one thing becomes something to cling to. The one thing of consequence I've ever made."

"That's not true," he said. She sighed in the dark. They said together, "The kids."

"They belong to themselves," Sarah argued. She repeated, "It's not enough."

"So it matters more, the blog?" He spat out the last ugly word.

"Of course not," she said. "You're a smart guy—surely you can understand this. You and the girls matter more than anything, but it's not enough. And I could learn to live without it, but I don't want to. I don't know why I should have to."

"Because you hurt people."

She admitted, "There is that." And then she asked, "You're still my one person, right?"

"I think you need to stop explaining," he said. "I don't know who you're trying to convince."

"You?"

He said, "I'm an easy target. You subsumed me too, you know."

"It's kept me from losing myself," she said. "Over and over again, it has."

"I get it," he said. He rolled onto his back. "They make books out of blogs?"

"They don't anymore. Except that one about what white people like."

"Did you sell more books than they did?"

She said, "Probably not."

He felt around for her hand and gripped it. "It's late," he said.

"What are we going to do about Frances?"

"You didn't put her in there, did you? On the blog?"

"Oh," said Sarah. "Just a little bit."

"Which means?"

"We're going to have some trouble."

"We?"

"Remember? Everything I own is yours."

From the Archives: Mitzi Bytes
Baby Love

The grand achievement of my yesterday is that I nearly managed to make it to noon without being puked on. Maybe I finally had this figured out, I thought, as the baby threw up over my shoulder, the mess contained by the perfectly placed burp pad on my shoulder, and my T-shirt was unscathed. Maybe I can really do this, I thought, bouncing downstairs with my ponytail swinging, holding the baby in one arm like a football and carrying a basket of laundry in the other. I'd had a shower that morning, and I was feeling awesome. And then to commemorate the occasion, I put down the basket and swung the baby up, dangling her in the air in an attempt to make her smile . . . and I should have seen it coming. I thought perhaps the peculiar expression on her face was the beginning of glee, a tooth-less gummy grin, but instead it turned out to be something more digestion related, and there came an explosion of vomit all over my face, right into my mouth, which had been wide open while I cooed inanities in her direction: "Who's a pretty little baby? Who? Who? Wha—? Bleurgh."

So that was the end of that, my clean streak. I had to rinse out my mouth, wash my face, change my shirt, and rinse my mouth again. And yes, I cried, because these days it doesn't take much, but then again, on the other hand, I'd just had somebody throw up in my mouth. You'd probably cry too.

I had toast for lunch and ate it on the kitchen floor beside the baby, who was kicking her fat legs furiously on her play mat. She takes her work there very seri-ously, reaching for the dangling toys and clumsily manipulating the overhead arch so that the star secured to it would start to play "Twinkle, Twinkle" in a tinny tone.

Another toy on the floor beside her was a plush ladybug with a mirror on its under-side, and I held it up before her so she could see herself, her favourite sight. She smiled at that, drool running down onto her chins. She made an approving noise, and I felt a little bit better, pleased with myself for having been able to pull that off.

And have you died of boredom yet? Yes, I'm well aware that I've become a documenter of abject tedium. Why bother documenting, then? To which I'd answer that if I didn't, there'd be no evidence that a day like this had even existed. I honestly feel that I've disappeared, been wiped off the face of the world entirely to exist in some bizarre no man's land overflowing with half-digested milk. And I am never alone, but I've never been so alone, which is a paradox, but the great open spaces of my days offer considerable opportunity to ponder such things.

I had a vision of what all this would be like. I would be the woman with the ponytail bounding down the stairs, the woman I was for all of seven seconds this morning before the deluge in my mouth. I'd seen the mothers, and I thought I knew what I was seeing. I'd overhear them in cafés, bleary-eyed with quiet smiles, saying things like "It really changes everything," and I thought they meant it in an existential sense, as though parenthood permits you to understand the world from a whole other plane. And in a way, it actually does, but I also know now that those mothers hadn't meant that at all. What they meant about babies changing every-thing is that after you have one, you'll never sit down to eat an actual meal again, let alone go out for one. That you can forget about consistently bathing or sleeping for more than an hour and forty-five minutes at a time (if you're lucky), and your glasses will perpetually be torn off your face by grubby fingers. Your nipples will erupt at the most inopportune times, and you'll get blisters on your areolae, and there will be times you'll want to run away from your entire life, never to return, and I never imagined that I could ever think such a thing about my home, my child, my life. After all, I made this thing. But like nothing else I've ever experienced before, having a baby has acquainted me with my limits. I never realized they were in such close reach.

This morning I took us to the library. Not because I necessarily wanted to go, because it was cold and it was raining and I had to get us bundled, strap the baby into her stroller, which she hates. But because I might have gone insane if we didn't go somewhere, even if just to the library's Baby Circle, which is a coven of fellow manic moms gathered together on a ratty carpet while our babies cry and scream. And we all come up with explanations for their baby behaviour, justifications. "He's hungry." "She's gassy." "He's grumpy because he was up all night." Nobody willing to admit that it seems to be a chronic condition, this baby thing. Nobody daring to mention the torture of meeting four o'clock in the morning, eyes wide open, over and over again. Mostly everyone is trying to be cheerful. And maybe some of us actually are.

But when I got to the library, it was closed. I'd forgotten that they'd cut their hours. It was raining, the baby sleeping sound and dry behind a plastic rain-guard, and all at once the futility of everything—the mechanisms and the manoeuvring to get to nowhere, another day just like the one that went before—was overwhelming. What a struggle it had been to arrive here, for a program I didn't even particularly want to attend, and now there wasn't even that—so what was I doing? And would the days just continue on like this forever and ever?

Of course, it's not all like this—the baby slept through an incredible coffee date on Wednesday with a friend of mine, and we celebrated with mammoth slices of chocolate cake, which I got to eat hands-free—a rare indulgence. There are the Saturday mornings with the three of us cuddled up in bed, a tiny universe unto itself with all the company I require in the world. There is every smile, every milestone, every time she does something new that suggests that things are changing, that she is evolving, and that it's all going to be so much better one day—although this is usually the point at which I start tearing up and saying things like "She's growing up so fast."

CHAPTER 14

· · · · · · · · · · · · · · ·

S arah and Chris at home and in bed, and everything is going to be all right. Mostly. If everything he told her turns out to actually be the truth, that is. A proviso.

Well, that was easy. Tidy. The End. Okay.

Except that with a blog, things just don't work like that. Chronology runs in reverse; the end of the blog (which is right now) perpetually the beginning of the story. Nothing is fixed. Now is ever present. And so here she rests, Sarah Lundy, beside her husband, who will always love her, her greatest blessing, and she contemplates the rest of the mess, the trouble into which she's written herself. Intractably. The terrible next steps. She knows exactly what's going to happen. She could practically write the tale. Because, after all, this is what she does.

On weekday mornings after drop-off, the mothers of Acorn Avenue Junior Public School tend to assemble at the Have You Bean, the coffee shop at the end of the road. They arrive pushing their deluxe strollers, sleeping baby brothers or sisters snug inside, or carting yoga mats in carrying cases constructed of organic hemp, for their classes at eleven. These are women whose part-time jobs are consulting for non-profits, pro bono law work, and/or shuttling kids to Mandarin, Hebrew, and competitive gymnastics. These are Sarah Lundy's people, her colleagues in the mother trade, and while many of them are not her friends *exactly*, and some (Claudia Kincardine) not at all, they are the world in which she lives, on weekday mornings in particular, and on this particular morning, she will be the topic under discussion. Today, joining dangerous crosswalks, that particular kindergarten teacher, GMOs, and third-world sweatshops, Sarah Lundy is the problem about which Something Must Be Done.

She sees them there in her mind, the shop's entrance cluttered with strollers, the group having taken over the big table by the window, the solid oak one that certainly once resided in some pioneer woman's kitchen and which is now marked with years of cup rings and scratches pressed too hard to earnest notebooks. Covered with saucers, espresso cups, sippy cups, and half-eaten muffins and scones. This is standing room only, Leslie and Claudia having rallied the troops.

What is Leslie doing there? She should be at work, plus she lives across town. And Claudia? But Claudia has emailed every parent on the Acorn Avenue listserv to notify them of Sarah's numerous crimes, of her duplicitousness, the threat in their midst.

Michelle is seated, out of place. She's never been on Acorn Avenue before, and the world of the mothers mid-morning is foreign to her. She's holding her phone, just for something to do with her hands. Allison and Naomi are lined up at the cash, waiting for their lattes. It's the usual morning rush at Have You Bean. Except it's all in her honour. *Honour* not exactly the word.

Here come Janie and Beth-Ellen now, not wholly invested in this meeting, Sarah supposes. She hopes, at least. Or else Janie is carrying with her a kit of explosives, and they're all rigging up something huge, the most shocking act of revenge ever to be exercised in Maplewood Village history. They'd put a plaque up after, like they did with the race riots during the 1930s in the park just farther west.

There is no way to tell. Sarah closes her eyes attempting to interpret the expressions on her best friends' faces. This is like sitting in on your own funeral, she figures. Or perhaps it's not like it at all, and this is exactly what this vision is. She looks around. Nobody is crying.

"Let's get started," Leslie says, and everybody quiets down. The crowd around the table is thick. Beth-Ellen and Janie linger in the back. The whole book club is there, and mothers from her daughters' classes. No Starry Fiske, though—where is she? No Frances either. It is telling that Frances's schedule is so busy and rigidly set that she can't even manage an appearance in Sarah's troubled fantasy.

"Call to order," announces Claudia. So it is going to be official. Leslie is making notes, or taking minutes. Sarah can't tell. She continues, "Approval of the agenda?"

"One item," says Michelle. "The matter of Mitzi Bytes." Moved, then seconded.

"Could we banish her?" asks Claudia. "Is there legal precedent for that?" She is looking at Leslie, who has the background, and one of the other mothers who is a human rights lawyer and has taken the morning off work.

"You mean socially? Or physically?" says Leslie. "Because it's really only the former that falls under our jurisdiction."

"What about slander? Or libel? I mean, what are our options

there? She's got her tit in the wringer, and we're going to make it worse." Sarah is disturbed by the words she is putting in Claudia Kincardine's pretty mouth.

"We could sue for breach of privacy," says Leslie. "That we were identifiable. I've looked into it. There is basis."

"Seems too polite," says Claudia. "Character defamation?"

"Do you think you were defamed?" Beth-Ellen calls out from the back, like a reporter at a press conference.

"We all were," somebody shouts. "All those lies."

"Really, lies?"

"Well, these weren't facts, were they?" asks Claudia. "The reality that she was dealing in."

"It's not about facts, though," says Leslie, who has somehow acquired a gavel and bangs it on the harvest table. The crowd settles down. Michelle yawns. "It's truth, which is a much less tangible thing. And it's about stories, and how she stole ours. How she profited from it."

Not so, Sarah thinks. Her ad revenue had plummeted, barely counting as profit lately. If there were an accountant here, somebody could make the case.

"It's about stories, and it's about justice," says Michelle. "But not *that* kind of justice." She stares at Leslie, and the gavel disappears with a *poof*. "I want her to be sorry."

"Oh, she's sorry," says Janie. "At least, I'm sure she is. Perhaps we're being a bit too harsh."

"She did it to you too, you know," says Leslie. "I read it. She couldn't even obscure our initials, and then there it was, your whole life laid bare. She . . . she *subjectified* us, is what she did."

"I've been objectified every other day of my life," says Janie. "This is better, hands down."

"It wasn't right," says Beth-Ellen. "But it wasn't evil either."

Sarah's heart soars. Her good name defended. Or at least declared not evil.

"She's an asshole," says Janie. "I'll give you that." The soaring heart sinks back to earth. "But is any of that really news to you? I mean—you know her. It's like confirmation of something instead of a surprise."

"So you're okay with it," says Leslie. "Being used. How she took your story because she didn't have her own."

"Not particularly," says Janie. "But I don't want to burn her at the stake either. It's complicated. I read what she wrote, though, and some of it was beautiful. It's hard to stare your own life in the face, but she was asking questions, trying to figure it out. She's not without sympathy here. She just showed her work, while the rest of us keep our process under wraps."

"I take issue with the duplicity," says Leslie. "This whole secret life behind our backs, and we're implicated in it. It's being *used*—so literally. I was her friend, I thought, but I was *material*. It's degrading."

"I think she's a sanctimonious bitch weasel," Michelle reports, her words at odds with the elegance of her posture. The cigarette holder between her fingers is a step too far, Sarah thinks. Have You Bean is non-smoking anyway, and Michelle is in danger of morphing into Cruella de Vil. So Sarah scrubs that detail out. "This is less complicated for me than it might be for you—I fell out with Sarah Lundy years ago."

"I've started a petition," says Claudia. "Ninety-seven names so far. Next step, get her banned from the PTA."

"But she never joined the PTA," somebody points out. Another mark against her.

"Demand a public apology?"

"An apology on demand sort of negates the entire point, no?"

"Well what, then?" Leslie asks the group.

"This helps a bit, doesn't it?" asks Beth-Ellen. "Getting together and talking some shit? She deserves that much."

Michelle says, "It isn't enough."

"What's going to be enough, then?" asks Janie. One of her spokespeople, Sarah thinks. She wouldn't be so alone in her corner.

Leslie says, "Some things are irrevocable."

This was a fact. The entire vision could end right here, because this was the point of the exercise. Sarah rolled onto her side and pressed her backside against her sleeping husband. Bent her spine around his shape, willing the terrifying space between them to simply disappear.

From the Archives: Mitzi Bytes
Women Are Closer Than You Think

When my second baby was born, my best friend B disappeared from my life. She stopped calling, didn't answer my calls, and I was overwhelmed by my own thing, so I didn't end up talking to her for a year and a half. I haven't written about it because up until now it seemed like part of a larger pattern; so many things have slipped through the cracks. I chalked it up to being one of the casualties of parenthood; there are friends you lose, and it's inevitable, though I regretted the loss. I wished it had been somebody who'd meant less to me, and it was surprising too—she'd seemed so on board throughout my pregnancy. But people are strange. I know that too well.

Our mutual friend got married last weekend, and I knew B was going to be at the wedding. Our friend was conscious of the rift, and we'd talked about it, although B still got along with her just fine. "I don't want things to be awkward," our friend said, "but you're both important to me." Luckily it was an informal wedding, her fiancé's second, so we didn't have to put up with any bridesmaid shen-anigans. I told our friend that it all would be okay, though of course I was incred-ibly nervous.

But everything turned out all right. B looked fantastic, and I felt so relieved when she saw me and smiled at me across the room. Her husband came over and started talking to us as though no time had passed—did he even realize that anything had happened? And then finally after the ceremony, we found each other. From the look on her face I knew she was the person I'd known for years and years, and I put my arms around her. I said, "I've missed you."

She said, "I'm sorry."

She said, "I've really been having the most terrifically terrible time."

It was a buffet, and we were free to sit where we liked, so we grabbed plates of chicken and rice and headed to the edge of the room. Everybody else was busy eating, and they left us alone while we sat down together, and I asked her, "What's been going on, then?" It was me, I'd supposed. I'd never considered any other possibility. I'd said something, or I'd done something, and she'd gone off on me altogether.

But she said it wasn't. She proceeded to tell me that in the last two years, she'd miscarried more times than she'd had her period. So many dead babies, she said, that she'd almost lost count. "And they weren't babies, of course," she said. "You know I know that. I never even once managed to make it to six weeks, but it's the idea of the thing. In my mind they were babies." And when my daughter was born, she said, she just couldn't face it.

"I kept waiting," she said, "for my own luck to change. For when I could call you up and give you my good news, and then everything would be okay, but then it started to be longer and longer, and nothing changed, and by that point I couldn't just call anymore."

She said, "I was out of my mind. I was furious and devastated, and I hated everything and everybody. And then I just stopped getting pregnant at all, which at first was almost easier, but then it wasn't." Doctors could find no medical explana-tion for any of it. She'd been to half a dozen specialists. "And my mother keeps reminding me that she never had any trouble like this. She keeps telling me it's all mind, and all I have to do is relax."

Things were better now, she said. "We've had our time to grieve, and I'm so glad to see you." She said, "I'm sorry." She was seeing a psychologist who'd put her on antidepressants, and they were helping. She told me that she hadn't actually unfriended me on Facebook, but she'd just quit altogether, because the whole thing was torture. Parades of pregnancy announcements, baby bump photos, and big kids with backpacks setting out on their first days of school. "It's like the entire platform was invented to destroy me. I'd literally spend hours on there scrolling through photos, crying. It made me miserable, but it was like a compulsion. I was looking for something, like a key, that could somehow get me where I needed to be."

So she deactivated her account. That helped too, she said. But she still snuck onto her husband's page from time to time. She said, "And I've been watching your baby and seeing her grow, and I'm so sorry I've missed it all. I feel terrible that I haven't been there. But there have been so many things, I guess you see, that have made me feel even worse."

I told her I'd had no idea. I said, "You know, it never even occurred to me. You have your work, and the way the two of you travel, and all you do—no one would believe there could be anything missing."

She said, "Well, we try to make it that way. When there's space to fill, you have to fill it with *something*. And there have been good times too these last few years. Places we've been and things that we'd seen that never would have happened if we'd had a baby. But still. I'm trying to make my peace with it, that it might never happen. And I think that's going to be an ongoing project."

My heart hurt, and I felt so stupid for never cluing in, but it was so good to have her there, to see her face in front of me. I dreamt about her all the time and anticipated chance encounters, but we'd never had one. I was terrified that we'd leave this place tonight and she'd be adrift again.

I said, "It doesn't have to be like this, you know. This space between us." And she'd told me how she'd spent these last few months feeling so apart from everything—from motherhood, and womanhood, and where she imagined herself being in her life. So I confessed to her how much I identified with that, and how Facebook photos were only a small part of the bigger picture. "In so many ways," I told her, "we're not so far apart at all." Women, they're always closer than you think.

Our friend, J, the bride, came up to us then. "If it isn't the anti-socialites." We said, "Come join us." She said, "I can't. I'm the bride."

She said, "But they're going to make me dance. There's a DJ, you know, and this whole night is about to go KC and the Sunshine Band. And I want you guys to come up and dance with me. I only like dancing when I'm dancing with you."

CHAPTER 15

. . . .

"The thing about me, though," said Sarah, "is that I never make the same mistake twice."

"That's not remotely true," said Andrea. "I've read your blog."

Sarah was quiet for a moment. "I guess it's more like an aspirational thing."

"Just because you say a thing," said Andrea, "doesn't make it so."

"I've heard otherwise," said Sarah. "From New Age people."

"Well, then."

They were on Skype, sorting out a course of action. Sarah had insisted on the video, meeting face to face. "I want to look at someone who doesn't hate me," she'd explained. She'd dropped the kids at school wearing her hat low over her face, hadn't even got out of the car. She'd seen them up the school walk from which they'd turned and waved before entering the playground, and then she'd driven away and hoped for the best. They needed her less than she liked to think they did.

She sighed and frowned at Andrea, trapped in a box on a pixelated screen. Andrea didn't really need her either but was kind enough to indulge her at a time like this. "It's what you pay me for," she'd explained to Sarah, which didn't serve to make her feel any better.

"Listen," Andrea told her now, "everything is going to work out all right. Sure, you might have rocked the PTA, but they'll get over it."

"So you don't think it's so bad?"

"The main thing is that Chris is on board."

"Or not so much on board as not bothered."

"Which serves the same purpose. I mean, you don't have to go looking for a new place to live."

"You think I might have to move?"

"A new place to live *alone*, I mean. Anyway you're the one who said traffic's been through the roof since this all started."

"It's all local."

"That doesn't matter. I say, ride the wave. See where it takes you. Don't let them knock you down."

"Everyone hates me."

"Yes, but they're obsessed with you. You can use that."

"I want to write a new book," said Sarah. "A different one, not like you said, about *Chicken Soup for the Soul*."

"So do it," said Andrea.

"With my name on it."

"Except no one knows your name. That's the problem."

But not the only problem. There were so many, and after the call had ended, Sarah remained at her desk, contemplating which one required tackling first. And before she'd come to any conclusions, it was time to get ready for her class that afternoon.

* * *

Candice wasn't there, the classroom dynamic off-kilter without her.

"So no one knows anything?" she asked the other girls. "If she had a baby? Is she sick?" They shook their heads. She persisted in asking.

"Listen, miss," said Lolo. "I don't even know the girl."

"Candice?"

"I mean, I know her. Like you know her. But not outside of here. It's not like we're friends."

"No?" Sarah looked at the others for confirmation.

Audrey was staring back at her, her expression crooked with disdain. "Well, I mean, other than that, naturally, we're all part of the same teen mom syndicate."

"Really?"

"Jesus Christ," Audrey answered. "Who do you think we are?"

Sarah had been standing before the group, and she sat down now, into the chair that Candice would have occupied had she been there.

"You'll have to forgive me," she said to the girls. She thought of her mother's advice: *You have to apologize.* This was what she owed them. If she told the whole story, would it lighten the load? She said, "I'm sorry."

"The last week," she said, "has been a shit show." And she imagined telling them everything—about Mitzi Bytes, Jane Q, her husband, the police, and the dumbwaiter. About Candice and the daffodils—"It was a poem by Wordsworth."

"No shit?"

"Think of it," Lolo would say. "A poet called Wordsworth."

Audrey would say, "Sounds more like a butler."

Tasvir: "What's your point?"

Sarah asked, "What?"

"Well, think of it," Tasvir would say. "If I were writing down this story for you, you'd be asking me that very thing. You were the one who told us that a story has to take its reader somewhere.

"Also, if I were *reading* this story, I'd suggest that the instructor was misusing the class as her personal therapy session."

Sarah sat up straighter and looked around. None of these girls really liked her. It was never quite as clear when she was standing before them, but now that she was sitting in the circle, she knew it to be true. She'd gone into this job thinking she'd be Michelle Pfeiffer in *Dangerous Minds*, or *Welcome Back, Kotter*, at least, but there were no Sweathogs here. And she was still very much herself, being stared down by a group of young women who were really unimpressed.

Was this always going to be her destiny?

Tasvir said, "Miss?"

"Okay," said Sarah. She had a plan, she did, but she'd let it get away from her. The girls weren't convinced, but she could win them back—she stood before them, pushed her hair off her face, and took a deep breath. "Sonnets," she said. "A poem, but with a framework. A-B-B-A."

They remained unconvinced.

"Okay, no," she said. "I want us to make a list instead."

"A list?"

"Words," said Sarah. "The best ones. Let's get down to the basics—it's why we're here. Tell me all the words you love in the world."

Lolo said, "Inferno."

Audrey said, "Tarantula."

Tasvir said, "Ubiquitous."

Audrey said, "Fucking."

Lolo said, "Obviously."

Audrey said, "Turbo."

"Nefarious."

"Millipede."

"Anagram."

"Amazing."

"I really love *skeeze*."

Lolo said, "Literally, we could write a book."

Sarah filled the whiteboard, and only partially with obscenities. She wrote down everything they told her, and then she gave them their assignment: to take the list of words and make a poem of them, a poem for which meaning was incidental. The point was euphony. She wrote down that word. *Euphony.* She said, "It means something that sounds good. I love that word too."

She stopped by Ashwin's office on her way out. Sunlight was peeking in the window through the broken slats of his venetian blinds, dust motes dancing in the air. He was on the phone but gestured for her to wait—just a minute, he mouthed, and then he listened to whomever he was talking to, rolling his eyes.

Sarah wondered what had brought him here, Ashwin, if it had been a passion for teaching that had led him to this dingy office, and a desk piled high with file folders, defying all bureaucratic measures toward paperlessness. She wondered if anybody ever ended up where they'd intended.

The call was done. "What's up?" Ashwin asked her.

"My plagiarist. Candice. Remember? The daffodils. She wasn't here this afternoon. I was wondering where . . . Her baby was due . . . If you know . . . ?"

Ashwin thought for a moment and then reached for a file behind him on the windowsill. "Yeah," he said. "Her social worker called yesterday. She's left the program."

"Left? Why?"

"Dunno," said Ashwin. "They didn't say. They don't have to."

"Really." Sarah came into the office and sat down in the chair before the desk. "So what do I do now?"

Ashwin looked confused. "Nothing. She's gone. You don't have to deal with it—the plagiarism, I mean. If you were going to."

"No," said Sarah. "I mean, what happens next? With Candice? How do we find out?"

Ashwin was shaking his head. "You don't. She's gone. Not your problem."

"Could we follow up? Why would the social worker let her do that? I mean, what about the baby? It's just, there's a lot of uncertainty."

"No," said Ashwin. "She's just gone. It happens."

"So suddenly?"

"It has to be. It's about the funding. We'd be billing them for a student who isn't even here. They don't want that."

"But—"

"It's got nothing to do with you," he said. "She's out of the picture. The daffodils. Don't sweat it."

•   •   •

Driving home, Sarah ended up behind the knife-sharpening truck on its long slow toll down the block. Nobody came out to meet it. The purple vehicle was so battered that the letters on the back of it were unreadable, if they'd ever been letters at all. The truck looked so much like how she'd envisioned it that she wondered if this wasn't actually the first time she'd ever seen it, this truck whose bell she'd heard tolling for years. It was all so familiar, and that was the most troubling thing about the first-person point of view—who was really to be trusted?

The truck turned left at the bottom of the road, down Sarah's street toward her house, and she elected to change her route then. She still had half an hour before she had to get the girls at school, just enough time if she didn't run into traffic. So she turned right instead and went back out onto the main road, speeding toward the east end and hitting only green lights. She arrived at Beth-Ellen's house in just seven minutes, which was a record, and parked in the driveway. Before she got out of the car, she called Chris. He even answered.

She said, "I'm going back into battle this afternoon. So if you don't hear from me again, well, you know I loved you. And you should probably get someone to come around and pick up the girls."

"This whole thing's going to blow over," he said.

"If you say so." She didn't believe him. She didn't think he believed it either. And then she walked up to Beth-Ellen's door and dared to ring the bell.

"You," Beth-Ellen answered. She was holding an economy block of cheese. Sarah couldn't see them, but she could hear the boys screeching, and evidence of their destruction was in abundance—toys scattered across the carpet, crayon scribbled on the mirror in the hall, a basket of shoes on its side, the shoes littered everywhere. Beth-Ellen herself looked composed.

"Can you talk?" Sarah asked her.

"If you don't mind disaster." She led Sarah inside to where the boys had invented a game of taking all the cushions off the couch and turning them into slides. "We'll have to sit on the floor." She put on a movie to keep them relatively quiet, and then they demanded crackers and juice, so she had to get them that, and finally she came back and sat down on the floor on the other side of the couch, away from the TV. The boys were paying them no attention, but Sarah still kept her voice low.

"Goddamn, am I in trouble," she said.

Beth-Ellen said, "Seriously. Is there anyone you didn't get in there?" She was still holding the cheese, but she had a knife now.

"Claudia Kincardine," said Sarah.

Beth-Ellen caught off a slice and offered it to her. "I don't think I know her."

"She's terrible." She accepted the cheese even though she wasn't hungry.

Beth-Ellen said, "Well, that's good to know." She was eating her own cheese.

"Do you hate me?" asked Sarah.

Beth-Ellen said, "It's not that simple."

"I really love *you*," said Sarah, "if that wasn't obvious. What I did, it wasn't an act of, well, otherwise."

"It was a violation."

Sarah said, "It just all got out of hand."

"I don't know," said Beth-Ellen.

"The boys are quiet."

Beth-Ellen peeked around the couch. She said, "They're fine. They're hypnotized." She said, "I got the link—Michelle sent it. She sent it to everybody. Janie told me it was coming. It wasn't nearly as bad as I'd been told to expect. I mean, they were talking like you were a monster. Like this was some egregious hack job, but then I went on the site, and it was a world I recognized. It was so totally you. And I felt better then. I know you, I do. I just didn't realize that half the world knew you too."

She continued. "And the first thing we all did when we got

the link was go in there and look for ourselves. And because you didn't use our names, we had to read through everything, and sometimes it wasn't clear who you meant, but sometimes it was. Sometimes it was horrible to read what you really thought, even if I already knew what you really thought. I think it was just hard for everyone to find themselves. But we wanted to too. I'm not sure I would have felt okay about the whole thing if you hadn't put me in at all."

"So you feel okay?"

"Hardly," said Beth-Ellen. "That's not what I meant. And I don't know, Sarah. You've caught me off guard here. Just showing up like this. It isn't exactly fair."

"I haven't lost a friend here, have I?" Sarah asked her.

"Oh man. You've lost more than one friend, I think. I read what you wrote about Michelle—it was kind of terrible. And then Leslie is livid. I don't blame her for that. The whole thing is really shitty."

"But you—" For these are the points that mattered.

"It all just makes it kind of hard to trust you. Even though everything you wrote was true—it doesn't matter. It's about your character. About how you treat people."

"So you're saying . . ." Sarah let her sentence trail off.

"I'm saying what I'm saying. Just listen."

"I'm sorry," said Sarah.

"That's a start," said Beth-Ellen. "Listen, I don't know. There's no precedent. It's a bit like a jet engine just fell out of the sky and landed in the middle of our friendship. I mean, there's a crater."

"But *only* a crater?" A crater was space. Therein was possibility.

Beth-Ellen paused for a moment. She said, "Not only. But I mean, there's a lot of damage."

And how do you fix a crater?

Sarah said, "You know, it's possible that you've never known me better in our entire relationship than you do right now. Speaking of trusting. Everything finally crystal clear. It's all out in the open. Do you see that?"

Beth-Ellen said, "Maybe I know you. But the thing is now, I'm not entirely sure if I *like* you." She was speaking carefully, watching Sarah's face. It was hard to breathe. "I'm going to need time, is what I mean. You get it?"

Sarah said, "Totally." She was trying not to cry. And while she could have sat there forever, waiting for her friend to say the one thing that would signal everything was going to be okay between them, there probably wasn't that much time left in the world, let alone before she had to leave to get her kids at school. She checked the time. She might not have such good luck with traffic lights on her way back. She got up and Beth-Ellen did too.

Sarah said, "You know, I want to help with the cleanup." Beth-Ellen looked confused—her messy house. "The damage. The crater. With the situation, I mean. Our friendship. However I can. And I don't know what else. What I can do, or even say, even? I mean."

Beth-Ellen said, "I love you, okay? But I can't just stand here listening to you filling in the silence. Plus, the movie's going to end."

"And this is not all about me."

"Bingo," said Beth-Ellen.

"I've got to go get the girls." She followed Beth-Ellen back to the door. She said, "I'll call you," and then, "or you can call me." Waited for Beth-Ellen now to state what she'd prefer, but Beth-Ellen said nothing. Which might have been intentional, or else circumstantial. One of the boys was calling her, demanding her attention, and she'd given Sarah more time than she deserved, anyway. More everything. There was reason to be hopeful. Sarah would insist on this fact.

* * *

For the past week, Sarah had slunk into the world feeling all eyes upon her, but she was sure she wasn't imagining it now. There would be no quick getaway—all the nearby parking spots were taken, so she had to park around the corner. On her walk toward the school, she smiled at familiar faces that turned to stone before shifting glances at the sidewalk.

Sarah was smiling the kind of smile that made her face hurt. Perhaps a neutral expression was the way to go, except that her own version of neutrality was so often interpreted as sour—not the impression she wished to convey. Adding insult to injury. It was awful to be so self-conscious.

But there was Cherry, motherfucking Mary Poppins herself, who looked ecstatic to see her. "You are in a fuckload of trouble" she was singing as she flew down the path. "But I'm sure glad to see you."

That was nice. "I'm glad someone is."

Cherry said, "No, I mean I thought you were dead. Claudia's out for fucking murder. She's even got a petition and everything. So it's good to know the assholes haven't got to you." A class of kindergarteners was flowing around them. Cherry was so loud, but Sarah didn't say a word—you don't want to alienate the only woman on the playground who didn't wish you dead. Cherry laughed. "Haven't got to you *yet*, I mean. Ha ha. Just joking."

Sarah turned her mouth up in a smile. A couple of mothers she recognized from Clementine's class walked past looking at her, and then they quickly looked away, whispering. Cherry saw her watching them. "One thing," she said in a very loud whisper, "is that they don't seem to be packing the heat."

Sarah looked confused.

"I mean, like, don't fucking worry," said Cherry, who then grabbed her hand and led her up the path toward the playground. "I'm just playing around. It's not a big deal. Claudia, she hates me, but she hasn't killed me yet. You'll be all right too."

Sarah was concerned that not being murdered constituted "all right."

"You look good today. Your hair looks different."

"I brushed it," said Sarah.

Cherry said, "Well, you're killing it." So much killing. Sarah wanted her to stop speaking now.

The kids weren't out yet. Even with the walk from around the corner, she'd arrived with extra time, mostly because she couldn't bear the thought of being late on top of everything, her poor girls waiting around after everybody else was gone. Having to contend with the judgment: "Can't even pick up her kids on time." "Probably pressing matters. Had to update her *blog*." All those whispering mommies, and how whispers do carry.

So she stood beside Cherry, who was back on her phone, hammering out something terribly important with her dexterous thumbs, and Sarah tried to imagine that none of it mattered. That she was cool with having had her good name ravaged on the school listserv. The name had never been all that good to begin with, and she'd done nothing she was ashamed of. Except. Except. Except.

She hated the way her certainty turned circles on itself.

And then the school bell rang, and children exploded from all the exits, such a swarm that Sarah didn't feel visible anymore, except to her daughters, who both spotted her at once and made their separate ways toward her, arriving together.

"Can we stay and play for a while?" asked Clementine.

"No," said Sarah, who had each one by the hand and was heading for the gate already, but not fast enough. A tap on the shoulder, and she spun around, the girls spinning with her. It was Naomi Lloyd, peering up at Sarah through her glasses.

"I can't believe you," Naomi said. "I've been rereading the blog since I heard, and it still doesn't make sense. Did you know I've been reading it since the very beginning? With the fish shop, and everything, and I was right with you then. I so identified with all of it, and I bought your books, or at least the first two, and all this time we were in the very same book club? I'm still stunned. Really stunned. Here's Mitzi Bytes, and it turns out I know you?"

Sarah shrugged, slight smile. She wasn't sure if this was a compliment. She anticipated Naomi spitting right in her face.

Naomi said, "I just don't know what to think."

Sarah said, "Me neither." They began walking down to the street together, Clementine and Gladys slightly farther down the path.

"So *you're* still talking to me," Sarah said.

Naomi said, "Obviously. And I want you to sign my books now. Even though I feel a bit stupid. Nobody likes being made a fool of. I've just got a thick skin. And I don't think you ever wrote about me. Nothing terrible, anyway."

"Nothing terrible," said Sarah, who was quite sure Mitzi Bytes had never written about Naomi at all, because she was mostly unremarkable, save for her stature, and Mitzi Bytes had one virtue, and it was that she didn't mock people for their physical attributes. Most of the time.

"Anyway, it's all such a shock," said Naomi.

"For me too," said Sarah.

"It's a bit like a witch hunt," said Naomi.

"Well, not much of one," said Sarah. "I'm right here."

"Because you're not a witch," said Naomi.

"That too."

"Although if someone proposed trying to drown you in a river, I don't think Michelle or Leslie would object."

"Or maybe I'd float?"

"You *are* funny," said Naomi. She was looking around for her own kids, who were hiding under the pine trees. "That should have been my first clue. Would you sign my books? Would you?" Someone hurled pine needles into someone's eyes, and a child started to cry. Naomi ignored it and called to someone over Sarah's shoulder. "Christine." She came over. The other woman looked familiar—she had a son in Gladys's class, Sarah thought. "You know who this is?" The woman shook her head. Naomi lowered her voice. "It's Mitzi Bytes. The blog. Like I told you?"

The woman still looked confused. Naomi looked back at Sarah and tried to explain. "I did tell her."

"I don't know," the woman said. "I don't really read blogs." She looked uncomfortable, but there was another mother by her side who'd just happened to overhear. "Mitzi Bytes? Seriously? I used to read your blog all the time." She and shook her head. "Crazy," she said.

"See?" said Naomi, enjoying her moment of glory, being a spreader of news. But now the child under the tree was hysterical, perhaps blinded. Naomi gave Sarah a quick hug and ran off to rescue. "It's all going to be okay," she was calling to Sarah and not to the kid. "Let them hunt for witches; whatevs."

260 • Kerry Clare

Her heart lightened, Sarah turned around to find Gladys licking the fence post. She switched back into gear. "Guys," she called. "That's disgusting. It's like barbed wire. You could sever your tongue. Seriously, Gladys stop it. Clementine, you know better than that."

Gladys said, "But I wanted to taste silver." Clementine was refusing to carry her backpack to the car. Sarah didn't want to be any more of a spectacle than she already was, so she picked up the backpack, grabbed the girls' hands and dragged her daughters along. They were both whining, but Sarah didn't really mind. Perhaps she would soon turn a corner after all, and she almost felt good.

Until she'd turned the actual corner and spotted her car where'd she left it, obscene scratches from something, presumably keys, etched down the length of the passenger side.

•   •   •

It might have just been a coincidence," Sarah said to Chris for the fifth time that night, once the girls were in bed and they were sprawled on the couch in an unergonomic fashion. "A random act of vandalism. Let's not connect dots too hastily."

"Maybe we can buff it?" he suggested.

"Sadly, not a buff job. It was a random act by a decidedly determined vandal." She told him, "I hate the way my certainty turns circles on itself." The phrase had been turning circles in her head, over and over.

He said, "There's a price to certainty. I think it is delusion. There's a wholeness to a circle, no?"

He said, "Anyway, what happened to the daffodils girl?"

Sarah sat up tall. She'd completely forgotten to tell him about the class, and Ashwin, and everything that had happened that afternoon. "I don't know," she said. "She quit—she did. She left the program. And we don't know why. She's just gone."

"She had her baby?"

"No idea," said Sarah. "She was due. But that didn't necessarily mean she'd have to quit. She hasn't finished the program yet. She could have taken a break—I don't know. I don't know anything. That's what's so annoying."

"The uncertainty."

"What happens next? What's happening at all?"

"And while you were pondering those existential questions, you were keyed by a vandal."

"I feel like I've lost control of the plot," said Sarah.

"Were you ever in control of the plot?" asked Chris.

"But you get it, don't you?" she asked him. "Of course you do—think of work. Of building an app, and chasing the bugs out of the software, and there's always another one, because the technology is fallible, and so are the people using it. Something is always out of place, going wrong."

"It's usually the people using it," said Chris.

"Isn't it always the people?" asked Sarah. "They ruin everything."

From the Archives: Mitzi Bytes
People Ruin Everything

It's fortunate that I'd never have enough charm to be elected into public office, because if I ever were elected, I'd be prone toward the most awful totalitarianism. It's just easier that way, and I actually have sympathy for the Bolsheviks and their determination to have the whole world conform to a system. Can't you imagine it? Such heavy boots, but clutching their battered copies of Karl Marx:

262 • Kerry Clare

"We have the solutions, and they're written in a book." What could possibly go wrong?

The problem with the systems is never the systems but the people. People are the worst. Whereas books are easy, contained, straightforward, or else they would be if they didn't continually get into the hands of people. People, like my neighbour across the road who believes that the Bible is literally true and that Harry Potter is a work of the devil—why is this woman allowed out of the house? If I had ruled the world, she'd be sent to a Borstal for stupid people and not permitted to have opinions until she'd been sufficiently reformed.

Anyway, at our school, we're currently having a problem with allergies. Peanuts have been forbidden for centuries—we're cool with that—but now a parent with a child with an egg and dairy allergy is calling for a school-wide ban on these items too. Naturally, some parents are a bit put out by this, and the parents of this child have not been placated by the school solution of having her eat her lunch in a supply cupboard with a table and chair and a light bulb hanging on a string.

A group of idiots have responded to the controversy by staging a Nut-In in the school foyer. Several families showed up with jars of Skippy peanut butter and loaves of bread, pulled their kids out of class, and proceeded to distribute slapped-together sandwiches, which they ate in a circle while singing "Kumbaya" and "We Shall Overcome." When the principal came out of a meeting to ask them to cease, they all stood up, sandwiches in hand, and started in with "We Shall Not Be Moved."

It was mortifying. I heard about the whole thing because newspaper reporters showed up to cover the protest, which was the last thing we needed. Our school is already semi-famous for having banned balls from the playground for safety reasons, and for the PTA's stand against hummus without fair-trade designation ("Because would YOU want to be a chickpea?"), so this was the sugar-free frosting on the whole-grain vegan cake.

"Nut-In Indeed." The headline for the right-wing rag actually said that. I almost bought it.

Anyway, it's only going to get worse. The parents of the allergic kid called the police, who finally disbanded the protest (though they were leaving anyway—lunch was over, and they all had to return to work), and then pulled the kid out of school and enrolled her in a Waldorf program, and now they're suing the school board for lack of reasonable accommodation, as well for child endangerment.

The organizers of the Nut-In sent out a school-wide email celebrating their supposed triumph. "It's a good day for personal freedom," the message told us, and then it went on to let us know that they were running a slate of candidates for the PTA on an All-Nuts platform, and I don't think they were even being funny.

What a fine message to be passing on to our children—that putting the life of a five-year-old at risk is just fine, that it's every man for himself out there, that we must not give up our right to bear peanut butter granola bars and send them in our kids' lunches.

I complained about this to someone, someone even who I thought was sane, who shrugged and said, "Well, I can see where they're coming from. What are we supposed to pack in their lunches, for god's sake?"

Sometimes I really do fear there is no hope for any of us. I despair at the idiots mightily, for they're all around us. And yet.

It's true that there are no easy solutions. You could probably say that about everything. And while it frustrates the hell out of me to see the nuts staging Nut-Ins versus the hysterical mother demanding the whole world become her fragile child's plastic bubble—couldn't somebody just be reasonable, please; be willing to give a bit—and while the tension forever wrought between the extremes makes my hair hurt . . . it's ultimately useful. Really, the idiots are useful—just not for the reasons they think they are. It's that eternal push and pull that stands to keep our minds in check, to forever be questioning, to never be too entirely sure.

It's a virtue, I think, having an open mind. It's not waffling or flip-flopping, but instead it's the gift of perspective, which is a far more complicated gift than obliviousness is. It means you never will be eating peanut butter in an elementary school foyer while a small child sobs in the office clutching her

EpiPen. It significantly lowers one's risk of being a total asshole. And when you have a personality like mine, you take these risk-lowering factors where you can find them.

It means I'm probably lying when I say I'd be a dictator, and that I'd just be a terrible politician for a whole host of different reasons, but I kind of think that being a terrible politician is a virtue too. It also likely makes one a good blogger, so here I am finally winning at something.

CHAPTER 16

. . . .

On Friday morning, she asked Chris to stay home from work. "Can't you please?" Sarah had asked him. "Taking the kids to school is making me crazy. All those people looking at me. And it's always better when it's you who takes the car in anyway. When I do, they talk to me like I'm stupid, and I don't want to deal with that today." She would even have cried appendicitis, except she no longer had an appendix. But Chris said no. That he'd been distracted all week, and missed enough time on Wednesday. The week was nearly done, and he couldn't cut out now. What would it look like? Things between them were completely back to normal, it seemed.

"It would look like you were taking care of your family," she said. "I need you." She was sitting up in bed, and Gladys hadn't even come in yet. She was talking in full sentences, and she hadn't had a shower, had her tea. Indeed, these were desperate times. "I was a victim of violence."

"Violence against a car door."

"Still."

Once he was dressed, he went outside to assess the damage, and he returned much less blasé about the whole thing. "That's no scratch. It's a gouge. Why didn't you tell me?"

"I did," she said. "But you just did the thing you always do, which is to make everything that's important to me seem silly and small. Rendered in miniature. You think I live in a dollhouse."

"So you're mad at me now too? I thought we were all right."

"I'm just really rattled," she told him. "And I need you and now you're leaving."

"I'm going to work."

"No, you're escaping. You could stay home if you wanted to. A sick day. A float day. People do that, you know."

"I *don't* know."

"You saw that gouge—it was brutal. Don't send me back out there." She was being hysterical, but anything less wouldn't capture his attention.

The girls were fighting in the bathroom. One of them was going to have to go in there and break it up.

"All right," Chris conceded with a heavy sigh. "I'll stay home." He wasn't happy about it. "And I'll take the car in. That bodywork's going to cost a fortune." He headed down to the hall, on his way to deal with the kids.

"Well, maybe you could ask Evan to lend you some cash?" she called after his retreating back. "I'm joking," she offered wanly when he didn't turn to give her an answer, but she wasn't, and she knew he knew it too.

. . .

While Chris drove the girls to school, Sarah finally called Janie. She hadn't called Janie in years, text messages and emails sufficing for their communication, but she needed to hear her voice, to express nuance with tone and inflection. She was calling her friend to clarify things.

"So, what's this about me being a terrorist?" Janie asked her. "That 'J' person, forever toting around a stick of dynamite. It's absurd."

"She's a character."

"A cartoon character," said Janie. "If I really were a mad bomber, you'd have never had the nerve to write me that way. If I really were that character, I would have blown up your house already."

"So you've thought about it," Sarah said. "I was not so far off the mark."

"Not at all," said Janie. "Anyway, I'm a conscientious objector. This whole thing has become totally insane. How did you ever pull it off? And you never said anything at all."

"My mother knew. I didn't know she knew, but she always did."

"Of course she did. But I had no idea. None. I'd even seen the books."

"But you hadn't read them."

"Well, no."

"Oh, it's all such a mess, Janie," said Sarah. The house was cold. She curled her feet beneath her body to warm her toes. "It was an innocent thing, just a bit of fun, and then it got bigger and bigger, and I didn't stop it while I could. I don't know if I could have stopped if I tried. The blog became a compulsion. A lifeline."

"You could have said something."

"But how?" asked Sarah. "'Oh, and by the way, there's this whole business I've been carrying on behind your back'? In the beginning, it was all kind of shameful—the sort of stories I couldn't even confess to you."

"I had no idea you had any stories you couldn't confess to me."

"Well, I didn't really," said Sarah. "There was exaggeration, some spin. I guess you would have recognized the stories, but it was embarrassing, whiling away my lonely Saturday nights on a blog, on the Internet. Nobody did that then. There wasn't even Facebook."

"It's just bizarre," said Janie. "I feel like that guy from the crappy '90s movie who's just realized he's spent his whole life on reality TV."

"Which one?"

"Which what?"

"Which movie. There were two. *The Truman Show* and the Matthew McConaughey one that was critically panned."

"Are you drunk?" said Janie.

Sarah said, "You don't want to know. But no."

"It's shitty," said Janie. "Like you were making furtive notes, and reporting on everything behind our backs. Even the nice things, the good moments—those were private. They were meant to be. I never thought I'd have to be explicit about that."

"I know that," said Sarah.

"But do you?" said Janie.

Sarah said, "Actually, yeah. I've had several conversations like this in the last few days, if you can believe it." This was testing her patience. Lately, it had been as though she were trapped in the very same day. And now the seasons were running backwards—flakes of snow were beginning to fall outside the window. Everything was wrong.

Sarah heard her mother's words again. She told Janie, "Listen,

I know it was wrong. And I'm sorry. I know I fucked up—but I can't stand to think I've ruined everything. Everything with me and you."

"Well, it helps," said Janie, "that you wrote me as Wile E. Coyote. Do people really believe that stuff?"

"It's a kind of truth," said Sarah. "Don't you think so? Stories always have their own particular slant. It's how they become stories, after all."

"But you don't need it all to be a story, right? That's my point. Sometimes a thing is just a thing. It doesn't need a spin, or a slant. Or a bomber."

"I just need to know you're still on my side. I'm in big trouble, Janie, and need all the friends that I can get."

"I am your friend," said Janie. "Especially considering the alternative."

"Not being my friend?" This was kind of lovely.

"Well, allying myself with those crazy women from your kids' school. With their petition, and somebody's trying to get a court injunction to have the whole site taken down. I've wound up on someone's email list, and I don't even know how. I've emailed twice to ask to be removed, but nobody's answered. And they only ever reply to all. If I'm ever been tempted to use my chemistry know-how to nefarious ends, it would be inspired by this."

"We could both run away and go underground?"

"Those women are fascists. They make you look nice."

"Thanks?"

"Listen, just don't press it, okay?" said Janie. "It's a lot to take in. But yes, I still love you. Mostly because you didn't call me a home wrecker on the Internet."

"I regret that post," said Sarah.

"No you don't."

"Not really."

"They're fuming, those women," said Janie. "And they've got a lot of time on their hands."

"You're saying this isn't going to just blow over?"

"It's unlikely," Janie said. "Chris is okay?"

"Oh, he's got problems of his own." He was back from school. She heard his heavy steps across the porch.

"Listen, I'm really lucky to have you," said Sarah.

Janie said, "Uh-huh. Listen, I've got to run."

• • •

She'd made tea, and they drank it in silence on either side of the breakfast bar. He'd been looking at her car again.

"It's brutal," he said. "And you've got no idea who could have done it?"

Sarah thought, man, I could draw you an elaborate flow chart. But she said nothing and just shook her head.

"And the kids got off okay?"

"Yes." He was irritated. "It's not brain surgery. I can drop off my children at school. I'm not an idiot, you know."

"I didn't say you were an idiot." She supposed he was suggesting that *she* was, for these inconsequential matters on which she spent her days. "It's just tricky sometimes. The parking. Or one of them starts kicking off."

"It was fine."

Sarah said, "You're angry at me."

He had to think about his answer, which was awful for her. He said, "No." Tentatively. He said, "About the money. I was thinking about it. Are you going to keep holding that over my head?"

It would be easy to deny it, but that wasn't her style. She had to think about her answer too. "It's a hard thing, you know," she said. "Everything I ever suspected laid bare."

"You knew about the money?"

"No. It's just a symptom of a wider thing. Like, I mean, what kind of a partnership is this anyway? I told you, I'd never spend our money like that without talking to you about it first."

"No."

"Which makes me think that it's not 'our' money anyway. It's yours."

He didn't say anything.

She continued, "Which makes me afraid that there's not even an 'us.'"

She waited, but he gave her nothing at all.

"Really?" she said. "You're not even going to answer that?" But denying wasn't his style either.

"Not everything is about money," he said. She started to interrupt him, to say "Don't you think I know that—" but he didn't let her. He said, "But if we're going to make everything about money, we could talk about yours. Your secret stash. Was that 'ours,' then, or do you hold yourself to a different standard?"

"It's different for a woman," she said.

"You've been listening to your mother," he said.

"Maybe I should have been," she said. "She knows a thing or two. Anyway, it's not the same thing."

"It's exactly the same thing."

She said, "It's not. Because I need you. And you don't need me one bit."

"Ah, come on."

"In practical terms, though, it's true," she said. "Admit it."

They were facing off now. The mugs between them had been drained.

272 • Kerry Clare

"Admit it." She was driving him to it. And what he needed to do was resist, to fight her. Not to give in with the acquiescence that had characterized his relationship to her since their first conversation. That had always made things so easy between them. "Admit it."

They were at a standstill.

And then he shrugged. She saw his shoulders move and felt the blood leave her face, rendering her numb and breathless. But it was not too late for him to take it back, to have the gesture mean something else. So she waited. But he didn't. He exhaled and offered it to her, the gift she'd never wanted, the knowledge that she'd been right all this time.

He said to her, "I guess."

•   •   •

She left. There was no other course of action. She was going through the motions, but the alternative would have been to collapse to the floor, a puddle of despair, but she'd given him far too much already, and this was the one way to leave her dignity intact. To rise without a word and grab her keys, her bag, and walk out of the kitchen, out of their house. She got into the car and backed down the driveway, not even looking properly for traffic as she sailed out into the street through the row of parked cars, but thankfully, the street was empty.

Where was she going? Theirs was a one-way street, so it was not as though she had a choice in the matter. She just went, and as she stopped at the corner, she realized she was still wearing her slippers. Which might have proved a deterrent on a less desperate day, but she kept going. The slippers were blue, woollen, and ugly, knit by Beth-Ellen during the four months she spent on bedrest when she was pregnant with her boys. She'd ended up giving a pair to everybody she knew, donating others to local women's shelters. Sarah had hardly ever worn hers—the yarn was acrylic and scratchy—but this morning the floors in her house had felt particularly cold. A lucky coincidence, perhaps, because were it not for the slippers, she might be driving barefoot.

Sarah changed lanes and almost mowed down a cyclist. They came to an intersection, and the woman had gotten off the bike and was banging on the hood of Sarah's car. Slamming it with her fist, shouting, "Are you completely fucking insane?" Sarah just stared at her, impassive. What was going to happen next?

The light turned green, and she realized she was shaking. The woman on the bike had relented, put off by Sarah's lack of response. The grocery store was right there, sprawling low and surrounded by an expanse of parking. At this time of day, it was never busy, so she pulled in. She'd get out of the car before somebody got really hurt.

This meant, though, that she was wandering the grocery aisles in Beth-Ellen's ugly slippers, only realizing this once she was inside, pushing a cart to keep her steady. A glimpse of other customers suggested that she was not the most eccentrically dressed among them, however; a man without a shirt, stinking of urine and coated in white plaster dust cruised on by her, his cart heaped with cartons of organic orange juice.

She felt numb. This was what it was, she decided, how she couldn't feel her cheeks, and how her heart would hurt if there were actually a heart in the empty space inside of her. Hollow. She was the shell of a somebody, and she'd been the very last to know. How had everybody else been so adept at seeing the nothingness inside?

In the frozen meats, however, she felt some relief. The chill from the freezers was something—she shivered. She felt the air on her face and was assured that she actually had a face. Closing her eyes, she breathed deeply and tried to calm her racing heartbeat. When she felt someone tap her on the shoulder. Opening her eyes to her worst nightmare, Claudia Kincardine, her little boy sitting in the front of her shopping cart, a seat he was too big for, his tiny nose running thick with yellow snot.

It was a showdown, like something out of the Old West, with shopping carts instead of wagons, and her in her slippers. Oh god, she was wearing her slippers.

But Claudia Kincardine did not even notice. She was too intent upon Sarah's face. "You look awful," she said. Her tone was approving.

Sarah said, "Thanks."

"We're nearly at two hundred signatures, you know." Her voice was low and confidential.

Sarah echoed her tone. "That's not really a lot."

"There's talk of filing a court injunction. We're taking you down."

But Sarah's attention had been caught on a place past Claudia, somewhere on the horizon. From where a squat man in a John Deere cap was coming down the aisle wearing a plaid flannel shirt, his jeans unbuttoned, the zipper wide open. She blinked, and still he was there.

". . . the law on our side. Your lack of regard has been appalling. And we've assembled a task force . . ."

The man stopped in front of the bacon and started fumbling with himself. And Sarah knew what was coming. It was almost as though she'd been expecting him, this funny little man in his distinctive cap. There wasn't much occasion for John Deere in the city. Sarah wondered if he drove in from somewhere, if he had a combine harvester back home. If this was some kind of political protest, maybe. *Farmers Feed Cities.* Getting his bits out in the frozen meats.

"Are you listening to me?"

Because there he was, his penis in his hand. A piddly member, one that seemed to suit his character. Certainly nothing worth displaying in public, she thought. He was holding it nonchalantly, looking up now for the first time since she'd seen him. Regarding her with a small, satisfied smile when he saw her watching him. *There you are*, his expression was saying. *I've been waiting for you too.* Waiting for her reaction, but she wasn't going to give him that. What would Mrs. Ramsay do?

". . . has been egregious. And your attitude since has only made things worse. I've never met anyone more uncooperative, anti-social. Do you have a community-oriented bone in your body?"

But Sarah couldn't answer. She was too stuck on the community-oriented bone that was coming closer, ever so slowly. The spell only broken by Claudia's little boy, who'd just sneezed, the yellow snot all over his face now, and Claudia was hovering over him, mopping up the mess with a tissue, her tirade unceasing. ". . . the benefit of having the law on our side. Plans are in place. It's all going to come to a head. Do you even realize what you're up against?" Stopping finally to await a response.

"Are you hearing a single thing I say?"

The man was so close now that Sarah could see the purple veins, the rest of it dappled with pink. It was bigger, more impressive, and now she could sort of see why he carried it around. A sad little thing hidden away inside his jeans, but out here in the open, it was flagrant and important. He was like a peacock. A bird toward whom, however, a person wouldn't want to get too close.

Sarah shook her head.

But Claudia couldn't see it. She had no idea of the scene that was unfolding behind her. As her son whined, she wiped his nose again, and Sarah Lundy continued to refuse to capitulate.

Sarah said, "No." He was right there. Staring at her, stroking his *thing*. Getting off on her defiance, her refusal to look away. But then something changed and his eerie peace was disturbed. He'd been distracted by the sight of Claudia Kincardine, Sarah realized, as Sarah was now too: Claudia brandishing a pork shoulder.

The man in the cap couldn't see Claudia's face, its angry contortions. "There's a special place in hell for women who don't support other women," Claudia was saying, waving the frozen shoulder for emphasis. And was the pork to be her family's dinner, simple as that? Or was it a weapon instead, about to be brought down with a wallop upon Sarah's head? Even the kid in the cart looked troubled by the prospect, and the exhibitionist put off his performance.

For the first time, Sarah flinched, raising her arm to stop a potential blow. Closing her eyes, which meant that she missed the entrance of Starry Fiske, who'd come breezing up the aisle with a basket in her hand, a single pomegranate rolling about inside.

"One could possibly misconstrue all this," she said, and Sarah opened her eyes. Saw Starry there, sizing up the situation. She'd placed her gentle hand on Claudia's arm, and Claudia lowered it, dropping the pork into her shopping cart with a thud.

Sarah looked around—the man in the John Deere cap was gone. But how could he have gotten away so fast? These aisles stretched for miles. It was as though he'd been an apparition, somebody who appeared out of the walls. Or freezers. Looking around—he was nowhere. "A person might think," Starry continued, "that you, Claudia, hon, were threatening our friend Sarah here with a pork product." She waited a beat. "Now, wouldn't that be funny."

"Our friend?" repeated Claudia, pale and shaking now. Her son, his nose now wiped, had stopped fussing and was watching the whole thing with interest.

"Oh, yes indeed," said Starry, deftly taking Claudia's arm, the one that had been brandishing the meat, and holding it in a careful grip. "Haven't you heard? Because, certainly Sarah, word is spreading. We sure are grateful. Right?"

"Yeah?" said Sarah, finding her breath. Wiggling her toes inside her hideous slippers. Blood was returning to her extremities with a rush, and the effect was jarring.

"Because," Starry continued, reaching out for Sarah's arm and joining her hand with Claudia's. "Because Sarah has agreed to be the Celebrity Ambassador for the year-end gala. Isn't that incredible? A big job, but I am confident she can do it. And we're honoured to have her, an author. Did you know, Claudia, that she was one of *Time* magazine's top bloggers of the decade?"

Claudia dropped Sarah's hand, stunned. She stuttered, "No."

"Anyway," said Starry, clutching her basket to her chest, "I am confident that with this gesture, we can smooth over any trouble between us, no? Such an excellent way of giving back?" She gave Sarah a satisfied look, and Sarah tried to convey something back that was gratitude. Sort of. "We're all looking forward to it," Starry went on. "The entire PTA." Then she actually winked.

Starry had her. There was no escape. It was amazing. Sarah shook her head, and Starry put her hand on her arm. "I'll be in touch," she said. She looked at Claudia. "So, how does that sound?" she asked her.

"Good?" said Claudia, still disoriented.

Starry let Sarah go. "Now you get going," she said. "Run along home and put some shoes on." Patting her on the shoulder, and as they watched her go, Sarah knew. She could feel their eyes boring into her back, taking in the full effect of her dishevelment, and Beth-Ellen's slippers. Some ambassador, Sarah thought, cringing, but also overwhelmed by the extent of Starry Fiske's pure genius. She hadn't had a clue. All the rest of them were merely players in Starry's steady hand.

• • •

Back in her car, she felt calmer. Reality had been reset, or at least some vital aspects of it. But not everything.

A text message from Chris: *Where r u?*

And right now the phone rang in her hand. "I need you," he said. And she could tell that this was not simply a rhetorical statement. There was an urgency in his voice that she'd never heard before.

"What is it?"

"It's Frances." But of course, Frances. With Chris, it usually came down to Frances, and there was going to be trouble. They just didn't know on which front. "I called her last night and this morning, and she hasn't got back to me. And I haven't heard from Evan." Evan, who Sarah had last glimpsed from the dumbwaiter, a memory that made her shoulders ache and her back hurt, though she realized now she'd been aching all along. "I called her office this morning, but they said she'd gone home sick. There was a crash, something smashing. I heard her yelling. I want to go over there, but I need you to come."

She said, "How does she do it?"

"Who? What?"

"Frances. How does she manage to get you all twisted in a knot? You never worry about me this way. Even after I've offended the entire PTA and been victim of an actual vandal. You're unruffled about that. But your sister doesn't call you for a couple of hours, and you're all about to call in the army."

"No one mentioned the army."

"You know what I mean."

"You're saying all this is a cry for attention? What you're going through?"

"No. But would you blame me if it were?"

Chris said, "But it's not the same at all. You—you're going to be okay. It's what you do: get yourself out of trouble. What else would you have to talk about when we got together with friends? So, I mean, I'm concerned, and the car is bad news, but Frances's trouble goes so much deeper than that. It's more than a gouge.

"It's all gone wrong for her," he said. "If it ever was right. And she's reached a point where I don't think she can pretend anymore." Out in the street, a car sounded its horn. "You aren't driving, are you?" he asked her.

"Not yet," she said.

"You've got to come," he said. "She won't answer her phone. I'm afraid that she's snapped, or maybe it's him."

•   •   •

She was home in five minutes, pulling into the driveway. He came outside to meet her, opening the car door before she'd had a chance to. "I need you," he said. But this wasn't just about

Frances and the moment at hand. "You cornered me before," he said. "Didn't give me a chance."

"A chance?"

"To answer your question right."

She undid her seatbelt, got out of the car.

"You're wearing slippers."

"I left in a hurry."

"I'm sorry," he said. And then he pulled her into the fiercest hug she'd ever been party to, his arms wrapped around her with superhero force. He whispered in her ear, "I need you." He sniffed. Was he crying? "You're everything. This whole life— you're the centre. You made it for me, the kind of life I never could have imagined for myself. And without you, none of it means anything. Like that song: If not for you. About not being able to find the door, or see the floor. I wouldn't have a clue. And I don't, really. Evidently."

She was crying too. "I love you," she said.

He let go. He looked down at her. "Never, ever go away. You just can't do that. Okay?" She nodded. "I need you to come with me," he said. "Now."

So Sarah and Chris went over together. She put on her boots. Even with all the recent traffic, the path between their property and Frances's was poorly trodden and hard to navigate—Frances was such a tough nut. Still, Sarah cared about her sister-in-law, if only for her husband's sake. Plus she was curious about what was going on.

The backyards were quiet. The snow was still falling, a few small flakes, but each one melted as soon as it touched down. Sarah had followed Chris through the backyard, past Eeyore's house, the two of them scrambling through the trees and the gap in the fence. They paused for a moment at the foot of the stairs, but could hear nothing going on over the garage.

"Do you think she knows?" Sarah asked. "About the charges?" The backup singer's husband's. And about Mitzi Bytes too, but she didn't want to mention it. She envisioned the scratch on the car.

"She's going to be pissed," said Chris. About the charges. About the blog. But then again, Frances was always furious about something. It was odd that they were each of them so fearful of her wrath, because they were both accustomed to it. Not necessarily to being its object, though, which was something different.

"It doesn't look like anyone's home," said Sarah, looking up at the empty windows. Chris was already making his way around to the side door—he had the key on his ring. He knocked first, and Sarah was beside him by the time Evan answered. He blocked their way inside.

"I told you to stay out of here," he said.

"Where's Frances?" Sarah asked.

Evan said, "Now's really not a good time."

Chris said, "Is she sick?"

"Later," said Evan. "Okay? It's for your own good, buddy. Trust me."

"Come on," said Chris, who was bigger than Evan, albeit less prone to playing up his physical prowess. "Frances?" he called out into the house.

Evan lowered his voice. "Now fuck right off," he said. "I told you. She's kind of lost it. You don't want to see her right now."

"Did she find out about the charges?" said Sarah. "Is that it?"

And there she was. Standing in the doorway beside her husband, they were the least likely match. Or perhaps the least likely mismatch, and now it had all come to a head. Her hair was pulled back in a headband, and she wore a black dress with pearl earrings, a pearl necklace. Everything as usual, except she had a towel wrapped around her wrist, soaked in blood.

She said, "What charges?" Evan shut his eyes and shook his head, inhaling deeply. Frances realized they were staring at her wounded wrist and said, "Don't worry. I didn't sever *those* arteries."

"What are you doing, Frances?" Chris asked her. "Are you all right?"

"He called your office," said Sarah, indicating Chris. "They said you were sick."

"She's not sick," said Evan, whose head was still shaking, but his eyes were open now.

Frances's mask slipped a bit when she turned her head to address him. "Don't tell me what I am," she said. "Or what I'm not." She looked out at her brother and sister-in-law. "He doesn't know a single thing."

"You okay, Frances?" asked Chris.

"I warned you," said Evan, his voice nearly as high as his eyes—he appeared to be talking to the ceiling.

"Do you want to come in?" she asked, and pushed Evan out of the way, gesturing for Chris and Sarah to come inside, and they came after her. They all went up to the kitchen. Then she turned around, faced them, and said, "Now. What charges?"

"There are no charges," said Evan.

"You," she said to Evan, "are not allowed to speak to me. I told you to go." She looked to Chris and Sarah. "He won't go."

"Go where?" said Chris.

"Like I care," said Frances. "What are the charges?

"He said there aren't any," said Chris.

Frances said, "That's not the point."

"Frances, what did you do to your wrist?" Sarah asked her. Gentle prodding. They would have to be careful.

She said, "I punched a window."

"A window?"

"Well, it was either that or his face." She gestured generally to the direction of Evan, who was lingering on the edge of things. "I wasn't thinking." She put her fist in the air, a gesture of power. "Rest, elevate, direct pressure."

Sarah sat down in the desk chair. This was the household management centre, a whiteboard just above detailing Charlotte's various appointments and activities and Frances's carpooling commitments. "Where is she?" said Sarah. "Charlotte."

"I took her to school," said Frances. Then she seemed to realize that her brother was out of place. "What are you doing home?" Chris started to explain, but she interrupted him. "Are you in on it too?"

"On what?"

"Whatever this is," said Frances. Is this an intervention?"

"But for what?" said Sarah.

"For god's sake, I don't know," she said. "Do I have to think of everything?" And then she started to cry—her stone face shattered. Sarah had long wondered about the process, tear ducts and sobs, and if Frances was physiologically like other people, and she seemed to be. It felt as though she were seeing something she shouldn't see—if she'd been hiding in the dumbwaiter now, she would have pulled the doors all the way shut, never mind the pain in her shoulder. Frances and Chris moved toward one another, and he put his arms around her. She fell into him like water, and he held her and didn't move again. Sarah's chair was on wheels, and she resisted the urge to roll right out of the room. It was so awkward. If she'd been standing still, she could have slunk out inconspicuously and hid around the corner, but now she was sitting and she was stuck.

Evan was gone—the creep could creep. It was his specialty. But it made it easier to talk. Chris said, "What happened?"

She said, "It's stupid. So stupid." The two of them sat down at the table, Sarah off to the side as always. Frances was talking, though she wasn't talking to her. She explained that first thing this morning, she'd had a visitor at work. Some crazy hippie man with a long ponytail, and he wouldn't go away no matter how hard her secretary tried to deter him. Finally, Frances came out of a meeting and saw him there, strode over, and tried to take control of the situation, but the hippie man refused to relent.

"He said we had some business. I couldn't imagine what kind of business he meant. I mean, this was a man who literally stank. He was a white guy with dreadlocks, and he had those bandages on his face. He looked like someone off the street, and I was dubious, and then he mentioned Evan." At his name, she looked around for him, briefly noticed his absence with a shrug, and then continued. "I thought the guy was a musician, that this was something about a gig. They owed him money maybe, but he told me he wasn't a musician. That music was the problem.

"His wife, he told me, was stepping out with my husband. That's what he said—I didn't know what he was talking about. I was thinking about dancing. The two-step. I was thinking about who in the hell would be this man's wife? What had happened to his face? And so he had to lay it out for me—Evan was sleeping with his wife, and she was the backup singer living over the garage. The girl.

"He was making a scene—everybody was pretending not to look, but how could they not? I couldn't have asked him to come into my office, though, because I didn't want to be alone with him, and he smelled so bad. The windows in there don't open. We could have gone downstairs for a coffee, but I didn't want to get in the elevator with him. So we stayed where we were in the corridor, and I tried to tell him that it was just about the music, but he kept insisting. Finally, I had to call security and have him taken out. It was mortifying. I couldn't stay there.

"So I came home, and Evan was sleeping. I woke him up and asked him about the girl, and he said it was hard to explain."

"How?" asked Sarah.

"That's what I asked him," said Frances. "I told him it was pretty straightforward, and it would be in his best interest to deliver an honest denial. He said, 'Do you want me to be honest, or do you want to hear what you want to hear?' I told him I wanted him to die, and then he went into this whole thing about how they were having an emotional affair. Nothing physical yet, but he's just in love with her. *Just.* As though there was some kind of honour in that. Like I should be grateful.

"He told me I shouldn't be angry at him. He said, 'The mind knows what the mind knows,' and I told him what my mind knows. He told me not to get aggressive. He said I was always so aggressive, and it had put distance between us. He said he'd gone to her for comfort, so it was basically all my fault. And then he told me I was getting aggressive again, so I punched the window out. Just a pane. Upstairs in our room."

She shook her head and ran her good hand through her hair, the same way Chris did. "It's a ridiculous story, I know it."

There was nothing to say. They could hear Evan walking around upstairs, like scurrying mice feet. The sound was embarrassing.

"The cuts aren't deep," Frances said, checking under the towel. "The bleeding's stopped. But now tell me. What about charges?" She was more weary than angry now, her edges worn away. Sarah had never known her to sit so slumped.

Nobody said anything. Sarah got up to put the kettle on. She said, over her shoulder, "Listen, do you want me to go? Leave you alone?" She looked back at the table. Frances didn't move. Chris shook his head. She proceeded to get mugs down from the cupboard.

"It's about his nose," Chris told Frances, and then he told her everything, except for the dumbwaiter. Frances was entirely placid now; her expression didn't change as she took in what her brother said. When Sarah put the tea in front of her, she wrapped her hands around the mug, even though it was hot. She held them there.

Chris kept trying to explain. Her silence was scaring him— he seemed to figure that he had to talk to break it, to stumble upon the one right thing to snap her out of her spell. He was saying, "And I was always on your side—you know that. I was helping you, helping him, or at least that's what I thought."

Finally, Frances said, "I can't believe Evan hit someone." She was broken; she was sad. Wholly without her shell, and Sarah had been waiting for years to see what this would look like, who would be the human being inside. The answer was awful. Her own discomfort tinged with guilt, as though she'd willed all this to happen. Hypothetical questions were one thing, but crossed over into the realm of actual just made her like the world less for the myriad ways in which a person could be defeated.

She'd counted on Frances—that there could actually be a person that hard, that tough. What did it mean for the rest of them that there wasn't, after all?

She left them there eventually. There wasn't a place for her in this tableau, and she wanted to go home. She said she'd pick up Charlotte after school and bring her over for dinner at their place. She resisted the urge to ask "What are you going to do?"

because she knew that Frances didn't know any better than she did. Frances, who stiffened just as usual when Sarah ventured to give her a hug. So not everything was changed.

Sarah checked her phone on her way back through the trees. Another reason she'd wanted to leave—it seemed insensitive to be checking her messages through somebody else's crisis, but then again, she had a crisis of her own. Which seemed to be ramping right back up judging by the volume of unread texts and emails she had waiting for her.

A series of them from Janie, beginning with *WTF?*

Followed by *What fresh shit have you stepped in now? You've sold out to pornographers????*

* * *

She went to her desk, and she went to the site. Chris later said that this was an entirely stupid move, and that right then she had compromised her whole computer and those of all her contacts, but Sarah didn't know how she could be any more compromised than she already was. She tried to log in to the back end first, but a pop-up window informed her that Access Was Forbidden. So then she typed in that familiar URL, the one she always took care to erase from her history when she left her computer. First the screen black, and then it started flashing—this was like no incarnation of her website that had ever been. A series of women in various states of undress, stuck in poses purporting to be erotic, but they were so far from sexy. This was a horror show. A banner ad for Viagra appeared on the screen.

I've been hacked, she texted back to Janie.

Russians? North Koreans? she responded.

More likely Claudia Kincardine's anti-social nephew, Sarah supposed, imagining him holed up in his teenage dungeon delivering justice to Mitzi Bytes. Cherry had told her about that guy. She remembered what Claudia had said: *The plans are in place. It's all going to come to a head.*

Or maybe it was just a coincidence.

The screen kept flashing—she couldn't make it stop. Later, Chris would have to reformat her hard drive, and so many files would get lost. Once they were gone, though, she couldn't remember what any of them had been, so she didn't miss them. The Old Lady Project—she'd have to start all over again. At least she had pictures of her kids on her phone. It turned out these were all that mattered—how nauseating was that?

But it wasn't really. She got that. The kids were changing all the time, so fast so often that from one morning to the next, they seemed like entirely different people. Sarah needed the pictures as proof of where the time went, but all the rest of it, everything else that mattered, were stories she kept filed away on her brain. It was an unreliable filing system, nothing ever turning up at the right moment and so much at the wrong time, but it worked. And it was possible that she didn't need an archive, that she could go forward now.

"I could start again," she was thinking as she watched her computer and her website simultaneously imploding right in front of her. Naked breasts and bums flashing like the world's worst strobe light, and it was all gone now, she realized. The most charitable act of revenge she'd ever been party to, if it was indeed such a thing. The damage wouldn't undo all the harm she'd done, but it might bring her troubles to a halt. She was thinking about Michelle, and Leslie, and Frances. Especially Frances. There could only be so many screenshots. Frances would never have to know—no need for Sarah to compound her problem.

A clean slate. That's the one thing a blog could never deliver, except this one time. A new blog, and she'd put her name on it. She'd show her face to the world. She should have done that all along. And here was the solution to everything. She would have it both ways after all.

God bless the hackers, the pornographers.

Sarah laughed and spun around in her chair. She looked out the window now to see Chris coming through the trees, and he saw her there. He waved to her, and then in an uncharacteristic public gesture (though no one was looking), he blew her a kiss. They were feeling tender, both of them, she supposed, after the carnage they'd just witnessed over at Frances's, the near disaster of their own morning and the evening before.

We can't let this get away from us, she was thinking, and she was thinking he was thinking that too as she returned a kiss in the air his way. He disappeared beneath the overhang, and she heard the sound of him coming inside.

She wanted to whoop, but she didn't call him. There would be time enough to present him with her latest catastrophe— because her troubles were his, after all, particularly those involving computer hardware—but she'd give him a break for now. For now she wanted to be alone anyway, just a few minutes to reflect on all she had and what she'd come so close to losing.

"This is a good life," she whispered to herself, still staring out the window, the glass reflecting the frenetic screen behind her. It didn't matter anymore. And maybe she'd never again be able to show her face in Have You Bean, but she'd never felt comfortable there anyway, among the overpriced lattes and hundred-dollar stretch pants. They hadn't been her crowd, which she hadn't been honest about, and perhaps that was the problem.

And now she'd get away with it; they'd hate her for it, but that part wasn't her concern.

"This is a good life," she said again. She was yearning to write about it, all of it. Because to put it down in words was to be sure that it had happened. And there were so many aspects of the story she still had to puzzle out, and she knew no other way.

The View from Here
Sarah Lundy, *The Maplewood Village Sentinel*

It's a long way from an olive to an acorn, but the distance is being bridged by Acorn Avenue Public School's spring fundraiser. This month, crates of fair-trade olive oil will arrive at the school and be sold door to door and through telesales.

"We wanted to do something a little different," said Starry Fiske, Acorn Avenue parent and head of the school's fundraising committee. "Everybody sells the chocolate almonds, and the magazine subscriptions, and the Christmas wreaths. At Acorn Avenue, we pride ourselves at standing above the crowd. And who doesn't need olive oil? It's a pantry staple. Cooks will feel good, knowing it's all sustainably sourced."

Not just environmentally sustainable, the olive oil is an ethical choice for other reasons. It's made from olives harvested by a collective of Palestinian and Israeli women, and proceeds from sales go toward peace projects and other initiatives throughout the region.

"It cooks at a medium smoke point," explained Fiske. "But it's helping keep Middle Eastern politics from reaching a boiling point. Who wouldn't be on board?"

However, there have been some quiet protests by area parents who are balking at the item's price. Some have suggested that $32 might be a high price to pay for a 100-millilitre bottle of the stuff.

But Starry Fiske is undeterred. "It's a beautiful oil," she said. "You get what you pay for, as well as the peace of mind of knowing your purchase has a positive effect on the world."

And not just in the Middle East. She goes on to elaborate the ways in which the raised funds will go toward supporting local students' educations through the purchase of new technology, library books, and sporting equipment for Acorn Avenue Public School.

"It's like the song goes," she tells me. "About believing that the children are the future. So you put your money where your mouth is."

And when the currency is olive oil, you literally can.

ACKNOWLEDGEMENTS

If I was not a reader first, I don't know that I'd have anything to write about. Obviously, this novel owes a debt to *Harriet the Spy*, by Louise Fitzhugh, and *To the Lighthouse*, by Virginia Woolf. I have also been influenced by Elisa Albert's *After Birth*, and the wonderful *Mommyblogs and the Changing Face of Motherhood*, by my friend Dr. May Friedman.

"Colleagues in the mother trade" is a phrase belonging to Grace Paley. Sarah's mother's advice about "two things you're going to have to do" is paraphrased from Ole Golly's in *Harriet the Spy*. The song Chris references is "If Not for You," written by Bob Dylan, but I'm imagining he was thinking of the George Harrison version. I borrowed the verb *farfetch* from Mary Ann Hoberman, and it really should be brought into wider use.

My students at the University of Toronto teach me so much about blogging and continually renew my passion for it. I have also learned so much from bloggers I've followed for years, who have been generous enough to share their experiences, wisdom, and foibles. I am grateful too to those who read my own blog—some since its inauspicious beginnings many years ago. Thank you for letting me grow and learn, and coming along for the ride.

Thanks to Samantha Haywood for being a most excellent champion of Mitzi. I don't think this novel could have found a better home than with Jennifer Lambert, who liked the book enough to want to make it better—I'm so grateful for your attention and expertise. Grace Yaginuma is amazing. Thanks to Noelle Zitzer, Kelsey Marshall, and everybody at HarperCollins Canada.

Many thanks to my friends and first readers Julie Booker, Maria Meindl, Rebecca Rosenblum, and Julia Zarankin. Thanks to the Salonistas and the Vicious Circle for being my literary communities, Craig Riggs and Kiley Turner for the best part-time job ever at 49thShelf.com, and to my friends who are the ground beneath my feet—among them, Heather Birrell, Anakana Schofield, Jennie Weller, Britt Leeking, Erin Smith, Kate Wilczak, Rebecca Dolgoy, Katie Doering, Nathalie Foy, and Kelsie Hernandez and the families Cruz-Blackman and Freitas-Peski for too much fun.

To the parents of my children's schoolmates, many of whom over conversations on the playground have become my friends— thank you for the warmth and kindness my prickly protagonist might have benefited from.

Thanks to my parents and sister—Joan Clare, Ken Clare, and Christy Massey—who have supported my literary aspirations since Grade 3. I am very lucky.

In addition to being a work of fiction, *Mitzi Bytes* is a love letter to my family. I started writing it one summer night after having supper together on our porch and discussing some ideas that had been floating around in my head. As is always the case, our conversation clarified my thoughts, and I am grateful to editorial contributions from my husband and eldest daughter—the youngest was then too little to talk. I found the time to write the book during the rest of that summer, because Carol Burnett and Aileen Quinn entertained the big girl daily as she watched *Annie,* while the baby napped. Perhaps you can even hear "So janitor, so senator . . ." playing in the margins.